FOAL

REMEMBER ME

Chelsea Bobulski

Feiwel and Friends

New York

To God, for giving me this book when I needed it most, and to Mom, Aunt Georgia, and Grandma, for giving me the trip of a lifetime that inspired it

A Feiwel and Friends Book
An imprint of Macmillan Publishing Group, LLC
120 Broadway, New York, NY 10271

Remember Me. Copyright © 2019 by Chelsea Bobulski. All rights reserved. Printed in the United States of America.

Our books may be purchased in bulk for promotional, educational, or business use. Please contact your local bookseller or the Macmillan Corporate and Premium Sales Department at (800) 221-7945 ext. 5442 or by email at MacmillanSpecialMarkets@macmillan.com.

Library of Congress Control Number: 2018955488
ISBN 978-1-250-18944-8 (hardcover) / ISBN 978-1-250-18947-9 (ebook)

Book design by Mallory Grigg
Feiwel and Friends logo designed by Filomena Tuosto

First edition, 2019

1 3 5 7 9 10 8 6 4 2

fiercereads.com

PROLOGUE

HE'D KNOWN SOMEHOW, AS HE pulled the trigger, that death would not be the worst of what he would face. Even before his finger slid across the cold curve of metal, he'd felt the curse weaving its way through the air, stitching and binding itself to the room, intertwining with every fiber and grain and molecule of the space surrounding him. Through the walls and ceiling and floorboards, down to the hotel's very beams and joists and stone-carved foundation.

Time had slowed to the pulsing, drumming beat of the blood that was pumping, seeping, crawling across the floorboards, as he placed the barrel against his brow. He watched the bloody meniscus spread like spilled honey, so thick, so dark, as to appear almost black, even beneath the glow of the crystal chandelier that beat its electric light down on him, filaments buzzing like locusts in his ears until he pulled the trigger—

And heard nothing at all.

He remembered everything as he stirred from his slumber, although he could not recall how long it had been since that memory took place, nor since he last awoke. All he knew was the hunger coursing through him, an ache he could never satisfy, no matter how many opportunities he was given to do so.

He no longer had a physical form, but he had no need of one. The hotel had seen to that.

As the sun broke over a new day, and the majority of the hotel patrons still lay sleeping in their beds, he stretched his presence from the dark, cold place where he'd been dwelling—waiting, *resting*—and slowly put on every wall and ceiling and floorboard, as if shrugging into a very old, very familiar coat.

Throughout the hotel, every open window snicked closed. Doors shook slightly in their frames, as if lovingly prodded by tender fingertips snaking across their polished grains. Hallway lights flickered like candle flame, too quickly to be noticed. Carpet fibers stood on end, and floorboards creaked where no one stepped. And in the soft blue light of early morning, in the interior, open-air garden that had been tucked into the middle of the hotel, a single red rose blossomed.

In the still, quiet hush of dawn, darkness seeped into the light, skittering across the walls in the form of shadows and chatter and lilting melodies of a time long past. Only one soul noticed, but there was nothing that could be done to stop it. Nothing to silence the ghosts, nor to send them back to their shallow graves.

All that could be done was to sit.

And to wait.

PART ONE

CHAPTER ONE

LEA

June 1907

IT'S A PITY THERE ARE so many boats on the water this morning. If I were to slip over the ferry's railing, I doubt anyone would leave me alone long enough to drown.

Although, if I'm being honest, I don't know that I would go through with it even if conditions were favorable. Mother likes to say I'm all dramatics with no follow-through, and perhaps it's true. Or perhaps Father merely trained the disobedience out of me long ago.

Whatever the case, I will not be jumping overboard today, so I force my gaze away from the waves lapping the side of the ferry and turn my attention to our summer residence.

The Winslow Grand Hotel.

The hotel had seemed an impressive-enough building in the brochure, but the pencil sketches pale in comparison to the real thing. A mammoth structure encapsulated in white wooden siding and capped by a sloping, copper roof, already turning green with patina, dominates the far side of the island, dwarfing the palm trees and other smaller buildings surrounding it.

"Isn't it magnificent?" The man standing next to me says, his hand slapping the slippery rail in front of us. "It's one of the country's largest wooden buildings, don't you know? Four hundred guest rooms! And the whole thing's been incandescent since '91."

"I heard it took ten million feet of lumber to construct," his little girl replies.

Her older brother scoffs. "More like twenty million."

She sticks her tongue out at him.

I close my eyes and will myself to absorb their excitement, to try to find the good and the magic inherent in this place, where so many people return, year after year, to summer on its sun-warmed beaches, but when I open them again, I cannot see the hotel for anything but what it truly is.

My prison.

As if reading my mind, Father's hand clamps down on my shoulder. It is a sturdy hand, strong and unyielding. I glance up at him, into the sunlight.

Shadows cloud his face.

"Aurelea."

"Father."

"You look troubled," he says, a note of warning in his tone.

I shake my head. "Merely lost in thought."

His grip tightens, a quick squeeze. "Try to look happier, won't you? You are meeting your betrothed here."

"Of course, Father."

He stares at me a moment longer. "We are very fortunate to be in this position, Aurelea. Remember that."

I glance at Mother, who smiles and holds Benny's hand as he

jumps up and down at the prow of the ship, pointing to a family of cranes wading along the shore.

"Yes, Father," I say.

The ferry docks and we are ushered into a streetcar with the name WINSLOW ISLAND RAILROAD COMPANY emblazoned across the top. Although it is a small car designed to transport hotel patrons to and from the ferry, Benny gapes at it just as he did the trains at the station in Philadelphia. His nanny, Madeline, nudges him into the car, and I sweep him onto my lap.

"Let go," he whines. "I'm too old for this."

"Is that right?"

He nods solemnly.

"Forgive me," I tease. "I did not realize you had become a grown adult at the ripe old age of seven. I suppose that means you won't want me sneaking you an extra dessert from the dining room tonight then, either?"

He screws up his face, pitting his desire for autonomy against his notorious sweet tooth. "Instead of sitting on your lap, how about a kiss on the cheek?"

I sigh. "I suppose that will have to do."

He glances around the car to make sure no one is watching, then pecks at my cheek like a bird, quick and sharp, before scooting onto the adjacent seat. Madeline chuckles softly, deepening the wrinkles around her eyes.

Once everyone is accounted for, the streetcar takes off, gliding along the rails toward the hotel. But while everyone else hangs out the windows to get a better glimpse of the Grand, I glance behind me, at the men unloading trunks and automobiles from the ferry, and beyond them, at the blue water and the life I left behind on its distant shore.

If everything goes according to Father's plan, I will not leave this hotel at the end of the summer as Aurelea Sargent, but as Aurelea Van Oirschot, wife of Lon Van Oirschot—entrepreneur and heir apparent to the Van Oirschot Steel Company.

Father clears his throat. "Aurelea."

I turn back in my seat.

The streetcar rolls through Canvas City, past rows and rows of striped tents that the brochure claims can be rented for the same amount of money a week that the hotel patrons pay per night. And if one does not mind a dirt floor and the absolute barest of necessities, the price drops to half that.

Men, women, and children wave at us from the street as we pass, some in their bathing suits, others dressed for lunch. I spot a group of girls around my age, perhaps a year or two younger, linked arm in arm as they head for the beach, their skin tanned and hair bleached from the summer sun. For a moment, I allow myself to imagine my arm linked through one of theirs, and I can see it—this alternate me, with hair wet from the ocean and skin caked in salt. The five of us are the best of friends; we've grown up together and we know each other's deepest, darkest secrets. We each have beaus of our own choosing, although whether or not we'll marry any of them is yet to be seen. We're arguing over what we'll have for lunch—ice cream to cool our sunbaked bodies, or something more substantial, to give us the energy we'll need to spend the rest of the day battling the surf. We would settle on both, I think, because best friends are good at compromising.

The streetcar flies past, and the vision fades.

I am no longer one of them.

We turn onto a long gravel drive lined with cypress trees, Spanish moss hanging from their branches like ghostly curtains, and glide to a stop in front of the massive hotel. The ocean breeze is even stronger here, cutting through the gaps in the palm trees dotting the beach and through the streetcar's open windows. In his excitement, Benny jumps out of the car as soon as the porter unlatches the door. He streaks up the hotel steps, his arms splayed out like bird wings.

"Benjamin," Father barks.

Benny freezes. Father does not have to say anything else. A stern look and a slight raising of his spanking hand is all it takes for Benny to walk dutifully back to Father's side.

"You're too old for that sort of behavior," Father mutters under his breath. "It's unseemly."

Benny nods.

"Yes, Father."

"It's all right, son. Just don't let it happen again."

But Benny does not look comforted. Father never lets things go so easily.

Mother takes my hand. "Come along, dear. Let's see if we can't find your beloved."

I square my shoulders and adopt the mask Mother has been training me to wear all my life. I do not need a mirror to know the lines furrowing my brow disappear or that my lips stretch into a well-practiced smile no one could spot as a fake—not when I can watch my mother go through the same transformation, her momentary concern over Benny vanishing as if it had never been there at all.

Mother waits for Father and Benny to take the lead, and then we follow them up the steps, toward the ornate wooden doors of the Winslow Grand Hotel.

CHAPTER TWO

NELL

June 2019

I SQUINT UP AT THE hotel through the front windshield as Dad steers our guttering '94 Corolla wagon up the curving gravel drive, past a labyrinth of cypress trees, tropical pink flowers, and Gucci-clad women carrying Coach purses.

"What do you think?" Dad asks, pulling the car under the porte cochere.

My brows arch. "Are you sure we aren't supposed to be using a servant's entrance or something?"

He laughs. "Not too shabby, huh?"

"It's like a castle," I say, my voice whisper-soft as I take it all in.

Unlike the square, cookie-cutter hotels Dad has worked in all his life, no two sections of the Winslow Grand Hotel look the same. It's like someone stuck a hundred Victorian houses together, enclosing them in the same white wooden siding and topping them with the same patina-green roof to hide all the seams.

The brakes squeal and the car slams to a stop. We both fly forward, our frayed, coffee-stained seat belts snapping against our chests.

I glance at Dad.

"Nervous?"

He smiles through the windshield at the family of blonds staring at our car, speaking to each other in rapid French. Behind us, a black Aston Martin keeps its distance.

"Nope," he says.

"Dad." I give him a pointed look. "The car's still in drive. You just pulled the emergency brake."

He frowns at the gear shift. "I did?"

I force a smile. "Don't worry. You're going to be great."

"Thanks, Nellie Bee. It's just . . . this is the big leagues, you know?"

"I know."

We don't mention the chest pains Dad had last fall—the panic attack that sent him to the ER thinking his heart was failing him—even though it was the scariest moment of my life, and I still remember the prayer that ran on a constant loop in my head as my ballet teacher drove me to the hospital after class:

Not him, too . . . Not him, too . . . Please, God, not him, too.

The on-call doctor told Dad that he was working himself into an early grave and needed to start taking it easy. Dad listened for a while. He actually made it home for family movie nights and Taco Tuesdays. He even came to my spring recital this year, even though it was on a Saturday and he hated leaving the assistant manager in charge on the weekends. And that was at a measly, thirty-two bedroom lodge in the Colorado Rockies, roughly a sixteenth of the Grand's size. Not to mention it was more of a quaint, small town, ma-and-pop kind of place. Not a luxury seaside resort with a reputation for excellence.

If I see Dad here at all besides at the occasional early breakfast, I'll count myself lucky.

The valet does a decent job of hiding his reaction to our beat-up car, only allowing himself a furtive glance at the crumpled bumper before taking Dad's keys. I get out of the car, slinging my duct tape–patched backpack onto my shoulder and stretching my legs. I absentmindedly turn my feet through each ballet position as another valet stacks our luggage on a cart and as Dad introduces himself as the new guest relations manager to every employee within a ten-foot radius.

I don't have to look back at Dad to know he's got his chest puffed out, his shoulders pinched back, and his lips pulled wide into the smile that turns his dimples into gullies. The Winslow has been his dream job since he first visited it as a kid during a two-night stay with his parents (two nights for which they'd saved up for years and that he still talked about as the most extravagant vacation they ever took).

Dad already loves it here, which means his workaholic tendencies are going to kick into overdrive before we even unpack our bags.

My back to the car and the parking lot beyond, I stare up at the wide, brick staircase leading to the front entrance. The doors—thick, old-fashioned things with fancy oval windows and giant magnolia blossoms, looping ivy, palm fronds, and fat-cheeked baby angels carved into the wood—stand open, and through the darkness beyond I can just make out the silhouettes of other guests checking in. *These* are the people Dad will be looking after. The people who will fuel his workaholic tendencies.

Be happy for him, I tell myself. *Remember what Dr. Roby said. Expect only good things to happen.*

"But what do you do when something bad happens instead?" I asked Dr. Roby at our first session four years ago, the backs of my knees sticking to the leather chair across from his desk. "Isn't it better to be prepared for the bad stuff so it won't hurt so much?"

He'd answered my question with another question.

"Why are you so sure bad things are going to happen to you?"

That was the moment I decided that Dr. Roby was of no use to me at all.

Dad puts an arm around my shoulders as one valet pushes our luggage into a queue by the hut and the other pulls our car away, its engine rattling like it has a jackhammer under the hood.

"Ready?"

I tell him what he wants to hear.

"You bet."

"That's my girl."

I try to swallow the fear clawing up my throat as we walk up the staircase—*Dad will be fine, this will be fine,* everything *will be fine*—but my heart pounds in my chest as we near the doors, and my head feels like a balloon floating above my shoulders, as if it isn't getting enough blood to weigh it down.

Expect only good things to happen.

The mantra keeps my feet moving, but as the yawning darkness of the lobby grows closer, another thought slams into my brain—

RUN.

I freeze.

Dad frowns at me. "Everything okay?"

No. I've never felt like something was more wrong in my entire life, but the feeling comes from nowhere, and I know it's rooted in a deeper problem. A deeper fear.

I hitch my backpack higher on my shoulder as Dr. Roby's voice echoes through my mind—*Call me if you need anything*—along with that look he gave me as I was leaving my last appointment, the one that said he didn't think I'd be okay, even though he didn't argue when I told him I wouldn't be looking for another therapist in South Carolina.

The look I gave back was stubborn, defiant. It said he would never be hearing from me again.

I'm finally going to prove to both him and Dad that what I went through after Mom died was temporary, a single ripple in an otherwise still pond—not a lifelong problem in need of constant intervention. It didn't define me then, and I won't let it define me now.

I will be fine.

I *am* fine.

"Yeah," I lie, my flats slapping the bricks as Dad puts his arm around my shoulders and steers me toward the front doors. "All good."

CHAPTER THREE

LEA

I ALMOST CANNOT WALK THROUGH the doors, even as Mother and Father and Benny urge me forward. They must sense the fear inside me, the knowledge that if I don't run now, I won't get another chance. But then Mother takes my arm with a firm hand and, like a captain steering a ship, pulls me into the lobby.

Mother stops as soon as we enter, laying a hand on her bosom. "Oh, Aurelea, isn't it beautiful?"

It is beautiful, with its tall pillars and paneled ceiling crafted from the same polished mahogany. The same designs of ivy, magnolia blossoms, palm fronds, and impish cherubim playing harps and lutes featured on the hotel's front doors have been delicately carved into each pillar. A gold elevator cage stands next to the staircase, and a second-floor gallery overlooks the main seating area and hotel entrance, which is probably why so many ladies are seated up there, watching the arrival of the Grand's newest guests. But it reminds me somehow of the Colosseum, as if I am entering through one gate and waiting for the lion to appear through another.

I spot him before he sees me, strolling into the lobby with three other gentlemen, all of whom wear white shirts and slacks and carry tennis rackets. I turn my face away and hide behind a pillar as Mother calls out, "Lonnie! Over here."

I squeeze my eyes shut, knocking my head against the pillar. *Just remember you love her*, I tell myself, *and that she means well*.

"Mrs. Sargent," Lon says, his voice thudding like a cannon in my chest. "Where's Aurelea?"

I take a deep breath, plaster on my practiced smile, and step out from behind the pillar.

"Hello, Lon," I say, forcing a cheer I do not feel into my voice. "Marvelous to see you again."

He takes my hand and brushes his lips across my gloved knuckles. I bite my tongue to keep from pulling it back.

It isn't that Lon is *completely* repulsive. My friends back home are all green with envy that I've snagged a handsome bachelor with a fortune to boot, but while I can appreciate his non-grotesque features in a purely analytical way, they do nothing to warm me to him.

"We'll be seeing a lot more of each other now," he says. His scent—a cough-inducing mixture of bergamot cologne, coffee, and cigars—invades my nostrils, sprouting a dull ache in my left cornea.

"I suppose so," I reply, the smell tickling my throat. Mother covertly pinches the inside of my wrist, and I widen my smile. "I couldn't be more delighted at the prospect."

"Neither could I."

Mother asks Lon about his tennis game and the men with whom he's been playing—business associates, Lon answers, who will also be summering at the hotel, allowing him to participate in both work and play whilst they're here. I take the opportunity to inch steadily backward, until the burning in my throat subsides.

"Of course, there will be no work on your honeymoon in September," Mother lightly chides him.

"Of course," Lon says, sliding his gaze to me. "I wouldn't dream of it."

He is expecting me to say something—perhaps that I am glad I'll have his full attention at that time, or that I cannot wait for September to come—but all I can think about is the fact that, in less than three months, I will be forced to share a bed with this man who bathes in cologne and smokes a horrendous amount of cigars and who is a complete and utter stranger to me.

So I say nothing at all.

Father returns from checking us in, appearing at Lon's side and shaking his hand. "Lon. Good to see you. Is your father around?"

"Taking a morning constitutional along the beach, I believe. He keeps a very specific schedule while we're here. In all the years we've summered at the Grand, he has yet to break it. Have you checked in?"

"Yes. I'm told our trunks should be along shortly."

"I won't keep you. I must change for lunch, anyway." He turns back to me, taking my hand once more. "Will I see you in the dining room in, say, an hour?"

I coyly tilt my head as Mother taught me, instantly despising myself for it. "I would not miss it for the world."

Lon grins. "Wonderful. If you'll excuse me."

Mother watches him go, her eyes traveling a bit farther south than a proper lady's should. "He is quite an athletic man, isn't he?"

Why don't you marry him then? I think, just barely catching my tongue between my teeth.

"Come along, ladies," Father commands us as he crosses the lobby toward the elevator. Mother and Benny slide into the elevator behind him, and then it's just me standing on the other side, but even at the urging of the operator, I cannot seem to step through the door. My heart quickens as I think of that song, the one about a bird in a gilded cage, and then suddenly my life is flashing before my eyes, my past and my present and my future all jumbling together, and one horrific truth stands out:

Not one day looks different from the rest.

I will live and die the same person, in the same gilded cage, as the day I was born, and even though I've felt the truth of that before this moment—felt it claw up my throat in the middle of the night when I couldn't sleep—the full effect of it does not hit me until just now, when I see a clear, visual representation of it: my parents and brother happily ensconcing themselves in the small, tight quarters of the elevator cage, and I on the other side of it, certain I do not belong there.

Father's eyes narrow. "Aurelea," he mutters under his breath. "Get on the damn elevator."

A man and woman step off the staircase and pass us with curious looks. Father smiles at them, saying, "She's deathly afraid of heights." Then he gets out of the elevator and takes my elbow. "It's all right, sweetheart. We don't have far to go."

"She could take the stairs," the operator offers.

Father glares at him.

The man shrinks under Father's gaze and gives me a pleading look. "Miss?"

I take a deep breath. "That's all right." Father's grip pinches my bones. "I must get over this fear someday."

I step into the cage, and the operator closes the door behind me.

I keep my eyes shut until it opens again.

CHAPTER FOUR

NELL

MY PANIC DIES AS SOON as we enter the lobby, as if that single word—*RUN*—had roared past me on the ocean breeze, sweeping me up in an undertow meant for someone else.

"Misplaced fear," Dr. Roby says, clicking his pen like a metronome, "is very common in those who have suffered a traumatic experience at such a young age. What we are going to learn here is how to control that fear, so that it will no longer control you."

"Well?" Dad asks, spreading his arms open wide. "What do you think?"

I shove the beige, square box of my therapist's room out of my mind and focus on the room I'm in now.

As the daughter of a man obsessed with hotels, I've seen my fair share of lobbies. Everything from affordable roadside franchises to big-city high-rises, rustic mountain lodges to gingerbread bed-and-breakfasts. I've seen contemporary lobbies with crisp, clean lines and modern lobbies that laughed in the face of feng shui. But this . . .

This is like walking back in time.

The huge space is broken up only by the pillars holding up the ceiling. The entire room, from the ornate reception desk to the second-floor balcony, all the way up to the beams crisscrossing the ceiling in a mesmerizing diamond pattern, appears to be sculpted from the same dark, polished wood, which gleams like amber in the warm light of the wall sconces and the antique chandelier hanging in the center of it all. It looks like something out of a dream, and all I can think is:

Mom would have loved it here.

I circle the room while Dad speaks to the receptionist, stopping at a pair of French doors leading to a large garden. I step out into the ocean-salted air, where the four interior sides of the hotel, lined in balconies and exterior hallways, rise around me, a square of blue sky arcing above it all.

The garden is like something from a fairy tale. Antique iron benches sit beneath a mixture of fruit, magnolia, and cypress trees, while a stone path winds its way through a variety of rose bushes and flowering, tropical shrubs. I follow the sound of rushing water to the other side of the garden, where a pond sits beneath a stone wall. A lion's face protrudes from the stones, a stream of water gushing from its mouth into the pond. Koi fish dart beneath the lily pads, their colorful scales glistening like rainbows beneath the water's surface. I stand there for a moment, watching them. Wondering if they ever find themselves worrying about things they can't control—things like whether someone will forget to feed them, or whether the water will evaporate and they'll suffocate on the air surrounding them.

The wind picks up, carrying with it the scent of lemon blossoms. I turn and head back the way I came, stopping halfway to the lobby as my eyes catch on a lemon tree sitting alone in a patch of grass. I walk across the damp lawn and press my nose to the blossoms. My heart squeezes at the fresh, citrus scent, the same way it does whenever I smell Mom's favorite flowers or her perfume on another woman. But we never lived anywhere near warm enough for Mom to grow lemon trees, and her perfume smelled like jasmine and vanilla, not citrus blossoms, so I have no idea why I would feel that same, heart-wrenching tug of familiarity at something that has nothing to do with her.

Frowning at the tree, I tuck my hair behind my ears and head back inside the lobby.

To my left, just past a gold elevator cage, a wide, opulent staircase ascends to the second level, off which steps a group of women wearing the type of clothing I've only ever seen on the cover of *Vogue*. I glance down at the jeans I've been wearing for three days and my favorite sweater, which now has a ketchup stain on the cuff thanks to those monster burgers we picked up in Nashville. Tugging the cuff into my palm, I move past the staircase, to a tall set of closed double doors crafted from the same dark wood as everything else. Above the door, the word *ballroom* is etched in looping gold letters.

String music drifts through the wooden seam.

The song is hauntingly familiar. I hum a few notes as I step closer, my voice rising and falling with the solemn melody as it weaves itself around my heart, but I can't remember where I know it from. Frowning, I grab my phone and open Song Finder, but as I hold my phone up to the doors, the melody tinkling around me like rain, a big red X appears on the screen, along with the message:

No Music Found. Try Again.

I glance back at reception. Dad's still talking to the woman behind the desk, no doubt getting her life story. He's always been good at that sort of thing. I sweep my gaze over the lobby, but no one's looking, and even though I'm not sure I should, I grab one of the handles and pull.

The door opens. I check over my shoulder one more time, then sneak inside.

Walking into the ballroom is like walking into a cathedral. The domed ceiling, crafted from the same dark wood as everything else, arcs above me in a mesmerizing starburst pattern. Four crystal chandeliers stretch across the expanse, lighting a space that appears to be—at least in its near-empty state, with only a vacuum cleaner sitting abandoned in the middle of the room—approximately the length of a football field.

Empty.

As in no string quartet, even though the music continues to tinkle through the air.

I step farther into the room, my shoes thudding softly across the blue-and-white Victorian carpet, past a small stage where a string quartet might set up and across the dance floor to a long bank of windows on the other side of the room. The windows overlook the foliage of the front entrance and, beyond that, the long, gravel drive that led us here, lined as far as the eye can see with trees covered in ghostly, gray ribbons of Spanish moss, gently swaying in the breeze.

The music swells, thrumming through me like a current, but I don't see any obvious speakers. I follow the noise back to the stage in the center of the room, figuring the sound system must be hiding up there somewhere.

I lift my phone again. The searching icon appears and then the app buzzes with the same red X.

"Impressive, isn't it?"

I jump.

A thirty-something woman with thick brown hair and an

off-kilter smile stands behind me, her eyes round like glass orbs behind her tortoiseshell glasses.

I clutch my hand to my heart. "Sorry, I— Should I not be in here?"

She waves off my concern. "They're just setting up for a conference. No harm, no foul." She holds out her hand. "I'm Sofia Moreno. General manager of the hotel."

I shake her hand.

"Uh, Nell," I say. "Nell Martin."

"I know who you are." She says this like she knows more than just my name, and I squirm a little under her owlish gaze.

She still hasn't let go of my hand.

"Nell?" Dad's voice echoes from the doorway.

"She's in here," Sofia calls back, though she doesn't take her eyes off me. She leans in, as if sharing a secret. "We were looking for you."

"Yeah." I twist and pull my hand out of Sofia's grip. "Sorry."

Dad's brow arches as he draws near. "What are you doing in here?"

"Uh . . . exploring?"

Dad gives me *that look*. The one that says he and I both know I was raised better than to go barging through closed doors.

Sofia clears her throat. "I thought I would show you to your room first and give you a chance to settle in before the tour."

"Sounds great," Dad says.

She hands us our room keys, her neon-orange fingernails glaringly bright beneath the chandeliers. I trace my thumb over the square card. On its face is a picture of the Grand lit up at night with huge, old-fashioned light bulbs—another key for my collection.

"Follow me," Sofia says.

She leads us out of the room and stops in front of the empty elevator cage.

"It should be along in a minute," she says, smiling at Dad.

On cue, unseen gears and pulleys whirr above us, and then the bottom of the elevator appears, descending into the cage and clanking to a stop. An interior cage door slides back, and then a white-gloved hand appears, retracting the exterior doors. A family of four steps out of the elevator, the smallest boy carrying a tiny beach bucket and shovel. They smile and nod at us as they pass, and then Dad steps into the cage.

"Good day, sir," the operator says, his downy white hair curling around the edges of his hat like cotton candy. "Going up?"

"Yes, please," Dad replies.

My toes hover on the edge of the cage. I tell myself to get in, but something about it doesn't feel right. My insides crawl beneath my skin as I stare into the tiny space. Dad gives me a questioning look, and I can feel Sofia's eyes burning holes into my spine, but my mind is completely blank.

I can't remember how to move.

Dad's brow furrows. "Everything okay?"

Misplaced fear. That's all it is.

"Yeah," I say, forcing a smile as I step into the cage, Sofia following behind me. "Everything's fine."

"What floor?" the operator asks.

"Fourth, please," Sofia replies.

The old man nods and closes the elevator cage. He presses a button and the gears above us grind together as the elevator lifts with a soft, murmuring *whoosh.*

Deep breaths.

Dad makes small talk with the operator as we ascend, asking him where he's from and how long he's worked at the Grand, but their voices are muffled, as if they're talking underwater. My gaze darts across the ceiling of the swirling gold cage, which suddenly seems a foot lower than it did when we first entered.

Sofia notices me staring up at it.

"Everything all right?" she whispers.

I swallow. "Yeah, just . . . tight quarters."

We pass the second floor, and the ceiling lowers again.

I could reach up and press my palm against it.

Breathe, I tell myself. *Just breathe.*

I close my eyes and run through Dr. Roby's exercises in my head, calling this hallucination out for what it is: claustrophobia, brought on by the stress and exhaustion of the move and by my fear that Dad won't be all right here.

The ceiling is right where it should be. None of this is real.

Something squeaks like a turning faucet.

I open my eyes.

One of the decorative gold curlicues slowly detaches itself from the cage. Its sharp edges flash like metal teeth beneath the overhead light as it twists.

I tilt my head. "Uh, guys—"

The metal lashes out, snapping across my arm. I cry out and press my hand against the cut as blood bubbles to the surface.

Dad turns to me. "Nell? What's wrong?"

"My arm—"

I turn it over, searching for the scrape, but there's nothing.

Not even a red mark.

I look for the sharp twist of metal sticking out from the wall, but the cage is perfectly intact, the ceiling back where it should be. I scan Dad's, Sofia's, and the operator's faces, searching for any sign that they saw the same thing I did. But they all look at me as if *I'm* the thing out of the ordinary here.

My mouth goes dry.

Oh, God. Not again.

When the operator finally says, "Fourth floor," and opens the elevator doors, I'm the first one out. I wait for Dad and Sofia to follow me, my hands on my knees as I gulp for air.

Dad's shoes appear next to mine. He puts his arm around my shoulders. "What's the matter? Talk to me."

"Motion sickness," I say, because I can't tell him I'm seeing things that aren't really there. I take one more deep breath before straightening up. "I'm fine now."

Dad doesn't look convinced, but Sofia's already walking away, leading us into one of the sunlit corridors overlooking the interior garden. I follow her and Dad around the corner, curling my fingers around my backpack straps.

I'm fine, I think. *Everything's fine.*

But my arm still burns where the metal sliced.

CHAPTER FIVE

LEA

AS SOON AS MOTHER CLOSES the door of our suite, Father scolds me for making him look so foolish in front of God and everybody over an elevator. Mother, who always keeps her eyes forward whenever Father disciplines Benny or me, comments on what a lovely sitting room we have and how nice it is to have a veranda overlooking the beach. She steps out onto the enclosed porch along with Benny and his nanny, completely ignoring the firm hand with which Father bracelets my arm.

"There is no point in you fighting this any longer, Aurelea. We are here now, and if you act like you are anything other than *ecstatic* about this wedding, so help me God, I'll—"

But I don't get to hear exactly what he will do. His speech is interrupted by a knock at the door.

I wrench my arm out of his grasp. "I'll get it."

His jaw clenches, but he lets me go.

I run a hand over my sleeve, smoothing the fabric, and open the door.

The first thing I see is a neck—a very tan neck with a sharp Adam's apple and a slice of collarbone peeking out from beneath a crisp, white collar. Underneath the neck is a bellboy uniform that appears as though it were hastily thrown together just moments ago, the jacket lopsided due to misappropriated button holes. My gaze returns to the neck, where the back of the shirt collar sticks up, and then higher, to a strong, square jaw, sharp cheekbones, and lips that curve into a charming half smirk. Straight, dark hair hangs over the bellboy's temples, framing his dark, slashing eyebrows. And those eyes—

I've never seen eyes so blue, like twin sapphires, and completely pure, without flecks of a different color or slightly different hues between the two. So unlike my own hazel eyes, in which patches of brown and green mix together. But it isn't just the color that's fascinating, although I'm certain I've never seen the sky look so blue. It's the way his eyes crinkle and soften as he looks down at me. There's something reckless and almost dangerous in these eyes.

Something *more*.

"Miss Sargent?" the bellboy asks.

I clear my throat. "Yes?"

"I have your family's luggage." He gestures to his left, where a luggage cart sits.

"Oh, right." I count four trunks and my frown deepens. "That's not all of them."

It's just an observation—Mother often accuses me of thinking out loud at the most inopportune times—but I don't realize the words might sound accusatory until they are already out of my mouth, as if I suspect him of running off with the rest.

"No, it's not," the bellboy agrees. "Someone else is bringing up the others, but we both could not fit in the elevator, could we?"

"Of course not," I say. "Silly me."

He smiles politely. "Not at all. I would be most concerned if I did not see all my belongings accounted for."

"You're too kind. Come in." I move to the side so he can slip past me. Then, thinking better of it, I jump in front of him again. "Wait."

He cocks his head, his lips twitching into another smirk.

"Your uniform," I explain. "It's rather disheveled."

He glances down at himself and swears under his breath. "Please, forgive my appearance."

"*I* don't mind," I say quickly, before he can get the wrong idea. I watch his fingers fly over the buttons, undoing his jacket, before promptly moving my gaze to a spot on the wall above his shoulder. "My father, on the other hand—"

"He doesn't take kindly to mismatched buttons?"

"Not exactly."

He buttons the jacket again, properly this time.

"Have you only just begun your shift?" I ask. "Or just returned from a break?"

He turns his collar down.

"Not exactly," he says, mimicking my words with a twinkle in his eyes. "I'm not really a bellboy, you see."

"Oh?"

"I'm a runner," he explains. "I can perform nearly every job on site—well, every job that doesn't require a college degree, anyway—so I go wherever I'm needed. I just came from peeling potatoes in the kitchen, and earlier this morning, I caddied at the golf course."

I lean my shoulder against the doorframe. "Well, then. I must say I am impressed."

He runs his hands over his pants, smoothing the fabric, then squares his shoulders in a perfect imitation of a soldier undergoing inspection. "Better?"

"Much."

He relaxes. "Thank you. Truly. You've saved me from utter embarrassment and quite possibly a demotion. I'm forever in your debt."

"Careful," I say, my smile growing. "I just may hold you to that."

His brow arches. "I hope you do."

I stare at him a moment longer, not entirely sure what to make of him, then step back from the doorway and announce, "Our trunks have arrived."

"Only four of them," the bellboy who's actually a runner says, winking at me as he passes, pushing the cart ahead of him, "but another bellhop is bringing the others as we speak."

Father sighs and removes his billfold, which looks a great deal thinner than I'm used to seeing it. He shoves a dollar bill into the boy's hand. "The two of you are to share that tip, understand?"

"Yes, sir," he replies.

I press myself against the wall as the boy carries our trunks, placing them in the bedrooms Mother has already assigned to each of us. A year ago, a maid would already be waiting to put away my things, but I'm sure I can manage on my own.

When he finishes, the boy takes his now-empty cart and starts for the door, but Father stops him. "What's your name?"

"Alec, sir," he says, turning back. "Alec Petrov."

Father's gaze narrows. "I'll be asking your manager about you, Mr. Petrov, and whether or not you shared that tip with the other boy."

Alec's jaw ticks. "Very good, sir."

He takes a final bow, his gaze sliding to me once more before pushing his cart into the hall, closing the door behind him.

I glare at Father. "What did you think he was going to do? Stiff the boy?"

Father's brow arches. "Language, my dear. I won't have Lon thinking we found you on a farm in Kansas."

Oh no. I won't let him off the hook that easily.

"Well, did you?"

He gives me a pointed look. "Sometimes I forget how naive you are, Aurelea. Boys his age, in his position—they can be downright feral."

I shake my head. "You don't even know him."

"And you do?"

"No, but I prefer to give people the benefit of the doubt."

Father stares at me a moment longer, then laughs softly. "Get dressed. Lon expects you in the dining room in half an hour."

I want to ask him if my *entire* summer is to be determined by Lon's various whims, but, of course, I already know the answer.

CHAPTER SIX

NELL

SOFIA LEADS US DOWN SEVERAL twisting, turning hallways that seem to go on forever, with short corridor offshoots leading to only one or two guest rooms each. Thank God for the signs posted on the walls. Even with them, I don't know if I'll be able to find my way back to the stairs on my own, but there's no way I'm taking that elevator again.

Sofia turns into a hallway that leads to two doors.

"Here we are." She swipes her universal key card through the door on the left. "Home, sweet home."

Our room is twice as long as it is wide, with a large bathroom, walk-in closet, two queen beds, and tall windows fashioned with white plantation shutters. Two of the windows face the patina green roof of the sprawling hotel, while the windows along the far wall overlook a decorative balcony railing half hidden by a massive tree, its branches close enough to scrape the window in a good gust of wind and its green leaves falling like a curtain onto the six-inch-wide balcony floor. I claim the bed next to the balcony windows by slipping my backpack onto the soft down comforter.

Our luggage hasn't arrived yet, and since we don't have any clothes to change into and nothing to put away, Dad tells Sofia that we'd like that tour now.

She claps her hands. "Wonderful!"

I tuck my key card into my back pocket, close the door behind me, and follow them to the end of the corridor. Sofia stops before entering the main hallway, turning toward a narrow flight of stairs I hadn't noticed earlier.

"Shall we start at the top and work our way down?" she asks.

Dad nods. "Sounds good to me."

Since Dad is going to be dealing with guest relations, Sofia says it's important that he learn the hotel's layout as quickly as possible, should any emergency crop up in one of the guest rooms. I try to keep up with their conversation as we weave through the narrow fifth-floor hallways—hallways that, Sofia tells us, once belonged to the maids and footmen who made the Grand their permanent residence—but my attention keeps drifting to the view through the windows overlooking the beach and palm trees on one side, and the front gravel drive and moss-covered cypresses on the other.

I wonder absently, the floorboards creaking beneath my feet, what it would have been like to have walked these halls a hundred years ago. I can almost see it. A different carpet—less contemporary, although not nearly as fancy as the carpets that would have been used on the lower floors—and fresher paint on the walls. And then, using what I know about the rough time period I'm picturing, I envision a man who, in my mind's eye, moves down the hall toward me, wearing tan trousers and a white shirt beneath a matching tan vest and brown coat. He smiles at me and tips his newsboy cap as we pass each other.

"Miss," my imaginary acquaintance says.

It feels so possible, this person and this greeting, and this stretch of space that has stood for more than a hundred years, with thousands of people passing through it in that amount of time. It's as if the air is heavy with their presence, every year and every guest superimposed on the other, all occurring in the same place, standing on the same floors, surrounded by the same walls.

The only thing separating us is time.

I stretch my hand toward the space where the man I conjured passed me by.

The dates and facts of history—the battles and documents and governments—never really appealed to me, but the pictures, the faces peering up at me from black-and-white photographs, always make me stop and wonder:

What's your story?

How did you live?

How did you die?

It only got worse after Mom, this need to know the point of it all. To see the threads of humanity intertwine through centuries and somehow figure out what it all meant.

Dad calls my name from the end of the hall. I drop my hand, dust motes shimmering like golden snowflakes in the sunlight, and hurry to catch up.

"And this staircase," Sofia says, "leads to our tallest tower."

"Can we go up?" I ask, my hand curling over the banister.

Sofia shakes her head. "It's really dark and not very clean. No one goes up there anymore, and for insurance purposes, we keep it locked. Sorry."

"That's okay," I say, although I can't hide the disappointment in my voice.

We continue our tour through the other guest floors, passing several more sets of stairs, which means I never have to go near that elevator again if I don't want to. The hallways widen the farther we go down, until we reach the second floor, which contains the widest hallways by far. If Dad, Sofia, and I stood next to each other holding our arms out, we *might* be able to span the width of the main corridor, but I don't want to ruin the professional mood of our tour by testing my theory. Sofia tells us this floor is where the wealthiest, most important Grand guests have stayed over the years.

Antique furniture original to the building is strategically placed along the walls, including long, delicate sofas with velvet cushions and ten-foot-tall vanity mirrors with cherubim and ivy protruding from their wooden frames. The sight of these pieces only adds to the feeling of the past coexisting with the present, and something about that makes me feel unsettled, as if a part of me is imprinting on the walls, sinking deep into the floorboards, adding a piece of my soul to this place just like the thousands that have come before me.

I wonder if Dad feels it, too.

I stand in front of one of the mirrors as Sofia and Dad look out over the garden. The glass is mottled with black age spots. The cherubim stare down at me as I take in my reflection.

Who else has stood in front of this glass over the years?

An image of a girl in a pink satin ball gown flashes through my mind, twirling and laughing inside the mirror. I reach for her, my fingertips brushing the glass. Her smile widens and her laughter clinks like falling crystal in my ears. Her mouth makes the shape of my name—"*Nell*"—and I feel the soft breath of it whisper across my knuckles.

My fingertips sink into the glass.

"Nell."

I pull my fingers away and glance at Dad, standing at the other end of the hall.

He gives me a bemused grin. "Coming?"

I turn back to the mirror, but there's no sign of the girl, and the glass is solid beneath my prodding fingers.

Mom always said I had an overactive imagination, but she said it like it was a good thing, something I should never lose. Dr. Roby said the same thing, using it to explain the nightmarish visions I started seeing after she died, but he said it like it was a bad thing, something to be dropped and never picked up again.

Still, I held on to my imagination during the beginning stages of my treatment, because Mom had told me to, because I knew she thought it made me special, and because the central theme of every single one of my visions was *her*. But it wasn't long before I realized that getting better for Dad's sake was more important than seeing Mom everywhere. The visions faded faster once I started forcing myself to focus on reality, and then, little by little, they disappeared completely.

Or, at least, I thought they had.

You're just sleep deprived, I tell myself in the same logical voice that got me through all this in the first place. *You and Dad drove across the country. You're allowed to be a little off your game.*

You still know the difference between what's real and what's not.

We end our second-floor tour in the gallery overlooking the lobby.

"Women used to sit up here back in the day," Sofia explains as we peer over the balcony. "They would watch the guests entering the lobby while they took their tea. From up here, they could witness every personal drama that passed through the front doors, like a nineteenth-century soap opera."

"Fascinating," Dad says, the crevices of his dimples sinking deeper than I think I've ever seen before.

I haven't seen Dad this happy in four years, and it makes my stomach flip. I don't want to be the reason he isn't happy here. Whatever's going on with me—relapse, withdrawals, exhaustion-induced paranoia—I need to get over it, for Dad's sake.

Sofia shows us the breakfast and dining rooms next and then a gift shop selling Grand-themed gifts, including pictures of Lottie Charleston, a 1930s movie star who frequented the hotel.

"And this," Sofia says, steering us into a hallway lined in black-and-white photographs, "is our Wall of History."

The pictures have been blown up and mounted on canvases, making them almost life-size. In one picture, a group of men and women wearing Victorian clothing stand in front of the garden, with a sign in front of them that reads, THE WINSLOW ISLAND HORTICULTURE CLUB. In another, a group of women sporting the hairstyles and dark eye makeup of silent movie stars sunbathe on the beach. In yet another, Lottie Charleston sings into an old-fashioned microphone, wearing a sparkly black dress and fur stole, while, in the picture next to her, Teddy Roosevelt sits on the Grand's wraparound porch, a dog at his feet.

But the picture that really captures my attention was taken in the ballroom. Judging by the women's circle dresses, I would guess it was taken around the 1950s. The old-fashioned light bulbs of the chandeliers glow like fat stars above the dancing couples, the vibrancy and excitement of that night preserved for generations with one shutter click.

I could stare at them for hours, these carefree, smiling faces, but Dad and Sofia are already walking back down the hallway, and there are other guests who want to look at the pictures, so I turn and follow them.

For the final leg of our tour, Sofia takes us through a promenade of shops selling everything from designer sunglasses, purses, jewelry, and clothing, to candy, baked goods, and children's beach toys. She finishes the tour with a peek into the hotel's restaurants and then a turn by the pool before taking us to the beach.

I leave Dad and Sofia behind on the concrete path as they finish discussing Dad's responsibilities. A cool breeze sweeps in on the crashing ocean waves, promising even colder water, but I don't care. I haven't had my feet in the ocean since the summer before seventh grade, when Dad took a temp job in the Outer Banks.

It's time to say hello again.

I slide off my flats, roll up my jeans, and let the sun-warmed sand push up between my toes as I make my way toward the tide line. The sun slips down the sky, painting the water in delicate, fiery brushstrokes. Down the beach from me, a mother holds her squealing daughter's hand as they wait for the water to return. The little girl sticks her other hand in her mouth and jumps up and down, trusting her mother to catch her if the tide tries to steal her away.

I stop at the water's edge, closing my eyes as I wait for the cold Atlantic to swallow my feet.

We're here now, Mom. We made it.

The water rushes over my skin, up my ankles, brushing over my calves and the rolled-up hem of my jeans.

Wish you were here.

My eyes burn, so I open them again and grit my teeth until the feeling fades. I turn my feet through the five basic positions, squaring my hips and straightening my spine as the water pulls away from me again. The familiarity of the positions centers me, forcing away the tears and bad thoughts and the reason we didn't fly here—the reason I'll never fly again—until it's almost like they were never there to begin with.

When I'm done, I turn my back on the horizon and try to fix my gaze on Dad and Sofia, but the magnitude of the hotel dominates my sightline, stealing the breath from my lungs. Everything else—every guest milling around the beach and the gardens and the patio, every bench and tree and sandcastle—fades away, so that all I see is a Victorian palace, its countless, gleaming windows watching me in the orange glow of a vanishing sun.

As per our moving day tradition, Dad and I order room service pizza for dinner, eating as we unpack. Most of our stuff is in a storage unit until we can find an apartment, and it isn't long before his suits are lined up on the left side of the closet. I stuff my jeans, T-shirts, hoodies, and dance clothes on the right side.

"You know," Dad says as I shove my empty suitcase into the back of the closet, "this may very well be the last time we move into a hotel room like this. I'm not planning on taking a job anywhere else."

"I know," I say. "Wasn't that always the plan? To work here until you die?"

"Well, maybe not until I *die*." Dad chuckles. "But certainly until I retire."

I close the closet door and grab my third slice of pizza.

Dad clears his throat. "I just wanted to make sure you knew that we aren't going anywhere this time. We're staying put for a while."

I sit cross-legged on the edge of my bed and stare at him, not exactly sure where he's going with this. "I know."

"So." He scratches his head. "So you don't have to feel like you need to keep your distance from people. You can actually make some friends here, get involved in the community. Maybe start thinking about your future, like where you want to go to college."

I ignore the first comment about making friends and focus on the one I have an answer for.

"I've already started thinking about it. I've done some research into local colleges and dance companies. Charleston actually has a really great reputation for ballet, and it's only thirty minutes away by ferry."

"That's wonderful," Dad says. He moves to the closet, hanging up his ties. "But there are a lot of respected companies across the country. I would hate to see you put all your eggs into one city's basket."

"We just got here and you're kicking me out already?" My voice is light and teasing, but his words feel like a betrayal.

Dad shakes his head. "Of course not, Nellie Bee. I just don't want you to feel like you have to plan your entire future around me. I'm really doing much better now."

If that's true, then that makes one of us.

"I just want to see you start putting yourself out there more," he continues. "You used to be so outgoing. Your mother and I were constantly trying to rein you in—" He pauses, and I know he's thinking of her, seeing her in some memory that belongs to him alone. "I guess what I'm trying to say is, you need to rejoin the world, sweet pea. It's time."

CHAPTER SEVEN

LEA

FOLLOWING A LONG LUNCH, DURING which Lon spoke of nothing but his business, and a tour of the grounds, during which Lon spoke of nothing but the countless summers he spent on Winslow Island throughout his life, I return to my room to dress for dinner and prepare myself to go through the same ordeal all over again.

Mother helps me change into an emerald, satin ball gown with a black-lace overlay, exchanging my day corset for an even tighter evening one. While most of our expensive belongings have been (discreetly) sold at auction, anything that could catch Lon's eye has remained. While Mother wears last season's gowns and Father clumsily repairs a rip in the seam of his tuxedo, I've brought along three trunks full of brand-new House of Worth dresses, even though I insisted they weren't necessary. Even though I'd rather Benny have gotten some birthday presents this year instead of budgeting all the money we had left toward keeping up appearances.

"We'll give Benny a hundred presents once you're married," Father told me one night after I'd confronted him about the ridiculous way he was choosing to spend our remaining finances. "*Two* hundred, if you'd like. But for now, *you* are what's important, so act like a normal girl and enjoy the extra attention, won't you?"

I only see Benny for a moment before Madeline whisks him away to take his dinner in the children's dining room—just long enough to learn he spent the afternoon on the beach, combing for seashells. He seems so happy here, his experience so different from my own.

Once Mother pulls my curls back into a fashionable updo (the only one in which her lady's maid had deemed her proficient before she'd been forced to leave for her new job) and Father has reassured both of us for the thousandth time that "It will all be worth it once Lon and Aurelea are married," we make our way to the dining room.

My parents take the elevator.

I take the stairs.

I pause at the second-floor gallery, wrapping my hands around the sturdy oak balustrade, and peer down into the lobby at the men in their tails and the women in their jewels, all congregating around potted palms as waiters in livery move around them carrying trays of champagne. I wonder, in a distant, doubtful sort of way, if the fall is high enough to kill.

Sighing, I turn and head for the staircase. My parents wait for me at the bottom, along with Lon and his parents.

"Oh, darling," Mother calls. "Look who we found."

"—dreadfully afraid of elevators, you know," I overhear Father explaining to Mr. and Mrs. Von Oirschot.

Lon offers me his arm. "Shall we go in?"

I place my hand on his arm and smile, though I don't actually say anything for fear that the words "Why? So, you can bore me with more of your insufferable stories?" will come flying off my tongue.

The dining room, which had been impressive in the middle of the day, is even more so beneath the full light of its electric lamps. The mahogany paneling on the walls drink in the amber glow, made even warmer by the darkness pressing in at the windows. The tables are covered in linens so pristinely white, they remind me of fresh Philadelphia snow. A string quartet stands on one of the balconies overlooking the room, playing us in to the notes of Debussy's "Rêverie."

Lon has taken the liberty of securing the same table for our two families for the entire summer, ensuring I will never be able to dine without him. It is a highly unwelcome surprise, although I suppose I'll have to become accustomed to sharing every meal with him eventually.

Everything is going as well as can be expected—the food is delicious, at least, and I can fake an interest in my future father-in-law's politicking with the best of them—until, suddenly, it isn't.

I pride myself on my ability to never show my true emotions, to never reveal how unbearably dull or self-important my present company is, but tonight, their arrogance and cruel wit suffocate me. The whole room feels stifling, filled to the brim with men and women wrapped up in their wealth and their power. They laugh and they snicker and they judge everything and everyone so that they themselves will appear above reproach. I'm ashamed to admit it was once my world, that I found myself just as self-important and influential as the lot of them, even though I'd never truly done anything remarkable with my life.

I'm not sure when the change occurred (sometime around the proposal, I think), but I've been finding it more and more difficult to act like I care about this world and these people—these walking, talking bank accounts who would turn judgmental, vehement eyes on me if they knew my true feelings. As if *I* were the joke here, and not them.

My head begins to ache and my muscles tighten as their conceited chortling and pompous comments echo through my ears. I can't seem to get enough air.

"Sweetheart," Mother whispers. "Are you well?"

"Not very," I reply.

The waiter sets down my fourth course, a filet of beef that sounded delicious a moment ago but the smell of which now turns my stomach. I stand abruptly, knocking my knee against the table.

All eyes turn to me.

"I'm so sorry," I fumble out. "I have a bit of a headache. All the travel, you know. Oh, please, don't get up." I wave all the men back down. "I just need to take a rest. Please, excuse me."

Father glares at me, but I don't have the strength to worry about the future repercussions of his anger, not when every ounce of my being is focused on putting one foot in front of the other. My breath comes in short, shallow gasps, and my chest suddenly feels as though it is caving in on my heart, but I keep a smile on my face, telling myself, *Just a little farther. Almost there.*

The lobby is nearly empty, but a few heads turn my way as I pass. My stomach sloshes, and my rings dig into my swollen fingers. I pick up my pace, my mind screaming at me to find a large open space where I can think, where I can *breathe*, before my panic swallows me whole.

CHAPTER EIGHT

NELL

I AM RUNNING DOWN THE fifth-floor corridors, my long cotton nightgown billowing behind me. A little boy with blond curls darts ahead of me, shouting over his shoulder, "You'll never catch me!"

I laugh. The sound bounces off the walls, high and tinkling. I follow him down hallway after hallway, through an endless maze lined with doors and small, attic-size windows, the pitch-black night pressing into the glass. Every time the little boy looks back at me, his eyes are a little brighter, his cheeks a little pinker, and my heart swells.

Even as I chase him, I know that this will come to an end soon. We can't do this forever. We will be ripped apart by circumstances beyond our control.

We will have to say goodbye.

But not tonight. Tonight, we are as young and free as baby birds, flying high above the world where no one will find us.

I round another corner. The boy is nowhere to be seen, but

a door in the middle of the hallway pulls shut. Smiling, I turn the knob and slip into the dark room. The door swings closed behind me, and the little boy giggles. My fingers splay across the wall, searching for a switch. I can hear the boy breathing behind me. My spine bumps into a metal coil dangling from the ceiling. I turn, clasp it in my fingers, and pull.

A single Edison bulb flashes above us.

The little boy stands in front of me, but he no longer looks young and vibrant. His blond curls are ashy and brittle, dead strands that look as if they would break with a single touch. The skin beneath his eyes is jet-black, and his rosy cheeks have turned into craters beneath his too-sharp bones. His lips are blue, the skin cracking as he speaks. Congealed, brown blood seeps through the fissures, lining his lips like railroad ties.

"It's happening again," he murmurs.

I press myself against the door, my heart hammering in my chest. "What is?"

"He's coming for you."

"Who's coming for me?" I ask. "What are you talking about?"

His spine creaks as he leans forward. And then, so softly I almost don't hear him, he whispers:

"Run."

———————————

I wake with a start.

I have no idea where I am.

Colorado?

A snore gurgles in the quiet, and it all comes rushing back to me. The valet desperately trying to hide his grimace at our car, the music emanating from the ballroom, the elevator, the dream.

I roll over and tap my phone.

3:01 a.m.

I try to lie back down, squishing the pillow around my head, but images from my nightmare flicker across my mind like an old movie reel. The dark closet. The little dead boy and that one word seeping through his bloodied lips.

Run.

Huffing, I slide out of bed, grab my key card from the bedside table and my backpack from the corner of the room, and head into the bathroom. I pull a pair of yoga pants, a tank top, and my worn ballet slippers out of my backpack. After changing into them, I throw my hair into a loose bun, then tiptoe through the room and out into the hallway, softly snicking the door closed behind me.

Walking through the hallways this early in the morning is like walking through a tomb. The silence has a presence, a heaviness that makes me feel anything but alone. Goose bumps prick my flesh, and I grit my teeth to keep from running as I pass closed door after closed door, the floor creaking beneath my weight. I take a wrong turn, ending up in a hallway with more doors instead of the back staircase.

The lights flicker off.

A cold wind whistles through the quiet, and the heaviness increases, as if someone is sharing the darkness with me.

Run.

A cold gasp of air tickles the back of my neck. My heart rams into my throat as I whirl around.

The lights flicker back on.

The hallway's empty.

I huff out a breath and mutter, "Stop being ridiculous."

I know the way to go; I'm just avoiding it.

Gritting my teeth, I turn around and head down two more hallways, marching through the exterior corridor overlooking the garden, painted silvery-blue in the waning moonlight, and then dart back inside the hotel.

The main staircase appears on my left, with the elevator cage next to it.

Tentatively, I reach out, curling my fingers through the decorative gold swirls, and peer down the shaft. The elevator sits at the bottom, where it has sat since the operator went home for the night.

"See?" I whisper around the knot in my throat. "Nothing to be afraid of."

A gear clanks. I jump back.

The elevator doesn't move.

Still, I keep to the far edge of the stairs, away from the cage, as I descend four flights to the lobby. One person stands behind the reception desk, but he's too busy laughing at something on his phone to pay me any attention. I sneak down the last staircase, cross the lobby, and, holding my breath, grip the handle to the ballroom.

The door opens.

I exhale and slip inside.

The room is dark, and it takes my eyes a moment to adjust to the dim light spilling in through the wall of windows on the other side of the room. I pad across the carpet, weaving around tables and chairs, and glance up at the long, curved ceiling, the chandeliers hovering above me like crystal ghosts in the darkness.

Reaching the dance floor, I pull my phone and earbuds out of my backpack and pick my favorite classical playlist. Then I begin my stretches, using the back of a chair as a makeshift barre as I run through the basic positions.

After Dad came home announcing his new job in South Carolina, my instructor in Colorado contacted the Charleston School of Ballet, explaining my financial need and setting up an audition for a possible scholarship in the fall, but all the teacher recommendations in the world won't help me if I don't stay in shape.

I try to pay attention to the time—the last thing I want is to get caught sneaking around in here again—but then the music swells, seeping through my pores, into every vein and valve and muscle fiber, until it's as if the melody is a part of me, the sole reason that my heart beats, and I forget all about watching the clock. My slippers swish across the hardwood floor and my mind clears, the world blurring around me as I spin.

Everything disappears when I dance. Nightmares. Creepy elevators. Weird general managers.

Mom.

Any thoughts or feelings at all, aside from thinking about the next move or feeling the rhythm of the music curving my bones. That's why I love it so much.

Dancing sets me free.

As the music ends, I dip into a low curtsy, placing my hand over my heart. And then, in the silent space between songs, a floorboard creaks.

I glance up.

The room is bathed in shadows and slices of moonlight.

"Hello?" I call, squinting into the darkness.

The door cracks open, cutting the shadows with a gold fissure. Someone steps into the light, his back to me.

The little boy from my dream.

No—it isn't him. This figure is tall and broad. A man. He steps through the door and into the lobby.

The man at the reception desk? Did he hear me dancing and come to investigate? How long was he watching me?

Although the logical part of my brain tells me that the man would've kicked me out if I wasn't allowed to be in here, the irrational part—the one that makes up nightmares about little dead boys and hallways that never end—takes over. I wrench out my earbuds, grab my backpack, and weave through the tables to the door.

The lobby is still empty, save for the man behind the reception desk, who's now reading the paper. If it was him watching me, he doesn't seem overly concerned about it.

That's because he doesn't care.

Still, something about it feels off to me. It isn't until I get back to my room that I realize why.

The man who slipped out of the ballroom wore a white shirt, the lamplight bleeding amber-gold through the fabric.

The receptionist's uniform is black.

CHAPTER NINE

LEA

I RUN OUT ONTO THE beach, my head pounding, my stomach pitching. The moon is full, painting the sand silver in its brilliance. Farther down the beach, the striped tents of Canvas City glow beneath streetlamps as far as I can see. Bonfires and electric bulbs fight the moon's light, gold sparks against silver rays, but on the hotel's stretch of beach, there is no one. Just me, the blue-black waves, and the oxygen filling my starving lungs.

The ocean looks so cool, so heavenly, and I am still in such a state of panic, I do not think about the sand that will cling to my dress as I walk to the edge of the surf and lie down by the water. I suddenly feel very tired and want nothing more than to fall asleep here, at the edge of the ocean, and put my life entirely in the water's hands.

I find myself doing this more and more lately—placing my life in the hands of a greater, more powerful force. Bartering my remaining heartbeats against the belief that there *is* a bigger plan for me, one I don't know or fully understand. If I am meant to be taken by the sea, then the sea will have me, and oh, I cannot think of a more peaceful way to drift into oblivion.

The cold, crisp water rushes up my calves, tickling the backs of my knees through my gown. I let out a breath, close my eyes—

And wait.

I wake to the sound of footsteps rushing toward me and a man's voice calling out, "Miss? Miss!"

I keep my eyes closed, thinking, *Oh, Great and Powerful Sea, if you plan to take me, please do so now, before it is too late.* It feels rather melodramatic, but sometimes circumstances call for such things.

Sand kicks onto my face as the man crouches next to me. I squeeze my eyes shut tighter against the grains. Fingers thread through my hair as he props my head on his lap. His hands circle my neck.

My eyes fly open.

"*What are you doing?*"

The man jerks back. "I was checking for a pulse. I thought you were hurt."

I push away from him. "I'm fine."

"Why didn't you say anything when I called?"

"I didn't hear you."

He looks like he's about to say something, but then he cocks his head, studying me. "I know you."

My brow arches.

"Your family checked into the hotel today. The Sargents."

I squint up at him, the moonlight edging his face in silver.

My eyes widen.

"And you're the bellboy who isn't really a bellboy."

"At your service," he says, breathless.

"Do you have a habit of accosting young women on beaches, Mr. Petrov?"

His jaws drops. "I wasn't *accosting* you. I thought you were dead!"

"If only," I say, but the words are faint, intangible, and drowned out by the crashing surf.

"What are you doing out here?" he asks.

I lie back against the sand once more and tuck my hands behind my head. My legs are icicles, my stockings damp from the surf and clinging to my skin, but I like the way it feels. The numbness of it.

"Being still," I say.

A beat passes.

"Do you want to be still with me?"

He opens his mouth.

Hesitates.

And then, with a sigh, lowers himself to the sand, lying down next to me.

"You might want to roll up your pants," I murmur as the waves rush to meet us.

He sits up, just barely pulling his pants above his knees before the water crashes over our legs. "Holy Mother of God, that's cold!"

I laugh and wonder how it is that I have met this boy twice now, and both times he has made me smile when I thought my whole world was crashing down around me.

"Please, forgive my profanity," he says through chattering teeth.

"I like your profanity," I tell him. "If you ask me, no one in my life has enough of it."

"Then will you also forgive me for saying that you, Miss Sargent, are one odd duck?"

"Only if you do not mean it as an insult."

"I don't."

"Then I won't take it as one." I stare up at the sky, breathing in the night air. "Aren't they beautiful?"

"The stars?"

"No, the rocks," I tease. "*Yes*, the stars."

"I used to think so."

"You don't anymore?"

He doesn't reply. The waves push against our feet, cascading higher this time, licking my hips. Then the words spill out of his mouth like hornets, fast and prickly. "My father died a few months ago. Influenza."

I close my eyes. "I'm sorry."

We don't speak for a while, the silence broken only by the rumble of the surf and the hush of the wind.

Finally, I say, "Lea."

"What?"

I tilt my head to meet his gaze. "My name. It's Aurelea, actually, but I prefer Lea."

"Lea it is," he says.

I take a deep breath and exhale as I sit up. "I should get back before my parents discover I'm not where I'm supposed to be."

"Would you like an escort back?" he asks.

"Now that *would* incite gossip," I say as I stand, brush the sand from my dress, and try to tame my unruly hair.

"Right." He stands and slaps the sand off his pants. "Of course. I should have realized."

I smile. "Thank you for being still with me."

And with that, I sweep around and half walk, half run back to the Grand. I don't know what I will find there, but it no longer matters. I had once again tested my mortality and found myself feeling more alive than ever.

At least for those few moments, I was not a woman trapped. I was a woman free, and I loved every fleeting second of it.

CHAPTER TEN

NELL

"SO I'VE BEEN THINKING ABOUT what you said last night," I say, pulling the wrapper off my blueberry muffin.

Dad pauses in spreading cream cheese on his bagel. It's still early, just a little after seven, and our breakfasts are hot from the bakery. We sit at a table overlooking the outdoor patio and the beach beyond, where white-capped waves pound the sand and swollen blue-gray clouds threaten rain.

"Which part?" he asks.

"The part about making new friends. Getting more involved. I was thinking I could get a job here."

"A job?"

"I thought it'd be a good way to meet people," I lie.

I have no interest in meeting people, or in making friends like Dad says I should, but I can't tell him I'm doing it for the money. We never have much to spare, and I have no idea how much of the tuition the ballet scholarship will cover, assuming the school even picks me for it in the first place. Dad's all for me working if it means making new friends or learning how to be a responsible adult—the typical parenty-type stuff—but he hates that there are things in this world he can't afford, things like ballet lessons at the most prestigious schools and a car to get me to said lessons.

I once reminded him that we didn't have a lot of money even when Mom was alive. Kindergarten teachers don't make nearly as much as they should, and Dad was still fairly low on the hospitality totem pole back then, but we got by. He said it made him feel better, but I could tell it made him feel worse.

I never brought up the issue of money again.

Dad finishes slathering on the cream cheese and takes a bite, thinking. Outside, the wind tears at the palm trees, and my nightmare-induced paranoia has me wondering if the incoming storm is some kind of omen.

"A summer job," Dad says finally, "sounds like an excellent idea." He checks his watch. "I've got a little time yet before I have to be in the office. Why don't we find Sofia and see if there are any positions available?"

I exhale. "Sounds great."

A flash of white leaps across the table as the first crack of lightning splits the sky.

Sofia's office looks like the gift shop threw up on it.

The built-in bookshelves behind her desk are loaded with Winslow Grand posters, travel brochures, and postcards—some new, some really old. Scattered among them are a variety of Grand memorabilia, from vintage Christmas ornaments hanging inside decorative glass boxes to coffee mugs, tea sets, and hand towels. A series of art deco paintings and black-and-white photographs of the Grand line the walls.

"That one's from right around the time the hotel first opened," Sofia says, catching me inspecting one of the pictures. It's an exterior shot of the Grand, taken from far enough away to capture nearly two sides of the behemoth structure, including a familiar decorative balcony outside a row of guest rooms. "See how there aren't nearly as many trees? A lot of them hadn't even been planted yet."

She stares at me like she's expecting a specific response, but I can't think of anything to say other than "Yeah. Crazy."

Her lips tilt into the same appraising smile she gave me yesterday, and I can't help but feel like I'm failing some kind of test.

Dad gapes at a frame on Sofia's desk. "Is this an actual menu from Eisenhower's visit?"

Sofia turns to him, and I feel like I can breathe again.

"It is," she says.

"Quite the collector's piece."

Sofia chuckles. "Well, I like to think I'm quite the collector."

Dad laughs, but it isn't his usual friendly laugh, the one he hands out to people like business cards. It's the adoring laugh—the one he reserved just for Mom. Sofia lays her left hand on Dad's arm, and I check the ring finger.

Clean. Not even a tan line from a missing ring.

"So what brings you by my office this morning, Oscar?" she asks, settling herself in the chair behind her desk and wrapping her ringless hand around a steaming mug of coffee.

Dad takes one of the seats in front of the desk. I gape at Sofia's overly familiar use of Dad's first name and stare at her hand a second longer, then sit down, my fingernails curling into my palms.

A few fat raindrops *plink* against the windows as thunder rumbles in the distance.

"Nell's interested in a summer job here at the hotel," Dad

explains. "So we thought we'd pop by to see if you have any available."

"Well, then, let me see what I can find." Sofia slides the tortoiseshell glasses hanging around her neck onto her nose and turns to her computer. "Do you have any previous work experience?"

"Some part-time waitressing last summer," I say.

I don't tell her it was at a twelve-table diner where excellence was defined by the crispness of the french fries, not the quality of the service, and the "homemade" apple pie was actually of the frozen, store-bought variety. Somehow, I don't think that kind of experience will help me here.

Sofia *tsks* her tongue against her teeth. "I don't see any serving jobs available right now."

Thank God.

"Actually . . ." Sofia glances at me sidelong. "How do you feel about working on a special project?"

"What kind of special project?"

"The hotel is working with a local historian to put together a museum featuring old photographs, ledgers, papers—even furniture, like the pieces you saw on the tour. Think the Wall of History, only much bigger. A completely immersive experience for our guests, in which they'll walk through each decade of the hotel's existence, starting with the opening in 1879 and continuing on through present day."

"Like walking through time," Dad marvels.

Sofia smiles. "Exactly."

They stare at each other for a moment, beaming.

I clear my throat. "So what's the job?"

"My son, Max, is cleaning out our storage room, organizing everything the historian needs to start putting the project together, but it's quite a big room, and it's taking him longer than

I thought it would. I can offer you the same amount of money I'm offering him—five hundred dollars upon completion of the project." She takes a sip of her coffee, eyeing me over the rim. "So what do you think?"

I glance at Dad.

"Sounds like a great experience, going through all that history," he says. "Frankly, I'm kind of jealous."

"Me, too," Sofia says. "I'd do it in a heartbeat if I had the time."

It wasn't what I was expecting, but it sounds pretty simple, and the money's more than fair, especially since I can't imagine it taking longer than two or three weeks, tops, which means there'll still be plenty of time left over to find another job and make even more money before the summer ends.

"All right," I say. "I'm in."

CHAPTER ELEVEN

LEA

I WAKE TO SUNSHINE STREAMING across my face, and I nuzzle into its warmth.

Last night's gown hangs in the armoire, meticulously swept free of sand, and my stockings are draped on the back of a chair to dry. Not for the first time since Father lost the majority of his fortune in a bad business deal, I am thankful for the privacy being without a lady's maid has afforded me. There is no one to spy on me—no one who feigns loyalty but really lives in my father's pocketbook.

I'd come up with an excuse for my parents last night as I walked through the near-empty lobby and deserted hallways, should they discover I hadn't returned to our suite as I said I would. I would tell them the truth. Or, at least, most of it—that I had needed fresh air and went for a walk around the grounds. They did not need to know I had spent time alone with a hotel employee. And if it appeared my parents had been waiting for me for a longer period of time than that excuse covered, I would add that I had gotten lost on my way back—which I almost did, anyway, so it wouldn't have been a complete lie. The hotel is so large, with so many twisting, turning hallways, that I ended up at the end of one before realizing the room numbers did not match up with where I thought I was.

How I planned on explaining the dampness of my skirt or the sand clinging to my stockings, I have no idea. Perhaps I'd hoped for a miracle of momentary blindness on my parents' part.

Luckily, an excuse was not needed. My parents were still out—Father no doubt drinking brandy with the men, while Mother took her after-dinner coffee with the ladies—and Madeline and Benny were fast asleep when I returned. I had enough time to not only change into my nightgown and robe but to clean all evidence of the beach from my gown and body before slipping into bed.

Now, I dig my face into my pillow as I stretch. With a groan, I push myself out of bed and change into a white muslin dress with a blue satin ribbon, hiding my ocean-scented stockings beneath my skirts. I pull my hair back into a simple updo, setting it with blue dragonfly pins that wink in the morning light and remind me, instantly, of Alec.

I smile as I think of him calling me an "odd duck." If he only knew half the thoughts that run through my mind on any given day.

Mother has ordered breakfast to our room. Silver trays piled high with croissants, hotcakes, eggs, bacon, sausage, and pineapple sit atop a table dressed in white linen. Mother is busy reading the society page, so I sneak into Benny's room to wake him, but both his and Madeline's beds are already turned down, and the only form of life in the room is the candle in Benny's light box, burned down to a stub. Shaking my head, I cross the room and blow it out. The Grand has a strict policy on open flames, what with the entire hotel being made of wood and all, but Benny can't sleep without the moons and stars that emanate from his little toy box, and Mother has always been the type to think the rules never apply to "our kind" anyway.

"Madeline has taken Benny down to the beach for an early morning swim," Mother says as I close Benny's door behind me, "and your father is playing tennis with Mr. Van Oirschot. So, since I did not know how you would be feeling this morning, I thought we could share a quiet breakfast together."

I take the seat across from her and dig into the hotcakes, careful to hide the pleasure I feel at the prospect of not having to share a meal with Lon.

"Do you think you would be up for a stroll after breakfast?" Mother asks.

"Won't Lon be looking for me?"

"Oh no," she says. "He's in Charleston all day on business. He told us last night after you left. But he promised he would be back in time to escort you to the ball tonight."

I cannot hide my smile at this news. An entire day without Lon and then a night spent dancing, in which it would be very difficult for him to speak at all? Instead of a miracle of momentary blindness, I've been granted a miracle of momentary solitude.

Thankfully, Mother misunderstands the source of my joy.

"Ah, see?" she says. "I knew that would make you happy."

CHAPTER TWELVE

NELL

SOFIA LEADS ME DOWN TO the basement, which I'm surprised to see has been renovated to accommodate several offices, with a marble tile floor, polished mahogany walls, and antique sconces emitting the same soft, amber-gold light as the rest of the hotel. Sofia notices me staring and chuckles.

"Not what you were expecting?" she asks.

"Not exactly."

I've seen my fair share of hotel basements, and the ones that are this old usually look like giant, creepy cellars, with cobwebs in the corners and a graveyard full of old papers and furniture. Even the modern ones usually look more like school cafeterias, with harsh, fluorescent lighting and poured cement floors.

"There's actually a walkout to the beach down here, as well as access to the front drive," Sofia explains as I follow her off the staircase. "We're in the planning stages of making this a main thoroughfare and adding a few more restaurants and shops down here. Budgeting the project has been my personal baby this past year, and I just got word that we'll be breaking ground on it next spring."

"Wow. Congratulations."

"Thank you. I'm sorry to say the storage room doesn't look as nice as this, though." She stops in front of a door and turns back to me. "Ready?"

She sounds like she's sending me off to a war zone instead of into an old storage room.

"Uh . . . yes?"

She smiles apologetically and opens the door.

At first, all I see is the single Edison-style light bulb hanging over the dark room, jolting me back to the linen closet in my dream. But then the weathered stone walls come into focus, along with the stacks upon stacks of ledgers, albums, dusty furniture, and beat-up boxes overwhelming the room. Two rows of metal shelving units along the far wall hold even more containers and old knickknacks, including a broken typewriter and stacks of old dining plates.

"Max?" Sofia calls out. "I brought help."

A shadow moves behind one of the shelves. A pair of Converse sneakers appears through an empty space on the bottom shelf, and then the boy attached to them rounds the corner. He's got a real Peace Corps–meets–James Dean kind of vibe, with an army-green shirt, slim-fit jeans, black boots, thick glasses, and mussed-up hair. He gives me a crooked half smile as soon as he sees me.

"New blood?" the boy asks.

"Nell, this is my son, Max," Sofia says. "Max, this is Nell Martin. She's going to be helping you organize this mess." She turns back to me. "Ignore him if he gets too charming. It's a nervous tic."

Max shakes his head. "Gee, thanks, Mom."

"Anytime, sweetheart," Sofia replies. "Go ahead and show Nell what you've done so far and see if you two can't come up with a system that'll make the work go faster."

"Aye, aye, Captain."

"All right, then. I'll leave you to it."

Sofia waves and closes the door behind her.

"So," Max says, "you're the girl who lives in the hotel?"

"Excuse me?"

"Mom was telling me about you last night. And your dad, too, of course."

"She was?"

He nods.

I don't know how I feel about Sofia talking about us like that. Not because I think she was saying anything bad, but because I'm worried that everything she was saying was good. As in, *very* good. As in, I-think-I-met-your-new-stepdad-today good.

"How are you liking it?" Max asks.

I think of the elevator, and the nightmare, and how that blueberry muffin this morning was almost worth being terrified of my own shadow. "It's . . . nice."

He nods. "I wanted to live here when I was a kid. I spent almost every day after school in this place."

"Doing what?"

"Oh, you know. A little of this, a little of that." His smile widens. "So you're in high school, right?"

"Yep."

"Junior? Senior?"

"Going to be a senior," I say. "You?"

"Same. Maybe we'll have a few classes together."

"Yeah, maybe."

"Want some water?" he asks. "I brought an extra."

"Uh, sure. Thanks."

He rummages through a green army satchel on the floor, pulls out an unopened bottle, and hands it to me.

"So the job is pretty straightforward," he says, taking a swig from his own bottle. "I've been going through everything in here and organizing it into five different piles: loose papers, books, pictures, artifacts—that'll be anything small, like eyeglasses, tea-cups, jewelry, that sort of thing—and trash. At the end of the day we take everything we've organized up to the front desk in those boxes over there"—he waves at a teetering stack of cardboard next to the door—"and the historian picks them up. Except the trash, obviously. That goes in the dumpster."

"So . . . that's it? We don't have to organize it anymore than that?"

"That's it."

I want to ask him why it's taken him so long to finish, but I don't want to be a brat, so I take a drink and try to think of something else to say instead.

My eyes lock on a Teddy Roosevelt biography peeking out of his satchel.

"So . . . you like history?" I ask, gesturing to the book.

"Love it," he says. "I'm planning on double majoring in college. History and screenwriting. I hold a very deep convic-tion that visual media is the best way to preserve history for the masses, or at least make it interesting to them again." He twists the cap back on his bottle and stuffs it into his back pocket. "That's actually why I was so stoked when my mom told me about this project. I've been working on this screenplay about the Grand for a while now, but I keep getting stuck. I thought getting up close and personal with some primary sources would jog a few plot ideas loose."

"Any luck?" I ask.

"Not yet, but there's always hope, right?"

"That's what they tell me."

———————————

I have no intention of staying in the storage room all day, breathing in the dust and decay of past generations, but as I flip through dry, crackling papers and stumble across old photographs and random objects—weathered billfolds and paper fans and vintage earrings—I find myself becoming consumed by these worlds that existed long ago. Hours melt into minutes, and minutes vanish into seconds. It's almost like Max and I have entered a space where the detritus of time has washed ashore, burying the passing hours in the debris so that time no longer feels linear or even makes any sense at all.

Even Max, who I thought for sure was going to ask me a million questions about my life as we worked, barely utters two words to me until his phone buzzes with a reminder for lunch. We each grab a sandwich from the café. Max offers to let me go for the rest of the day, but it's still raining, so it's not like I'm missing out on a great beach day or anything, and my feet start back toward the basement before my lips can even form an answer.

At four o'clock, Max takes the first box up to the lobby while I start packing up a second.

"Careful out there," Max tells me when he returns. "Floor's wet."

I finish packing the box and hoist it up, leaning back and propping it against my stomach. The ledgers reach so high, I can barely see over them. I shift the box's weight to my right hip and lean my head to the left as I slide through the open door and into the basement hallway.

I make it up the stairs to the first floor by keeping to the right-hand side of the wall. The hall twists and turns in a serpentine labyrinth in front of me as I weave through the crowd of shoppers perusing window displays, my pace slow as my feet navigate the slick, rain-dampened floors.

I'm too busy watching a group of kids running for the toy store to notice the puddle beneath my feet, and by the time I do, it's too late.

My heel skids across the floor and I let out a small shriek as the box slams into something hard. The wall? No, walls don't make "oomph" noises. The ledgers shoot up, their leather covers and the yellowing pages inside them flapping like chickens trying to fly. The box drops from my hands, and someone reaches out, their hands circling my arms, trying to steady me, but our limbs tangle together, and we both fall. One of their hands cups the back of my head, pulling my face to their chest. The clean scent of sandalwood, lemon blossoms, and fresh linen envelops me a second before the person lands on top of me. The hand holding my skull cracks against the floor.

Time slows.

I feel nothing but the splaying of fingers in my hair, the soft fibers of a shirt against my cheek, the careful weight of someone's body on top of mine. I hear nothing but the jagged edges of our breathing and the echoing thuds of ledgers smacking the floor.

And then I look up.

His eyes, ringed in thick lashes and framed by straight, dark hair that hangs over us like a curtain, blocking out the rest of the world, widen in shock. His lips part, and his arms tighten around me. My gaze roams his face, over his sharp cheekbones and square jaw, stopping on a small dimple in his chin. I frown at that dimple, and at the sudden, overwhelming urge to run my fingers across it.

I must have a concussion.

"Are you okay?" he asks.

I take a deep breath. "I think so."

His arms harden into stone around me. The worry lines crinkling his eyes disappear, and his gaze turns cold.

"Watch where you're going next time," he growls.

I'm so taken aback that I don't say anything as he pulls me up. Slowly, as if coming out of a trance, my brain registers several things at once. A dry mop lying on the floor—the edge of a gold name tag on my rescuer's shirt—the puddle that took me out, which he must have been mopping up. Which would make him a . . . what? Janitor? He doesn't look much older than me, maybe eighteen, and I wonder why an eighteen-year-old boy would choose a janitorial job over something more glamorous, especially when said boy looks like a Calvin Klein model.

And then my brain registers the fact that he's gathering up the ledgers and stuffing them back into the box while I'm just standing there, gawking at him.

"You don't have to do that," I say suddenly, crouching down next to him.

He grabs the last ledger and slams it on top of the others.

"It's already done," he says, picking up his mop and heading for the lobby.

"Thanks for the help," I bite back, an edge to my voice that sounds nothing like gratitude.

I have no idea if he hears me. He just keeps walking, rounding the corner and disappearing out of sight.

"Jerk," I murmur under my breath.

I wait a few more seconds, just to lessen my chances of running into him again, then pick up the box, my arms shaking under its weight, and head for reception.

CHAPTER THIRTEEN

LEA

AFTER TAKING A TURN AROUND the hotel's first floor, passing the ladies' billiards room, the library, and the chess room, Mother stops at the reception desk to ask after the hotel's Monday afternoon bridge club. I wander toward the doors leading to the interior courtyard, my gaze sweeping over the various fruit trees and tropical plants, stopping on a hotel worker planting a lemon tree. He wears brown corduroy pants and suspenders over a white shirt that sticks to his broad, muscular back. He sweeps his forearm over his brow, pushing back his hair—

Alec.

My heart speeds up. I glance back at Mother, but she's surrounded by a group of women now and not paying me the slightest attention. I take a deep breath and walk through the open doors.

"Another one of your many occupations, Mr. Petrov?" I ask.

Alec glances at me. "I am a man of many talents, Miss Sargent."

"I can see that."

He sets down his shovel and smacks his dirt-stained hands against his pants. A bead of sweat rolls down his neck to the pit of his collarbone, disappearing beneath his shirt. My eyes try to follow it instinctively, and I am surprised to find I can detect the hard ridges of his stomach muscles beneath the thin, damp fabric.

My cheeks warm.

"Did you make it back to your room undetected?" he asks, lowering his voice.

Even though I know we did nothing wrong—not *really*, anyway—the question makes our time together sound so much more indecent than it actually was, especially if overheard by someone out of context. I turn my head, searching for anyone within earshot.

"We're alone," he says.

He's closer now, his breath warm against my neck. A tiny, indescribable thrill shoots through me at the vibration of his voice against my skin.

"Yes," I say. "Our secret's safe."

His eyes twinkle at that. "Good."

"Why? Do you want to do it again?" I ask, only half teasing.

This takes him by surprise. He inhales roughly and surveys the courtyard once more, but there is no one hiding among the trees and no guests watching from above. He swallows. "Actually . . ."

"Yes?"

"Never mind."

"Don't be silly," I say. "What is it?"

He studies me. "My friends and I are going dancing in Canvas City tonight." His breathing, rough from the work and the heat, shakes slightly as he speaks. "Would you want to go?"

"With you?"

"And my friends," he clarifies. "We wouldn't be alone, so it wouldn't be improper."

"Except for the fact that I would need to sneak out of my room and lie to my parents to do it."

He winces. "Right. Of course. I shouldn't have asked—"

I lay a hand on his arm to stop him, realizing too late how inappropriate it is.

I quickly snatch it back. "What time?"

"After the ball," he says. "I'm working as a footman tonight."

Of course he is. Is there a single job in this hotel he doesn't do?

"That's perfect, actually, seeing as how I'm supposed to be attending the ball."

His eyes widen. "Are you saying you'll go?"

I don't know what I'm thinking; perhaps I'm not thinking at all. Lying to my parents last night was risky enough, when I was still on hotel property. Now I'm actually considering not only lying to them, but sneaking out in the middle of the night. If I get caught . . . I don't even want to think about the punishment that would follow.

But if I don't take every opportunity to make my own choices now, while I still have the chance, I know I will regret it for the rest of my life.

"Yes," I say, the word shooting from my lips the moment my brain pulls the trigger. "I'll go."

"Aurelea?" Mother's voice calls across the courtyard.

I wink at him, then turn and head back into the lobby.

"What were you doing out there?" Mother asks, taking my arm and leading me toward the staircase.

"I saw that worker planting a new tree," I reply. "I wanted to see what kind it was."

She squints out the window. "Looks like a lemon tree to me."

I chance one more look at Alec.

He's still watching me, his shovel lying forgotten at his feet.

CHAPTER FOURTEEN

NELL

MAX IS HALFWAY THROUGH PACKING another box when I return. He glances up at the sound of the door shutting.

"What took you so long?"

I roll my eyes. "You will not believe what just happened to me."

"You tripped?"

I glare at him.

He throws up his hands. "Don't look at me like that. I told you the floor was wet!"

"It's not that I tripped," I grind out. "It's that I tripped *into* someone who wasn't very nice about it."

He cringes. "A guest?"

"No. A janitor. At least, I think he was a janitor. He was mopping up the floor."

"Let me guess," Max says. "Tall, dark hair, scowly kind of face, maybe a year or two older than us?"

"Yeah. How'd you know?"

"You met Petrov."

"Who?"

"Alec Petrov," he explains. "He lives here in the hotel, like you and your dad."

Weird. Wouldn't Sofia have mentioned someone else living in the hotel?

"And he's not a janitor so much as a do-everything kind of guy," Max continues. "Mostly, he gardens and fixes things. Sometimes he'll fill in as a waiter or a cook if someone calls in sick and they can't find a replacement."

"So he doesn't have one specific job?"

"Not that I know of."

"Do his parents work here, too?"

"If they do, I've never met them. I've asked my mom about it before, but she just says other people's personal lives are none of my business. Never mind she's asking us to go through the personal property of a bunch of dead people *specifically* so that she can put them on display." He shakes his head. "Talk about hypocrisy at its finest. Hey, hand me that old diary, would you?"

———————————

After dropping off the last boxes of the day, Max and I head for the first-floor offices.

"Favorite movie?" Max asks me.

"That's easy," I reply. "*Center Stage*."

"Excuse me?"

"You know, the ballet movie? It's what made me want to be a ballerina."

"Well, I can't really knock it then, can I? And it does have a solid arc, at least."

"You've seen it?"

"I've seen everything," he says, his hands curling around the satchel strap crossing his chest. "So you're a ballerina?"

"Yep. Or at least trying to be."

"Is that what you want to go to school for?"

"That's the plan."

"Very cool. Maybe we can make a ballet movie together someday, when we're both rich and famous."

"We could," I say, "but there's no way you can top my favorite."

"Watch me." Max stops next to my dad's office. "So will I see you tomorrow?"

"Yeah, I'll be there."

"Okay, great!" He clears his throat. "That's, uh . . . great. I thought maybe you were bored out of your mind. I know most people would be."

"No," I say. "I actually thought it was pretty cool."

"That's awesome. I mean, I know Mom will be happy to hear it. She's been on my back about finding someone to help for weeks, but none of my friends were interested." He tilts his head and gives me the dopiest-looking smile. "Well, anyway. See you tomorrow."

"See ya."

He turns on his heel and heads back the way we came, toward his mom's office.

I shake my head and laugh a little at his geeky, adorable enthusiasm, then turn and knock on Dad's half-open door.

Dad sits at his desk, typing something on his computer.

"Hey, Nellie Bee! How was your first day of work?"

I plop down in one of the chairs across from him. "Good," I say, even though what I want to say is *I met one really nice guy and one jackass who apparently doesn't know the meaning of the word* accident. "Busy. How was yours?"

He grins. "Good. Busy."

"Are you almost done?"

"I've got a couple more things to finish up, but what do you say we get some dinner in about an hour?"

"Sounds good."

He turns back to his computer.

"Hey, Dad? You're really happy here, aren't you?"

He takes a deep breath and nods. "Happier than I've been in a long time, kiddo."

That's all I need to hear. His happiness is worth dealing with nightmares and a cocky janitor. And besides, it's not like I haven't found things to like about the Grand in the past two days.

Kickass bakery. Awesome job. Max.

Things could be worse.

I fish my key card out of my pocket and open the door to our room. It's quiet, almost eerily so, and for the first time I realize I haven't heard the telltale signs of any other guests around us. No TV mumbling through the walls, no drawers banging shut, no conversations carrying on in the hall. Which means either the room adjacent to ours isn't occupied, or nineteenth-century construction is way more soundproof than I would have thought.

I head into the bathroom, turn the shower to hot, and peel off my dust-caked clothes. The mirror fogs, so I open the tiny window near the ceiling, since our room is too high up for anyone other than the birds tiptoeing across the green copper roof to see me.

I step into the shower, rolling the kinks out of my neck and inhaling the steam as the water beats against my sore muscles. I close my eyes and hum to myself, a familiar melody. It takes me a moment to even remember where I heard the song recently, and then the answer comes to me.

The ballroom. Pumping through those insanely well-hidden speakers.

A floorboard creaks on the other side of the shower curtain.

"Dad?"

No answer.

I draw the edge of the curtain back with my fingertips. A fog of steam blurs the vanity and the outline of the door, but I can see enough to know there's no one in here with me. I frown before remembering the open window.

A gust of wind must have rattled the shutters.

Still, I finish up quickly. It's possible the creak came from Dad on the other side of the door, and I don't want to make him wait too long to get a bite to eat. I turn off the water, grab my towel from the shower rod, and pat my skin dry before wrapping it around myself and swiping the curtain aside.

I scream.

Every single drawer underneath the sink has been wrenched open, hanging haphazardly on their hinges, as if someone was looking for something and didn't have time to close them.

Dad?

I glance at the door—

It's locked from the inside, but I don't remember locking it.

Which *should* mean the person who did this is still in the bathroom with me—the window's too small for anyone to climb through and too high up for anyone to reach—but there's no one.

I'm alone.

My eyes lock on the mirror. Letters are scribbled in the fog, condensation dripping down the glass.

Heart hammering, I jump out of the shower, flip the lock, and open the door. The steam coils out of the room at the sudden burst of fresh air. I glance back at the mirror, knowing it was just my imagination, that my name won't be written on the glass.

The fog is starting to bleed away, so that only the tops of the letters are visible, but it's still there.

Nell.

And then that disappears, too.

CHAPTER FIFTEEN

LEA

THE BALLROOM IS PACKED.

Men in tuxedos and women in ball gowns that sparkle like stardust beneath the chandelier's warm, golden glow twirl to a musical compilation of Wagner, Strauss, and Mendelssohn. I am thankful for my full dance card, on which Lon has only been able to procure three dances. An improper amount, really, if we weren't engaged, making me miss the days when he was merely courting me.

I pick Alec out from the crowd almost immediately. He is positioned against the far wall, holding a tray of champagne flutes and looking marvelously handsome in his uniform and white gloves. I watch him over the shoulders of my dance partners.

Sometimes I feel brave and shoot him a grin or a wink, and sometimes I am so taken by his handsomeness, by the intensity in his gaze as he watches me back, that I can do nothing but stare and count the minutes until I can leave.

At half past eleven, I complain of a headache from the

champagne and inform Lon I will need to take my leave early. Mother looks worried—it isn't like me to leave a party before midnight, especially not one in which my dance card is full. I give her a reassuring pat on the arm before making my escape. She's been such a worrier since Father lost more than half of his clients, and guilt burns like a hot coal in my stomach, but each step I take away from the ballroom suffocates it a little more, until it is a flickering pile of ash beneath my excitement.

Once again, Ben and Madeline are already asleep when I return to our suite.

I change into a simple navy skirt and white blouse, then take my hair down from its expensive comb and braid it, tying it with a ribbon that matches my skirt. Finally, I place my pillows beneath my blankets in the rough shape of a sleeping body and turn out the light to inspect my work. The glow of moonlight pouring through my curtains bathes the bed in silver-lined shadows that only add to the farce. As long as my parents don't look too closely, I am certain they will not be able to tell the difference.

By the time I get to the beach, the moon is hidden by a dark cloud, its pale light outlining the puffy ridges, and it takes a moment for my eyes to adjust to the darkness. At first I don't see Alec, and fear grips me. Could he not get away? Or was it all a joke? Is he now laughing with his friends over the stupid rich girl who thought she had actually found a friend in him?

But then the cloud moves, bathing the beach in the moon's glow, and I see him sitting on the rocks. He's changed from his footman uniform into the corduroy pants and suspenders he wore in the garden, pairing them with a blue chambray shirt. He hasn't seen me yet, and I wonder if the same questions are running through his mind. If he thinks maybe I am off somewhere having a laugh at his expense.

I step out of the shadows.

His entire body relaxes at the sight of me.

"Part of me didn't think you were coming," he says as I draw near.

"Part of me thought the same of you," I admit.

He jumps off the rock and offers me his arm. I take it, surprised at how different it feels from the countless other arms I've taken over the years. Wider and firm with muscle—not the kind of muscle a gentleman procures from a round of golf, but the kind a man gets from working hard for a living.

"So," he says. "Are you ready to see Canvas City?"

CHAPTER SIXTEEN

NELL

MOM LEANS OVER MY BED, tucking the covers around me. She smells of roses and lilacs, of summertime and moist garden earth.

"Just three days," she says, "and I'll be back."

The faint traces of moonlight spilling through the plantation shutters spotlight the suitcase next to our hotel-room door. Dad snores in the other bed, and it startles me.

He shouldn't be here.

I'm twelve years old and in my own bedroom.

But when I look up, expecting to see shelves draped in dance trophies and team photos and feather boas, I see only a stretch of white. To the right of my bed, where my computer and textbooks should be sitting on a turquoise desk, is a bank of long windows with plantation shutters, overlooking a balcony that is just for show, and tree branches that slap the windowpanes.

And then I remember.

I'm not in my bedroom in Colorado because I'm in a hotel

room on Winslow Island. Because Dad's working here now. But the other person who's supposed to be here, the third person who made up the tripod that was our family, isn't here with us because she left for a teaching conference and never came home.

"Mom—"

She kisses my forehead. "I'll try to come back early if I can."

I fight against the sheets, but they cling to my skin, tightening against the bed, holding me down. "Mom, don't go—"

"It's my job." She gives me a sad, knowing smile. "I have to go."

"No." The sheets dig like ropes into my skin, flattening me against the mattress. "You have to listen to me—"

But she pulls away just like she did that night. Like this isn't goodbye forever.

"Sweet dreams, Nellie Bee."

"Mom!"

She grabs her suitcase.

"Don't!" I thrash against the sheets, but it's no use. "Mom, please!"

She opens the door. Glances back at me. "You have to be strong now, baby girl."

"Mom—"

The windows crash open, letting in a gust of wind that sounds like a jet engine failing.

She blows me a kiss. "I'll miss you."

And then she steps through the door, closing it behind her.

"No!"

The sheets go limp in my hands. I throw them off and run for the door. I wrench it open and scan the hallway, but I'm too late.

She's already gone.

"*Psst.*"

The little boy appears at the end of the hall.

"Follow me," he says.

I wipe the back of my hand across my tearstained cheeks. "Why?"

He giggles. "We're playing a game."

His voice crackles like radio static. He's standing in the middle of the hall now, even though I didn't see him move.

I swallow and press back against the doorframe. "What sort of game?"

I blink, and he's standing right in front of me, the light catching in his dull, brittle hair.

"We can't let him find you," he whispers, sliding his small, cold hand into mine. "Hurry."

He pulls me down the corridor, the hem of my night dress whispering around my ankles. Pink silk ribbons lace around my wrists and scooped neckline. I knot my hand in the thin, unfamiliar fabric.

The little boy looks back at me.

"Don't worry," he says. "I won't let him find you."

"'Him' who?" I ask.

"The man," he replies.

He leads me up a narrow flight of stairs to the fifth floor.

"We can hide in here," he says, opening the door to the linen closet.

I pull my hand back. "No."

The lights flicker.

"Hurry," the little boy says. "He's coming!"

Heavy footsteps thunk up the stairs.

The little boy holds out his hand. "Please."

The footsteps grow louder.

I take the boy's hand and plunge into the darkness.

I bolt awake.

The sheets are cold, damp, and wrinkled around me. The giant hole Mom left in my heart has been ripped open again, bleeding into my lungs, impossible to breathe around. Tears burn my eyes and sharp, choking sobs slice my throat. I try to tell myself it was just a dream, but my bones ache from thrashing, and the skin beneath my eyes is caked in salt from my tears.

I have two choices. I can wake Dad. Tell him about my dream and about what happened earlier in the bathroom. Find solace in the one parent I have left and, in the process, taint the happiness he's been able to find here. He'll give me that look that says he doesn't think I'll ever be okay, and then it'll be harder for me to believe it, too.

Or I can shut off my emotions completely.

I grab my backpack and head for the ballroom.

––––––––––––––

My indie-rock playlist pumps through my ears as I practice my *jeté* across the floor. It isn't traditional ballet music, but the power in the instruments and the emotion in the vocals give me the boost I need to jump higher, stretch farther, work harder. I lose myself in the stories of the songs and in the beat coursing through me. The music makes me brave, makes me want to put on a show for this room and anyone who might be in it. Person or imprint.

Alive or dead.

I'm only vaguely aware of my footing as I circle the room. *Grand jeté, pirouette, arabesque. Grand jeté, pirouette, arabesque.* Around and around I go, until my body is moving without thought.

I am like the air, and the air feels nothing.

It's only when my lungs can no longer pump fast enough to give me the breath I need that I slow. My hair has long since escaped my bun, cutting across my eyes and sticking to the sheen of sweat on my neck. The song ends with a falling hush, and I curtsy for my imagined audience.

In the silence, I hear the faint notes of another song. I check my phone, but the playlist is over.

The music isn't mine.

I tug the buds out of my ears. It's the same song from yesterday, the one I caught myself humming in the shower. Only, this time, it's crowded with a bunch of other sounds—the clink of crystal, the purr of muted chatter, the bubbly pop of champagne corks—all reverberating throughout the empty room. The melody is distant, and all I can think is that it must be bleeding through the walls from another room.

The dining room?

I put my earbuds in my backpack and head for the door, my ballet slippers swishing across the carpet.

I step into the lobby—the receptionist is working on a sudoku book this time—and cross to the dining room. My fingers lace around the door handle. The music and chatter grow louder, buzzing through my ears. I open the door—

The music stops.

Frowning, I step inside, but it looks just like the ballroom. Completely empty, aside from the bare round tables. The staff hasn't even started getting it ready for breakfast yet.

I step into the lobby, closing the door behind me, and walk back to the ballroom, my ears perked for the song, but there's nothing. Just the sound of the receptionist's eraser, smudging out a mistake.

CHAPTER SEVENTEEN

LEA

WE WALK ARM IN ARM past countless rows of tents. The night is golden from the light of streetlamps and cooking fires. Alec steers me toward the dance pavilion, out of which the ragtime beat of the Canvas City Band washes onto the street.

"Are you ready for this?" he asks, the uncertainty in his eyes belying the teasing lilt in his voice.

"I've never been more ready for anything in my entire life."

He grins. "Well, then. Let's not keep you waiting a moment longer."

In the ballroom, the air had been ripe with the smell of money—it pulsated from every bejeweled neck and stale conversation. The music was strictly classical, the alcohol strictly champagne. Here, inside the dance pavilion, the hardwood floor is sticky with beer and sweat, the air laced with the smell of pomade and cheap perfume. Shoes bought at the five-and-dime stomp across scuffed-up boards as the band bleats out a frenetic tune.

It's exactly what I need.

"Alec!"

Alec turns. A tall, skinny boy who looks like a red-haired coat rack pops out of the crowd carrying a drink. He drapes an arm around Alec's shoulder and says, "We were starting to think you weren't going to make it." His gaze flicks to me. "And who's this lovely?"

"Lea Sargent," I say, holding out my hand.

The newcomer takes my hand with a sturdy grip. "Fitzgerald O'Brien," he says, his breath smelling of alcohol and juniper. "Friends call me Fitz."

"Fitz is an old friend," Alec explains.

"It's a pleasure to make your acquaintance," I say.

Fitz turns my hand and kisses my knuckles. "The pleasure is all mine."

Alec clears his throat and looks out at the crowd. "We're really testing the fire code tonight."

"Aye," Fitz agrees, keeping his eyes on me.

"And if there's a fire?" I ask.

Fitz grins. "At least we'll die dancing and liquored up."

A girl with blond hair as thin and shiny as corn silk appears at Alec's side, bumping his shoulder with a frilly pink sleeve. "Hey there, stranger."

"Clara," Alec replies, not quite meeting her gaze. "Having fun?"

She speaks to him but stares at me.

"Aren't you going to introduce me to your friend?"

Another couple approaches us from the dance floor before Alec can respond: a boy with jet-black hair and a girl with freckles across her nose.

"We're doing introductions?" the new boy asks. "With whom?"

Fitz hangs his arm around my shoulders. "Don't come any closer, Tommy, my boy. I saw her first."

"Oh, God," Alec mutters, pushing his hair out of his face and knotting his hands behind his head.

I stifle a giggle.

"Well. Hello there," Tommy says, hooking his thumbs in his suspenders as he takes a step closer to me.

The girl beside Tommy elbows him in the ribs.

"I'm Moira," she says. "Tommy's *date*."

Alec nudges Fitz and Tommy away from me.

"Maybe this wasn't such a great idea," he whispers in my ear.

"Why?" I ask.

"It's okay," Alec says, his hair hanging low in his eyes. "You don't have to pretend you like this. We can get out of here."

"I'm not pretending." To prove it, I take Fitz's drink out of his hand and chug the remaining gin. Alec stares at me, slack-jawed, as I run the back of my hand across my mouth. "How about that dance?"

Alec's mouth parts slightly. "As you wish, Miss Sargent."

I grab his hand and tug him onto the dance floor. The band starts up another song that's fast and loose. I turn to Alec, placing my right hand on his shoulder and threading my left hand through his. Slowly, as if he's not sure he should, he places a hand on my waist. He watches me with wary, uncertain eyes, but then the music speeds up, and our feet start moving, and my laughter eases his concern.

He spins me around the floor, and I match him step for step. I imagine this is what a comet must feel like, streaking through the universe at impossible speeds. I am vaguely aware of the people around us. During one pass around the floor, I spot Tommy, Moira, and Fitz hooting and clapping their hands as they watch us. Clara stands off to the side, her hands on her hips.

Alec twists me away until we're holding on to each other

by our fingertips, then pulls me back into his chest. His friends whistle. I move to put space between us again, but he presses his hand to my back, keeping me against him, and then we're flying around the room, our feet hitting the floor for only half a second at a time before shooting up again. I know nothing but the music and the scent of the lemon tree still clinging to Alec's skin and the feeling of his body pressed against mine.

We only slow when the music slows. Only stop when the music stops.

"Let's give a big round of applause for the couple," the band leader announces, gesturing to us, and for the first time I realize we're the only ones left on the dance floor.

The crowd applauds.

Alec leans into my ear. "Thirsty?"

I nod.

He grabs two mugs of beer from the bar and leads me to a table.

I gulp down half my glass, then slap it on the table and lean back in my chair. "You are such a surprising creature, Mr. Petrov."

"*Me?* I'm not the one who just drank half of Fitz's gin."

I shake my head at him. "Where on earth did you learn to dance like that?"

"My parents invested in lessons when I was a boy," he replies. "My father said it would be easier for me to find the right girl if I knew how to dance."

"I think I would have liked your father."

Alec's lips twist into a sad smile. "He would've loved you."

"And your mother?" I ask. "When do I get to meet her?"

His brows shoot up. "You want to meet my mother?"

"I have to thank her for the lessons," I say. "If you didn't notice, I just had the time of my life."

"You can meet her anytime you want, really," he replies. "She works at the Grand, too."

"She does?"

He nods. "She's a laundress."

I place my elbows on the table, partly because it's comfortable and partly because I know Mother would hate it.

"And your father?" I ask. "Did he work at the Grand, as well?"

"Stable master. Worked his way up from a lowly stable hand. My parents were sixteen when they married. Instead of a honeymoon, they put all their money into emigrating from Russia to the United States. My mother was pregnant with me when they arrived at the Grand. It's all I've ever known."

"No wonder you know how to do all the jobs there."

He smiles, all humility, and twists his glass on the table.

The band switches to a slower set. I down the rest of my beer. "Ready for another spin?"

Alec does the same, plopping his empty glass on the table. "You bet."

When Alec takes me in his arms this time, my hip gently swaying underneath the direction of his hand, it's like a slow burn deep inside my chest. He stares down at me through a veil of long, dark lashes, pressing me closer, the shape of his body melding into mine. I can feel myself losing something as I stare up at him, but I have no idea what it is.

It terrifies and fascinates me in equal measure.

I can't look away.

CHAPTER EIGHTEEN

NELL

IT'S A QUARTER PAST FIVE when I start back to our room, and even though most of the hotel is still asleep, there are now signs of life in the forms of early morning runners crossing the lobby in their spandex and neon tennis shoes, televisions murmuring from behind closed doors, and the smell of freshly brewed coffee wafting through the hallways. It's easier to be brave now, surrounded by these sparks of life—easier to search for reasonable explanations rather than to believe music could come from nowhere, or bathroom drawers could open by themselves and a bathroom door could lock on its own.

My favorite explanations for what happened in the bathroom include a seismic shift, a strong gust of wind, and me being so tired that I don't remember locking the door or opening the drawers looking for . . . something.

Soap maybe.

Okay, so that last explanation is a little flimsy, but still.

I must have looked pale when Dad finally did return to the room last night—an hour later—because he asked me what was wrong, and looked confused when I asked him if he'd been in the bathroom.

"No, I just got back from the office. Why?"

I told him it was nothing, that I thought I heard something. I don't think he believed me, but I don't think he would have believed what really happened, either.

And what about the music? a ghostly voice whispers in the back of my mind. *That song you keep hearing?*

I scoff at the voice. That one's easy. Clearly, someone in the hotel is practicing the song just like I'm practicing my ballet. I just can't figure out which room they're in. They might not even be nearby—the music could be traveling through the vents from the other side of the hotel, just making it seem like it's in the same room as me.

What about the voices you heard with it?

What about seeing your name in the mirror?

What about the dreams?

Those have a much simpler explanation, one that works for the bathroom incident as well. But it's the one I'm most avoiding, because it's also the most plausible and because it would mean that I am not as fine as I want to be. Because it would mean running back to Dr. Roby with my tail between my legs if I can't figure out how to fix it on my own.

I'm so caught up in my own thoughts as I turn into the exterior corridor that I don't notice the ladder until my foot bumps its base. I fling my hands out and grab the metal sides, steadying myself and the ladder. There's a deep sound of agitation above me. I glance up a pair of long, khaki-covered legs and a white T-shirt to a muscular arm reaching for a light fixture. One tanned hand grabs the fixture while the other stretches out for balance.

"Sorry!" I say, wincing.

The man's head slowly turns in my direction. His dark hair brushes his temples, and his square jaw stiffens. He huffs out a breath.

"You have *got* to be kidding me," he mutters, rolling his eyes at the ceiling.

Alec. Petrov.

I push away from the ladder. It wobbles, and his grip tightens on the light fixture once more.

"What are you doing up there?" I ask.

"Changing a light bulb," he says through gritted teeth. "Is that all right with you?"

I narrow my eyes and seriously contemplate telling him where he can shove that light bulb, but I don't want to give him the satisfaction. I'm actually glad I ran into him—well, I'm not glad I *literally* ran into him. Again. But if we're going to be living under the same roof, we might as well come to some sort of peace treaty, and this seems like the perfect opportunity to extend the olive branch.

"I really am sorry," I say, forcing the words out. "It was an accident."

He places a new light bulb in the socket and twists. "Accidents seem to be a habit of yours."

I cross my arms over my chest. "I'm not clumsy, if that's what you're implying."

"Could've fooled me."

My nails dig into my skin. "Is there anything *you* want to say to *me?*"

He climbs down the ladder. "Nope."

"Seriously?"

He doesn't say a single word as he heads back the way I came. Not even a goodbye.

And that *really* pisses me off.

I run ahead of him, cutting him off at the door.

"I'm Nell," I say, thrusting my hand out. I try to bring the warm smile back—*if all you want to do is strangle someone*, Mom used to say, *you're better off killing them with kindness*—but my teeth clench and my mouth twists into a snarl. "Nell Martin. It's nice to meet you."

A muscle in his jaw ticks. "You have a problem with people not liking you or something?"

"No," I reply. "But I do have a problem with bad manners."

His brows arch. Not by much. Just enough to know I've surprised him before his face hardens again.

"Funny," he says, taking a step closer, his low voice rumbling across my skin. "Coming from a girl who doesn't know how to say 'Thank you.'"

My eyes narrow. That's not what he's so mad about, but if he wants to play it that way, fine.

"Actually, I said, 'Thanks for the help,' but you were throwing too big of a temper tantrum to hear me."

"Is that it?"

"Is that what?"

"Is that everything you have to say to me?" he asks, staring me down. "Because *some* of us have work to do."

I snort. "Yeah. That's it."

He moves around me. That clean, citrusy scent tickles my nose, smelling way too good for someone so awful.

"And try not to get in my way again," I shout at his back.

He barks out a laugh.

Fuming, I turn on my heel and march the other way.

Just who in the hell does he think he is? The prince of Winslow? The king of the Grand? I've never met someone so annoying, so infuriating, so horribly awful in my entire—

I stop next to the narrow fifth-floor stairway, my fingernails digging crescent moons into my palms. Ever since I got here, I've felt out of control, and I don't know if it's the move, or the hotel, or that look that Dr. Roby gave me that keeps flashing through my mind, but all I can think is:

Screw it.

I climb to the top of the stairs and take a right, following the path I remember from my dreams. I'm going to prove that there is no linen closet, because if there is no linen closet, then there's no dead boy, and if there's no dead boy, then the dreams I've been having, as real as they feel, are just that—dreams. A subconscious manifestation of my anxiety, as Dr. Roby would say, and then, once I see for myself that *none* of it is real, I'm going to forget about the open drawers and my name scribbled on the mirror and the elevator and the song and, most of all, Alec Petrov.

I'll go back to being okay. I just have to *see*.

I take a right, followed by another, and another. Outside, the sky is lightening into a cobalt-blue canvas smudged with gray clouds. A floorboard creaks behind me.

I whip around.

The hallway's empty.

I keep walking, taking one more turn, and—

There it is. The door to the linen closet.

My heart stops.

That doesn't prove anything, I tell myself. *You obviously remembered this door from the last time you were up here. It doesn't mean it's what you think it is.*

My anger makes me brave. I stride toward it, looking for a guest-room number, but there isn't one. I grip the knob and count:

One . . . two . . . three!

I wrench open the door.

Inside, the walls are stacked with shelves holding freshly laundered towels and linens. A metal chain swings in front of me. I follow the chain up to a single Edison-style light bulb. The only thing missing is the little dead boy, blood dribbling from his cracked lips.

Heart pounding, I slam the door shut.

CHAPTER NINETEEN

LEA

AT HALF PAST THREE, CLARA suggests a bonfire on the beach.

Fitz points at her, his eyes glazed over with drink. "Yes, good. We shall dance around the fire like cavemen and howl at the moon. Tommy," he yells. "Get your Irish arse over here."

Alec whispers in my ear, "We don't have to go. I can take you back to the hotel if you'd like."

"That," I tell him, "is the last thing I want."

It seems we're not the only ones in Canvas City with this idea. There are several other bonfires on the beach already, so instead of taking the time to build our own, we join a party playing banjo music and dancing around five-foot-tall flames in their bare feet. Moira smiles at me encouragingly as we dance, but Clara eyes me like I'm a thief and Alec as if he's the treasure I've come to steal.

"I think someone's sweet on you," I mumble out of the side of my mouth when I catch her watching us.

Alec sighs. "We courted for a few months. I think she's hoping we'll eventually find our way back to each other."

"Was there an intention of marriage?"

He bites his lip but can't quite hide his laughter. "It was never that serious. Clara and Fitz were my first friends. I can't recall a single memory without them in it. It only seemed natural that one of us would court her, but it never felt right. I thought it was the same for Clara. She was always looking at Fitz when we were together, anyway."

My brow arches. "Well, she's looking at you now."

He gives me a secretive, sidelong glance. "She never did like sharing her toys."

We spend hours dancing around that fire, howling up at the moon like a pack of wolves, just as Fitz said we should. As the sky lightens, signaling the dawn, Tommy lifts Moira into his arms, spinning her around. Fitz grabs Clara around the waist and storms her into the sea. She squeals and smacks his back, shouting, "Just wait until I tell your mother!"

I take Alec's hand and whisper, "Thank you."

"For what?"

"For inviting me tonight. You have no idea how much this means to me."

"Well, then. Consider this a summer-long invitation. Anytime you want to get away, just let me know."

"Do you really mean that?" I ask.

"Of course."

I turn back to the moon and close my eyes, my skin drinking in its fading light and the cool sea air. His hand cups mine in the darkness, and we stay like that, alone by the dying fire, until the sun breaks over the horizon.

The orange-gold light of dawn follows us as we walk back to the hotel's beach, leaving our footprints behind us in the damp sand. I glance back at the incriminating trail we've made from Canvas City, but the tide is rising, and I am comforted by the knowledge that the only evidence of our night together will be washed away before breakfast is served.

I dangle my shoes by the hooks of my fingers with one hand and hold my skirt up with the other. I am thankful now that I changed from my ball gown into day clothes, even though Moira and Clara and the other girls at the pavilion were wearing their best dresses. If my parents are awake when I come in, I can explain away my absence as an early morning stroll on the beach, so long as they never discovered the pillows beneath my sheets.

Alec, his hands in his pockets, keeps stealing glances at me when he thinks I'm not looking. It gives me the strangest feeling that he's waiting for me to disappear, as if I had never been real to begin with, which is so odd seeing as I've never felt *more* real in my entire life.

"Tell me about the ring?" he asks suddenly.

I'm so lost in studying this boy, who makes me laugh by day and dance like a comet by night, that I don't fully understand what he's asking, but then he gestures to the gigantic emerald Lon gave me, saying it matched my eyes, even though my eyes are hazel.

"Oh. That," I say.

"It's an engagement ring."

It isn't a question, but I answer anyway. "Yes."

"Aren't you a little young to get married?"

"Our wedding is set for the first weekend of September," I explain. "I'll be seventeen by then."

"That's still young."

"Yes, but there are mitigating factors."

"Do you love him? Your fiancé?"

I'm supposed to lie now. I'm supposed to say yes, of course I love him, and that I have never looked forward to anything as much as I'm looking forward to our wedding day. I've said those words so many times that they come easily to my lips, except . . . I don't want to lie to him.

"No," I say. "It's a marriage of convenience. Nothing more."

"For whose convenience?" he presses. "Yours?"

"You ask a lot of questions."

"You avoid a lot of questions."

I drop my voice to a scandalous whisper. "I'm avoiding the question because it's a dreadful family secret."

"Well, if you hoped to intrigue me with that declaration, Miss Sargent, you've succeeded."

I don't want to smile, but I can't stop my lips from twitching. "Let's just say my family is not as well-off as we used to be, and this marriage will solve a lot of problems."

He is quiet for a minute, thoughtful, so that the only sounds are the surf crashing next to us and our feet padding lightly across the sand. "So you're marrying him for the benefit of everyone else?"

I don't answer.

He wraps his hand around my arm, stopping me. "What about what you want?"

Behind him, the sky is turning pink and orange. With his face in the shadow of the rising sun, his ocean eyes are so dark that I feel I could tell them anything and they would bury my secrets deep in their inky abyss.

"I'm ornamental," I say. "What I want doesn't matter."

He shakes his head, taking my other arm and turning me to face him. "It matters to me."

"Why?" I ask, the word barely a breath on my lips. "Why would you care about someone you met just a few days ago?"

"I don't know," he says. "But I do."

I don't make a conscious decision to kiss him. The whole night has felt like something from a dream, and if I am dreaming, then I don't have to worry about the rules of decorum that govern my reality. In a dream, if you want to kiss someone, you simply do it, and I want to kiss Alec here, now, on this beach, with the sun rising on a new day behind us.

I drop my shoes into the sand and let go of my skirt. I lift my hands slowly, threading my fingers through his hair and pulling him to me. Alec kisses me first, his mouth devouring mine, as if he's been waiting his entire life to kiss me. I've never been kissed by anyone like this before, and I am momentarily stunned by the raw power of him, the way his arms wrap around me, his broad shoulders blocking out the rest of the world.

My very first kiss was a peck from my next-door neighbor at the tender age of thirteen, after our parents had taken us to see *Romeo and Juliet*. We left the theater wondering what all the fuss was about, pressing someone's lips against another's. We were left wondering after we tried it for ourselves and found nothing useful in the venture.

My second and last kiss before this one was given to me by Lon, on the day he proposed. It was the only time we'd been without a chaperone in our six-month courtship, and Lon hadn't even asked my permission. I guess my saying yes to his proposal was good enough, even if it was a timid yes that made me feel as though I was about to hurl my breakfast on his shoes. He'd pushed his tongue against my lips, forcing it into my mouth. It had been, without a doubt, the most unpleasant sensation I'd ever experienced, like a slippery eel wriggling between my teeth.

I still hadn't understood what all the fuss was about, and I'd had to wipe my mouth free of his spit when he wasn't looking.

I understand kissing now.

I curl my fingers around the back of Alec's neck, pulling him closer. Alec's hands move around my waist and then lower, pressing my body against his until we snick into place, two halves of a whole.

I don't want to stop, but the sun is up, and the hotel is blinking awake, and we can't be discovered here, like this. Alec seems to have the same thought. Reluctantly, we break apart, both of us gasping for breath.

I laugh, then pick up my shoes and the hem of my dress. "Good night, Mr. Petrov."

He bows his head, his eyes sparking like blue embers. "Good morning, Miss Sargent."

CHAPTER TWENTY

NELL

I'M DISTRACTED THE REST OF the day. I try to concentrate on my work in the storage room, sifting through personal letters, newspaper articles, and old journals from the first few decades following the Grand's opening, but I can't stop thinking about the linen closet. Sofia hadn't shown it to us on the tour—why would she?—so how did it wind up in my dreams?

Lucky guess?

After mom died, I saw her everywhere. Sometimes she looked just as real and solid to me as Dad, and I would think everything had just been one giant mistake, because Mom was home, alive and happy and *whole*. Sometimes she was just a bright, flickering shape at the foot of my bed, watching over me, a specter in the shadows, and I knew she'd never be whole again. Sometimes she was a mangled corpse, blood dripping from the place where half her skull had been ripped off.

I'm not sure what Dad thought. Maybe that it was a stage of grief, something that would pass if he ignored it. But after three months with no change, he reached out to Dr. Roby. At my first session, the doctor told me hallucinations were a possible side effect for children who had gone through a recent emotional trauma.

A side effect. A symptom. Nothing that couldn't be cured with twice-a-week therapy.

I fought Dr. Roby on it for a while, because admitting he was right, that Mom was just a figment of my imagination, felt like losing her all over again. It wasn't until I noticed what it was doing to Dad—the heaviness that dragged at his shoulders until he looked like a broken clothes hanger, the blue-black craters forming around his bloodshot eyes, the streaks of gray in his hair that hadn't been there a few months before—that I agreed to Dr. Roby's recommended treatment plan.

It didn't happen right away, but the more I saw Dr. Roby, the less Mom came around, and I knew he was right. She wasn't real.

She was *never* real.

Once I'd gone a year without seeing her, we dropped back to once-a-week sessions and then, eventually, once a month. Which was why, when I found out Dad was taking this job and Dr. Roby offered to help me find another therapist in the city, I told him I didn't need it. I hadn't seen Mom in more than three years, and even though I knew this was only because of Dr. Roby's treatment, a small, defiant voice inside me wanted to prove that I'd never needed him in the first place. That I would've been fine on my own back then and that I would certainly be fine on my own now.

I'm not so sure of that anymore.

Maybe Sofia did show us that linen closet on the tour and I just don't remember—there were a lot of gaps in my memory in the weeks following Mom's death, so it's not like these little "blackouts" haven't happened before. And maybe I did open those bathroom drawers and lock the door, and maybe I am just hallucinating that song.

I don't want to believe my brain is still this screwed up over Mom, but the only other explanation I come up with (other than ghosts, which is just too ridiculous to comprehend) is that it's all stress-related—from the move, from trying to stay in shape for the audition, from trying to come up with tuition money in case they pick someone else for the scholarship. And if it is stress-related, then I can control it. If it's stress-related, then it's *temporary*. Which means there's nothing to worry about and absolutely *no* reason to call Dr. Roby.

Sofia stops by the storage room after lunch to invite Dad and me to the hotel's bonfire tonight.

"It's mostly guests," she explains, "but Max and I try to make it to a few of them throughout the year, and I couldn't think of a more perfect way to welcome you and your father to the Grand."

"Thanks," I say. "I'll see what he thinks."

"You have to come," Max tells me after Sofia leaves. "Mom won't let me live it down if I can't convince you. For the past three days, all I've heard about is how we have to make you and your dad feel welcome."

I frown. "Does she talk about us a lot?"

He shrugs. "It's not, like, *all* she talks about, but yeah, she keeps asking how you're doing, and she keeps mentioning how impressed she is with all the ideas your dad is coming up with for new guest activities. To be honest, I think she kind of likes him."

My stomach twists. "Really?"

"Yeah," Max says, wiggling his eyebrows. "This time next year, we could be siblings."

I sit there, stunned, realizing too late he meant it as a joke. I try to recover with a laugh, but it's forced and the timing's all off.

Turns out Dad's all for the bonfire—no surprise there—so once Max and I finish up our work for the day, I head upstairs to change. I think about taking a shower, but even though I know the whole scene with the drawers and my name scribbled across the mirror didn't really happen, I'm not quite ready to face it again. Instead, I pull my hair into a low, messy bun and change into a pair of capris and a sleeveless blouse. I think about putting on some makeup, but it isn't like there's going to be anyone I want to impress at this thing.

What if Alec's there?

Then there *definitely* won't be anyone I want to impress.

Dad takes his favorite outfit into the bathroom to change. I try to watch TV to pass the time, but my stomach tightens at the thought of him getting ready for *her*, like it's some kind of date or something, until I can't take it anymore.

I leave a note on his bedside table, grab my key card, and head downstairs.

———

Along the lobby's far wall is a display featuring a brief history of the Winslow Grand Hotel. I read about the hotel's founder, August Sheffield, who built the hotel on Winslow Island following the Civil War reconstruction, in hopes of enticing Northern money to return to the area. I read about how people traveled from far and wide to enjoy Winslow Island's warm weather and restorative ocean air, and I read about Canvas City, a sort of campground for those who couldn't afford the hotel. An artist's rendering shows a row of striped tents in the shadow of the hotel, and there's something—

Four girls walking arm in arm, their heads tossed back in laughter, their hair bright and shining in the summer sun.

—so familiar—

An ache, somewhere deep inside me, to be one of them.
—about it.

I reach my hand toward the picture, the tips of my fingers ghosting over the tents. A rush of sound echoes through the room, quiet at first, then growing louder, like an incoming freight train. The hum of the ocean mixes with the excited shouts of a crowd and the *clank-clank-clank* of wheels against a steel track—

"Ready?"

I jump.

"Whoa, easy there, champ," Dad says, grabbing my shoulders. "You okay?"

"Yeah," I say, "You just—"

A figure moves behind Dad's shoulder, casting a look back at me before disappearing into the crowd. I'd recognize those hard, calculating eyes anywhere.

Alec Petrov.

How long was he standing there?

Dad waves a hand in front of my face. His cologne brings tears to my eyes. "Hello? Earth to Nell."

I shake my head. "Sorry, I was just, um, really into what I was reading."

"I can see that." He holds his elbow out to me. "Ready to go?"

I nod and thread my arm through his.

"You're wearing cologne," I say.

"I always wear cologne."

Not this much, I think. "And your favorite outfit."

He glances at me. "Is there something you want to ask me?"

Yes.

"Nope," I say. "Nothing at all."

CHAPTER TWENTY-ONE

LEA

MY PARENTS WERE STILL ASLEEP when I returned, and though I heard Benny moving around in his room, his door was closed. I changed quickly into my night robe, hiding my sandy stockings beneath my bed. I unplaited my hair and mussed it up a bit before sliding under the sheets. I closed my eyes, intending to get a little sleep, but my heart was racing, and I still felt the pressure of Alec's lips against mine, and when Mother opened my door half an hour later, I was wide awake.

Now I stand next to the fence of Winslow Island's newest attraction: an emu farm.

"Isn't it marvelous?" Lon asks. "I was here last summer when the emus first arrived. They came all the way from Australia in giant packing crates."

I cock my head as I study the funny-looking creatures. They're all barrel chests and skinny legs, too-long necks and too-large beaks. I glance at Lon and decide there is a definite resemblance.

"Yes," I murmur. "Marvelous."

"Here, step closer," Lon says, pushing me up against the fence until the middle railing digs into my hips. "They won't bite."

I have a difficult time believing that, considering the red-faced ten-year-old boy who passed us going the other way when we walked down to the paddock, holding his arm against his chest, his father comforting him with the promise of an extra-tall ice cream.

I try to push away from the fence, but Lon puts his arms around my waist and lifts my feet onto the bottom railing.

"There," he says. "That's better, isn't it?"

"Lon." An emu snaps its gaze to me, tilting its head and taking slow, tentative steps toward the fence. "Lon, put me down."

"Don't worry, sweetheart." His grip around my waist tightens. "I would never let anything happen to you."

The bird lifts its wings.

"Lon, I'm serious—"

The emu starts running, a roar gurgling in its throat.

"Let go!"

I elbow Lon in the chest. His breath rushes out in a loud "*Oof!*" and he stumbles back. I jump off the fence just before the emu crashes into it, snapping the top rail like a twig.

"Go on, Bessie, git!" A worker in denim coveralls yells as he runs for the fence. "Git!"

Bessie the Emu cocks her head and blinks her long lashes at him, then slowly steps back from the fence.

"Dumb bird," the worker shouts. "Sorry about that, folks. Bessie's a mite aggressive. More trouble than she's worth, if you ask me. Are you all right, miss?"

"Fine," I grind out through my teeth.

"Sir?"

Lon's still sitting on the ground, his hand rubbing his chest. He pushes himself to his feet and smacks the dirt off his pants.

"Yes, yes, I'm fine," he bites back. "The lady was startled."

My jaw aches from the force with which I clench my teeth. I don't think it would go over well if I told Lon that *the lady* was not startled—the lady merely took matters into her own hands, for which he should be eternally grateful, considering the injuries could have been much worse than the one to his pride had she not done so.

The worker looks over the fence and shakes his head. "She really got a hold of it this time. Third fence she's broken in as many weeks. If you'll both excuse me, I've got to grab my tool-box."

Lon still hasn't looked at me, which suits me just fine. I don't exactly want to look at him, either. Not until he apologizes for being such an overbearing brute, and possibly not even then.

"We should return to the hotel," he says. "I forgot I have a meeting with one of our investors."

"Very well."

We walk back to the hotel in silence, our unspoken words suffocating the air between us. Finally, we reach the doors to the lobby. I start climbing the stairs, but Lon grabs my arm, stopping me. For a moment, I think of Alec doing the same thing this morning, only Lon's touch isn't gentle. It's firm, unyielding. Too much like Father's.

"Are you really not going to apologize?" he spits.

My jaw drops. "You want *me* to apologize to *you*?"

"For humiliating me in public? Yes, I do."

"If anyone was humiliated, it was *me*. Holding me up against that fence even though I *told* you to put me down—"

"And I told you I wouldn't let anything happen to you."

"That isn't the point!"

A few guests turn to stare at us.

Lon pulls me away from the hotel entrance, his grip pinching my bones.

"Lon, you're hurting me—"

He loosens his grip, but he doesn't let go. He leads me around the ballroom's rotunda and shoves me behind a group of trees, away from prying eyes.

He takes a deep breath, tugging on the fit of his waistcoat as I press myself against the wall.

"I hope you know," he begins, his voice tightly controlled, "that I will not put up with such insolence when we are married."

I know this is when I'm supposed to beg his forgiveness. That's what Lon is expecting—what Father would want me to do. But my blood is pounding in my ears and my arm aches from the manacle of his grip, and maybe some of the fire around which I danced last night has seeped into my bones, because when I open my mouth, what comes out instead is "Neither will I."

His jaw drops. "What exactly did *I* do that was insolent?"

"You mean aside from forcing me into a situation in which I was not comfortable and then completely ignoring me when I told you so?"

"You need to learn to trust me," he says, taking me by the arm again. "Or I will make you learn."

"What are you going to do? *Beat* me into trusting you?"

He lets go of my arm, moving his hands to my shoulders. His fingers dig into my flesh. "What has gotten into you? You've never acted this way before."

Apologize, a voice that sounds exactly like my father's echoes through my mind. *Do it. This is your chance.*

"Lon, I'm not going to tell you again. Let. Me. Go."

He finally does as I say, exhaling sharply and swearing under his breath.

"Perhaps we should take some time to cool off," he says. "Re-evaluate."

I pick up my skirt and move around him. "Sounds like a fine idea to me."

"Aurelea."

I stop.

"I need you to understand something," he says. "I am a very busy, very important man. I need my wife to support me—to submit to me fully in all things. If you don't think you can manage that, then perhaps we should reevaluate our engagement as well."

He doesn't give me time to respond, which is fine, since I'm not exactly sure what I should say. He storms past me, striding out of the shadows of the tree grove and toward the lobby. A momentary thrill of freedom thrums through me as I watch him go.

Maybe I can finally do it. Maybe I can finally run away. I could hop the next ferry, pawn my ring, and take a train somewhere no one would ever find me—Montana, maybe, or Wyoming—some small town in the middle of nowhere. The money from my ring alone would probably keep me comfortable in a place like that for months, and I'm not afraid of hard work, even though I've never really experienced it, unless you count the dancing lessons when I was younger that calloused my feet or the headaches I received from walking around with a book on my head for hours at a time.

I could do it. I could go now. Start over. No one would even think to look for me for at least an hour. Except—

I can't leave Mother and Benny behind to suffer Father's wrath over my selfishness. And if I were forced to be completely honest with myself, I would also admit that the thought of running away terrifies me, although I don't know why. It's not as if I have anything left to lose, aside from the comfort and familiarity of staying exactly where I've been put. Still, I'm more afraid of what's *out there* than of Father, even as furious as I know he will be after he discovers Lon is "reevaluating" our engagement.

I take a deep breath, sparing one last look at the bay and the possibilities that lie beyond it, then step onto the concrete path. I nod at a passing couple as I walk toward the lobby.

Toward my familiar and comfortable fate.

CHAPTER TWENTY-TWO

NELL

THREE FIRES DOT THE BEACH. One has camp chairs around it and seems to be dominated by older couples drinking wine and martinis. Another has been overtaken with families roasting s'mores and shouting at their children not to get too close to the fire. The third has been commandeered by teens, college kids, and a sound dock pumping music from its speakers.

Max and I make our way toward that one, while Dad and Sofia head off to join the more sophisticated crowd. Sofia was right—the people around the bonfires are mostly guests, but a few employees and their children are here. Max introduces me to a friend of his, a waitress in one of the hotel's restaurants named Tara. She's just come from a shift, wearing black pants and a white blouse, her braids pulled into a neat top bun.

"Nell's going to be a fellow Winslow High prisoner come September," Max tells her. Then he looks at me and hooks a thumb at Tara. "Tara's going to be a senior, too. She's a shoo-in for homecoming queen, though, so she'll probably be too high and mighty to talk to us—"

Tara elbows him. "*You*, maybe. I can tell Nell's cool."

"I don't know what hurts worse," Max says, clutching his side. "My pride or my rib cage."

Tara rolls her eyes. "He's so dramatic."

The darker it gets, the more people show up. One of the underage guests sneaks open soda cans filled with beer. Max shakes his head. "Someone always pulls something like this," he tells me. "No one's gotten caught yet, but it's only a matter of time, especially if people get sloppy and start puking everywhere."

The guy offers me a can, but I decline. The one and only time I tried it, I was sluggish in ballet class the next day and all too aware of the fact that I smelled like a brewery. Not to mention I came *this* close to being that sloppy drunk Max was talking about and vomiting all over the studio's shiny hardwood floor.

Not exactly a feeling I want to re-create.

Besides, I don't need beer to have fun. Not when there's music blasting out of a sound dock and stars shining down on us like camera flashes. Someone starts dancing around the fire, and then everyone's doing it, jumping up and down to the beat. Tara grabs my hand and we dive into the throng, kicking up arcs of sand with our feet, and it's—

The hem of a dress, thick with petticoats, twists around a slender ankle.

—almost like—

A mess of blond curls spinning in the firelight.

—I've done this—

Another girl dances next to me, but where the brunette smiles, the blond watches me with wary eyes.

—before.

A log cracks in the fire like a gunshot, and the vision disappears.

My head spins. I reach out for Tara, steadying myself.

"You okay?" she mouths.

I nod. "Just dizzy."

Her brow furrows. She can't hear me over the music. I mime taking a drink, and she gives a thumbs-up.

I walk away from the fire, my skin hot and my throat parched. Tara follows me, and we each grab a water bottle from one of the coolers.

Max is sitting by the tide line, typing something into his phone.

"Texting a secret lover, Maxie?" Tara asks, plopping down beside him.

I catch a peek of a notepad app before the screen goes black.

"Got an idea for my screenplay," he says. "Had to write it down before I forgot."

"Oh yes, *the screenplay*," Tara says, sprawling out on her back. "Is your writer's block finally cured?"

Max stuffs his phone in his pocket. "Maybe."

Tara twists her body to glance up at me. "Has he told you what it's about?"

"Not yet," I reply, taking a seat on Max's other side.

Tara sits up. "Ooooh, can I tell her?"

"Be my guest," Max says, then fake-whispers in my ear, "She loves the limelight. Future drama major if I ever saw one."

Tara slaps his arm.

"Shush," she says before turning back to me. "Our story begins with the legend of Alec Petrov."

My eyes widen. "Wait, Alec Petrov? As in—?"

"The guy you attacked?" Max asks. "One and the same."

Tara arches a brow at me. "You attacked Alec Petrov?"

"I didn't *attack* him. We ran into each other. It wasn't a big deal."

"You sure made it sound like a big deal," Max says.

I smack his other arm.

"Ow!"

Tara shushes him.

"I'm sure Max told you that Alec lives in the hotel?" she asks me.

I nod.

"Well, according to local legend, he isn't exactly a *recent* tenant. In fact, some people say he's lived in the hotel for more than a hundred years. As in, he checked in, but he never checked out."

"He didn't 'check in,'" Max says. "He worked here."

Tara waves off his comment. "Same difference."

"So what's he supposed to be?" I ask. "A ghost?"

"Maybe," Tara says, her eyes huge. She waves her fingers in the air as if enacting a spell. "Or *an immortal*."

I lean forward, catching Max's gaze.

"You don't actually believe that, do you?"

"Of course not," he says. "Petrov's kind of an easy target. It was only a matter of time before someone started a rumor about him."

"What do you mean?"

Max stretches out his legs.

"No one knows much about him, which is kind of rare in a town like this. Add in the fact that he almost never talks to anyone and . . . well . . . people can be assholes."

Tara shakes her head. "Not everyone thinks it's just a rumor. My uncle worked here when he was in high school, like, a million years ago, right? Well, *he* says Petrov worked here then, too, or at least someone who looked *exactly* like him did."

"Maybe it was Petrov's uncle," Max says, "or some other relative. Did your million-year-old uncle ever think of that?"

I nod. "That's much more believable."

Tara pushes off the sand.

"Ugh, forget it. You guys don't know how to enjoy a good story. I'm going back to the party."

Once she's out of earshot, I turn back to Max.

"Don't tell me you actually believe in something like that. It's impossible."

"Of course I don't," he says. "But it is a pretty neat idea for a story. Just think of it—all the things a person like that would've seen, all the things they would've missed. It's the classic immortality conundrum. Yeah, you get to live forever, but is forever worth it if you're the only one? If everyone you meet in your life will die and you'll still be here? I mean, what's the point?"

"So if you have your story, what's the writer's block about?"

He grips a fistful of sand and lets it run through his fingers. "I can't figure out *why* someone like that would live in a hotel, or why *this* hotel."

"The legend doesn't explain it?"

He shakes his head. "That's why it's such a shoddy legend. I mean, there are theories, but they're all dumb."

"Like what?"

"Well, there's the theory you mentioned. That he's a ghost."

"I can attest to the fact that he is *very* solid."

Max laughs. "Yeah, I don't buy that one, either."

"What else?"

"There's the theory that he's an alien whose spaceship crash-landed on the beach outside the Grand a century ago and he's been biding his time ever since, waiting for a rescue ship to arrive."

"Seriously?"

"The best one," he says, "is that he's cursed, but no one knows why. Looking through the storage room has given me a couple ideas I want to explore, but I'm still hoping something in my research will jump out at me." He smirks. "Who knows? Maybe I'll even find an old picture of Petrov one of these days. Prove the rumors are actually true."

I shake my head. "You know, if you really want to know if any of this is true, you could just go to the source."

His eyes widen. "Are you kidding? That guy would knock me into next Tuesday! And, I mean, urban legend aside, there is something a little . . . off . . . about Petrov."

I roll my eyes.

"I don't think he's immortal or a ghost or anything," he adds quickly. "But I do think he's hiding something."

I think of Mom, of Dr. Roby, of the very real possibility I'm losing my mind and the one phone call I could make to stop it from happening.

"People are allowed to have secrets," I murmur.

"Yeah, I guess." He takes out his phone. "Mind if I finish? I had a real stream-of-consciousness thing going here."

"Go for it."

I lie back on the sand, closing my eyes while he types. The keys click and the waves crash, but my thoughts are louder than Max and the ocean combined.

CHAPTER TWENTY-THREE

LEA

"HAVE YOU GONE COMPLETELY MAD?" Father shouts, slamming the door shut behind him as he stomps into the suite. He drops his tennis racket on the floor. He was out playing with Lon's father again—or, at least, that had been the plan. The brevity of his departure suggests he went down to the tennis courts to meet with Mr. Van Oirschot, only to discover that Lon had called off the engagement and, therefore, Mr. Van Oirschot really had no reason to put up with Father and his subpar tennis skills any longer.

Mother stands. "Edmund—"

He hushes her with a look as he crosses the room, kicking Benny's tin soldiers. Benny jumps to his feet in protest, but Madeline shushes him and, taking his hand, leads him out of the room.

Father stands in front of me, shaking, his face as red as a turnip. "You are to go straight to Lon and apologize. I don't care how you do it, I don't care what you have to say to make it happen, but you are going to beg him to take you back, understand?"

"Do you not care why he called off the engagement?"

"Oh no, Aurelea, I care. When my daughter publicly humiliates her fiancé, the man who holds her family's entire well-being in his hands, I care a very great deal."

Fear grips my belly under his hard gaze, but I hold my ground. "You don't even want to hear my side of the story?"

It's the wrong thing to say. Father curls his hands into fists. The veins in his neck throb. "Do I need to remind you yet again," he says, "the fate that awaits our family if you do not marry Lon? Do you want to see your mother working in a shirtwaist factory? Do you want to see Benny with soot on his cheeks and a chimney sweep's broom on his shoulder? Do you want to see me begging in the streets?"

I take a deep breath. "No, but there must be another way—"

"There isn't. This is the way, Aurelea. So stop being so damn selfish, swallow your pride, and apologize." He does not have to say the words: *Or else.* They are implied in the tightening of his fists and in the memories of bruises hidden where no one could see.

"Yes, Father."

———————

I find Lon at the tennis courts with Mr. Van Oirschot, Lon's athletic form a long, rippling line against the horizon. His shirt sticks to his back as he tosses the ball up. The ball hovers in midair for a moment before shooting back down to Earth. Lon swings his racket with a terrifying show of force. The ball zooms over the net, nearly bruising his father's jugular.

"Slow down, *damn it*," Mr. Van Oirschot shouts.

Lon runs the back of his hand across his nose, where sweat puddles in the crevice beneath his nostrils.

"Again," he says.

His father sighs. "We've been at this for hours."

Lon glares. "Again."

Mr. Van Oirschot takes a deep breath and shakes his head, then sends the ball into the air. His form is not nearly as powerful as his son's, and fatigue has weakened his muscles. The ball barely clears the net.

The *crack* of Lon's racket echoes across the court and, for the first time, I truly notice the muscular build of Lon's body. Not in an appreciative way, like Mother or my friends, but in the way a person who's had fingerprints leave bruises on her skin would notice. Lon's barbaric demonstration this morning proved he has no problem pushing a woman around, and if Father can discipline me like he does with minimal muscle to back it up, what will this man, with his long, jungle-cat body, do to me?

My stomach turns and I lurch forward, my hand splayed against the papery trunk of a palm tree.

Oh, God. This man is going to be my husband.

It's not the first time I've had this realization, or experienced the panic that follows it. The first time it happened, I thought I was dying. Even now, even knowing it's just my body begging me to run, a small part of me still wonders if this is it—if this is how I'll go. Beneath a warm, summer sun with the sound of the waves crashing in my ears. People would scream and Lon would run to me, but I'd already be out of his reach, flying high above the clouds.

Steady, I tell my heart. *Steady.*

I force breath into my lungs and push it out like bellows. The smack of the ball against the court ticks the seconds away in my ears. After ten strikes, I don't have to try so hard to breathe. My heart slows, and my stomach calms, and my body pieces itself back together. Finally, I force my reluctant feet forward.

"Lon."

He turns. His nostrils flare at the sight of me. My hands shake at my sides, and I quickly knot them behind my back.

"May I speak with you?"

CHAPTER TWENTY-FOUR

NELL

I DON'T SLEEP.

I can't get the linen closet out of my head, or the little dead boy, or the sheets pinning me to the mattress as Mom said her goodbyes, or the bathroom drawers hanging open, or my name scribbled across the mirror. Every time I close my eyes, I feel like someone's watching me, and even when my eyes are open, the darkness at the foot of my bed looks thicker than the rest of the room, a shadow the moonlight can't penetrate.

You're imagining it, I tell myself. *None of it is real.*

I try to run through some of the exercises Dr. Roby had me do when I first started seeing him, in the most grueling weeks of treatment. The ones where, when I saw Mom standing in the corner of my room, or when she appeared on the playground at recess, or when she stroked my hair as I studied at my desk, I told her over and over again that she wasn't real, that she was dead, that she was never coming back.

But that damn linen closet being real makes me think other

things could be real, too. My mind is like a carousel, spinning faster and faster. I can't hold on to any one thought long enough to tell it that it isn't real, because the words *it might be* keep whispering through my mind, and my muscles are bunching, and the sheets feel like they're tightening around me again even though they aren't stretched thin and puckering like they were in my dream, and I know there is only one thing that can help me now.

At a quarter to four, I give up trying to sleep and head to the ballroom.

I can hear the somber, lilting melody seeping through the closed doors before I'm even off the staircase. I glance at the receptionist playing a game on his phone, but if he hears the music, he doesn't act like there's anything unusual about it. Glaring at the door, I stuff my earbuds into my ears, crank the volume as high as it will go, and blast my "Eclectic" playlist, a mixture of heavy metal, top 40, rap, and Latin pop—basically anything with a loud, driving beat. The perfect music for when I want to forget about technique and lose myself completely in dance.

I push myself hard as the music takes over, spinning around the room like a cracked-out Energizer bunny until my legs shake and my knees threaten to buckle and my vision starts to blur. Sweat slickens my arms, dripping down my temples and the nape of my neck. I push past the point where my body says I can't do anymore, because my mind is clearing, and once I get past the physical pain, there's nothing. Just me and the music, my body bending to every beat like the moon pulling the tide.

I don't stop, even when the sky turns pink. I know I should—anyone could walk in at any moment and find me—but at the end of each song, I think: *One more.*

One more song and I'll start to feel like myself again.

One more song and I'll have proved I don't need therapy to be okay.

One more song and everything will go back to normal.

But when the song changes this time, it isn't mine. The first haunting strains of the melody I was trying so desperately to block out start pumping through my earbuds. I glance down at my playlist. My phone says it's playing the Red Hot Chili Peppers's version of "Higher Ground"—the minutes on the track are even running like it's playing. But the song that's coming out is classical piano and strings, not even in the same universe as "Higher Ground."

I rip the earbuds out, but the music only gets louder.

Voices murmur around me. The lights along the walls and in the chandeliers start to flicker. The clink of glasses returns, along with bursts of laughter and popped champagne corks.

And then a voice separates itself from the others.

"Nell."

The voice is low. It slithers in my ears. Down my spine.

I take a step back.

"Nell," it says again, this time from behind me. My skin prickles as something brushes my shoulder. A lock of my hair lifts and spins in the air as if someone's twining it around their finger. "We've been waiting for you."

I whirl around. The lock of hair tugs, as if it's being held in place, but there's no one there.

I'm alone.

Goose bumps prick my flesh.

The flickering lights shut off completely.

I suck in a breath.

The lights turn back on at full blast as translucent silhouettes of men wearing tuxedos and women wearing ball gowns burst out of the walls. The couples glide toward the center of the room, waltzing arm in arm with each other.

The lights turn off, and they're gone.

My breath comes out in a long stream of silver-blue fog as I start to shiver.

Electricity sparks like old wires connecting, blasting the lights back on. The silhouettes move closer, circling me as they dance. One man separates himself from the crowd, extending his hand. He has no distinguishable features, but something about him makes my skin crawl.

"Come," he says. "Join the party."

I scream and sprint for the doors.

"Nell." All the couples stop dancing and turn to me as the lights shut off. "Don't leave."

The lights flicker back on, and every single one of them lies on the floor, blood pouring out of their cracked and mangled bodies. More blood is splattered on the walls—long lines of red where handprints clawed and dragged. Only the man who separated himself from the crowd stands apart from them, his features beginning to come into focus.

A cruel smile twists his lips.

"Join the party, darling," he says again.

A high-pitched whine screeches across the room as the bulbs burst and shatter.

I hold my hands over my ears as I run, blocking out the voices and the explosions of glass.

I reach the doors, grabbing both handles and swinging them open. I dart past the sunrise joggers, the caffeine addicts heading for the café, the groggy tourists still operating on West Coast time. Every single one of them stares at me, open-mouthed, as I bolt past. I hear one woman mutter "Is she all right?" to her companion, but I ignore her. My heart drums in my ears, and all I know is I need to get as far away from that ballroom as possible.

The garden doors are open, letting in the dew-dampened breeze and blue-gray light of early morning. I sprint into the grass, intending to use it as a shortcut to the other side of the hotel and, beyond that, the beach, even though I'm pretty sure I could put the entire Atlantic between myself and that ballroom and still not feel safe, but my body was already at its breaking point before I started running, and my legs give out as soon as I reach the koi pond.

I collapse into the grass, my forearms pressed against the old, weathered rocks rimming the dark water. A flash of silver scales glides near the surface before disappearing back into its depths.

I glance up at the water pouring out of the stone lion's mouth as I try to catch my breath.

Not real, I tell myself. *Not real, not real, not real*—

So why does my scalp still burn where my hair tugged?

You caught it on something, and you imagined the rest.

But I wasn't near anything it could have caught on. Only the chandeliers, and the very bottom crystals of those were still a good six feet above my head.

I stare into the lion's eyes.

"What's happening to me?" I mutter.

Someone coughs. I glance over my shoulder.

Alec Petrov stands behind me, wearing a pair of khaki pants and a white undershirt already damp with sweat, holding gardening shears and a bucket half-full of thorny branches.

I hang my head. "Perfect."

"I just wanted you to know someone was here," he says. "Before you kept talking to yourself."

"Yeah, thanks." I push myself up, even though my legs are screaming at me and my heart feels like it's doing somersaults in my chest. "I'll get out of your way."

I start to go, but he surprises me by murmuring, "You're not in my way."

"What?"

He clears his throat. "I just need to get to the rose bushes behind you."

My brow furrows as I glance over my other shoulder, where branches thick with thorns have begun swirling up the decorative pillars and second-floor balconies. Odd—I don't remember the roses reaching that high a couple days ago.

"Right," I say, moving out of his way. "Sorry."

He walks past me without meeting my gaze and immediately gets to work, pruning the branches at the source, then ripping them off the pillars, his thick gardening gloves protecting his skin from the thorns. My gaze catches on the muscles in his arms and back, rippling and tightening as he works.

I look back at the fountain.

"Those things really sprang up from out of nowhere, huh?" I ask, my mouth dry from running. I reach instinctively for the water bottle in my backpack and curse.

Alec glances back at me.

"Something the matter?"

He asks it in a way that makes it clear he doesn't really want to ask, but there's too much concern, too much trepidation in his voice. He wants to know the answer even if he doesn't want to ask the question, and that realization throws me off, because I have no idea why he'd care.

"I left my backpack in the—" I stop myself before saying "ballroom." It's probably not the best idea to admit to a hotel staff member that I've been dancing every morning in what's probably an off-limits space.

"Somewhere," I finish lamely.

He doesn't respond.

I'll have to go back before someone discovers it, but I can't make my feet move toward the lobby. I just keep feeling my hair twisting in midair, keep hearing the bulbs shatter, keep seeing those bodies lying on the floor, drenched in blood, and the man standing over them, asking me to join them.

Alec grunts as he pulls another branch off the pillar, its thorns clinging to the wood.

"Need some help?"

He looks back at me, his dark brows sweeping low over his blue eyes. There's something about them that reminds me of a wolf, so much so that I nearly take a step back. But there's no aggression in those crystal-blue depths; only curiosity and, now that I'm really paying attention, a sadness that catches my breath.

"I don't have another pair of gardening gloves," he says.

"I don't need any. I'll just cut the branches and let you handle the rest."

He wipes a sheen of sweat from his brow. "Why would you want to do that?"

"I need the distraction."

He stares at me a second longer, then holds out the gardening shears. I take them from him and slide in beside him, clipping the branches where they begin to veer onto the pillars.

Adrenaline still courses through my veins, and I hope he doesn't notice my hands shaking.

We work for a few minutes in silence before I see him glancing at me out of the corner of his eye. He pulls another branch off the pillar, his muscles straining from the force, and throws it into the grass.

"You like getting up early or something?" he asks.

I think about the fact that I haven't slept in thirty-six hours.

"Or something," I reply.

He grunts.

"What about you?" I ask. "Why are you out here so early?"

He makes a *hmm* sound in the back of his throat, like he's not sure he wants to keep talking. "I try to get jobs like this out of the way early, before it gets too hot." He grabs another branch. "And I don't sleep well."

"Me, neither."

He nods like he already figured that out.

There's something a little . . . off . . . about Petrov.

The diffused morning light around us softens as we work, shifting to a hazy, orange-pink color as the sun climbs the sky. I really should grab my backpack and get back to the room before Dad worries, but I want the hotel to wake up a bit more before I do. Safety in numbers and all.

I clear my throat. "Do you like working here?"

No answer.

"Do your parents live here, too?" I try, even though he's giving me every clue possible that small talk is *not* his thing. "Or is it just you?"

He hesitates. "It's just me."

Footsteps echo along the stone path as a bellboy appears. Alec nods at him, and the bellboy gives him a little half wave, but he doesn't meet Alec's gaze as he picks up his pace, scurrying into the lobby.

I clip another branch.

"How long have you been working here?"

Alec growls, soft and low.

"So," he says, not looking at me. "You've heard the rumors."

I wince. "Crap. I mean, yeah, I have, but I didn't—" I huff out a breath. "I wasn't trying to pry."

He's quiet for a moment. Then, soft as bird wings, he asks, "Do you believe them?"

"Of course not. They're ridiculous."

He hesitates again, then pulls the last branch off the pillar and throws it onto the pile at his feet.

"Thanks for the help," he says, holding out his hand. "I'll take those back now."

I swallow and hand back the shears. "I'm sorry if I—"

His hand brushes mine. My heart stops as I meet his gaze, completely forgetting what I was about to say. For the first time since the day we met, when he cradled me to his chest and threaded his fingers through my hair, he doesn't look at me with annoyance or anger. He looks at me with a hunger so intense, I feel it radiating down to the tips of my toes. He looks at me like I'm the only thing he wants.

The only thing he's *ever* wanted.

But then he looks away, and I know I must have imagined it. He takes the shears and starts cutting the branches on the ground into smaller pieces, shoving them down into the bucket.

I take a step back.

"Okay," I say, my mouth dry for an entirely different reason now. "Well. See you around."

He keeps working as I walk away.

And even though I watch him over my shoulder, he never once looks back at me.

CHAPTER TWENTY-FIVE

LEA

LON WIPES HIS FOREARM ACROSS his brow as he bounces the ball against the court, over and over again. "I think we said everything we needed to say."

"Well, I didn't."

He laughs, a harsh sound. "What more could you possibly have to say to me?"

I want to spit in his face. I want to tell him I'm glad our engagement is off and that I never wanted to marry him to begin with.

Instead, I say, "I would like to apologize."

"Oh really?"

I grit my teeth. He isn't going to make this easy.

"Yes."

"Why? Because your father told you to?"

I'm so surprised he says this, I almost blurt out the truth. But I harness it before it has the chance to escape.

"No," I lie. "I want to apologize because"—I take a deep breath—"because I realized I was wrong."

His gaze narrows. He's searching for something in my eyes, and I try to shape them into a convincing mixture of sorrow and guilt. It must work, because he tells his father to take a break, and Mr. Van Oirschot nearly collapses from the relief of his words. Lon hands his racquet to a court caddie, puts his hands in his pockets, and starts walking toward the beach without saying a word to me, but I follow anyway, turning my prepared speech over in my mind.

Lon walks until the people fall away, until it's just us and the sand and the ocean. He places his hands at his hips. "All right. Apologize."

I narrow my gaze against the brightness of the sun.

"I don't know what was wrong with me this morning. I'm— I'm terrified of heights, you know that," I say, thinking of the way Father used this excuse our first night here, when I took the stairs instead of the elevator, "and you lifted me up on that railing, and then the emu came at me, and I—I was out of my mind with fear." He isn't softening. I need to flatter him. "I should have known you wouldn't let anything happen to me, but, well, this is relatively new, what I"—the words are thick as sludge in my mouth—"what I *feel* for you, and you have to understand, when a woman is used to looking out for herself, it can be difficult to remember in times of duress that she now has a man who can look after her." I force a smile. "I'm certain I will get used to it by the time we're married, especially since we'll be spending the summer together. That is, if you still want me."

He hesitates.

"What about your father?"

My brow furrows. "He still approves the match, of course."

Lon scoffs. "Of course he does. No, I mean, wasn't he there for you growing up? You said you aren't used to a man being there to look after you, but isn't that what your father's been doing all these years?"

I don't care how you do it, I don't care what you have to say to make it happen, but you are going to beg him to take you back, understand?

Lon almost looks like he's pitying me, and I know I can use it to my advantage.

Very well, Father. If my entire life with Lon is going to be a lie, I can at least give him this one truth.

"My father has been a somewhat absent figure in my life. When he isn't at the office or shut up in his study at home, he's out of town on his business ventures. This is the most time we've spent together as a family in years. So, you see, I've never had such a . . . a *strong* male force in my life. You make me flustered when you"—I cannot believe I'm about to say this—"when you put your hands on me like that, and I lashed out instead of doing what I wanted to do."

"Which was?"

I look up at him from beneath my lashes. "Explore the alternative."

His shoulders soften slightly, and his eyes, dark with anger moments ago, are now liquid smoke. He takes a step closer, until our chests are nearly touching and my nose is in his collarbone. "What's the alternative?"

I hope he mistakes the warmth of the sun on my cheeks for embarrassment. "Please, Lon, don't make me say it—"

He captures my fluttering hands in his and kisses them both. "Say it."

I look away, out at the traitorous waves crashing onto the beach. So volatile, and yet so unwilling to take me when I offered myself up to them. A still, small voice swims through my head. *It wasn't in the plan.*

Stuff the plan. If the ocean had taken me, I would not be forced to degrade myself like this now.

You also would not have spent last night with Alec.

Oddly enough, it is Alec's face, clearer than the sun-bleached landscape surrounding me, that gives me the strength to say, "Kiss me, Lon. Help me get over my fear."

He needs no further prompting. His mouth crushes mine, swallowing my words. He slides his tongue through my lips with a groan, pressing his hands against my backside and lifting me up.

Alec. Think of Alec.

I imagine it is Alec's hands on me, Alec's body against mine, Alec's tongue gliding along my teeth. It isn't the same as this morning—I do not melt into Lon, nor do I *snick* into place as if he's the other half of me—but considering how the only other time Lon kissed me, I tightened up like a statue, it must feel like I'm at least somewhat interested now that my muscles have relaxed.

He keeps one hand on my backside, steadying me against him, and pushes his other hand up into my hair, making a fist at the base of my scalp. He wrenches my head back and kisses the underside of my jaw, his stubble burning my skin.

"I would rip this dress off you now if I could." He nips at the collar of my gown with his teeth. "Perhaps I will anyway."

I glare at him. "Don't you dare."

He laughs and puts me down. "Not an exhibitionist, darling?"

"Lon, I've never been naked in front of anyone, let alone an entire beach full of people," I say. And then, softer, to appease the sudden challenge in his eyes, "I want us to be alone the first time you undress me."

He groans again and sucks my lower lip into his mouth. "You

have no idea what you're doing to me, Aurelea. I don't know how I'll survive the summer."

My heart panics, flooding my veins with ice. I don't like the direction this conversation is heading. If I'm not careful, we'll be married before the week is up.

I push away from him and twist my face into a look I hope resembles regret. "Yes, but we must find a way. Our mothers have already sent out the invitations, and we cannot risk upsetting our guests, especially considering so many of them are business associates. We would not want them thinking the Van Oirschots are a flighty people, ruled by emotions rather than decorum."

He sighs. "You're right. Of course you're right. See? This is why we make such a great match, you and I. You know exactly which way to steer me to keep me sailing straight and true."

"So does that mean our engagement is back on?"

He sets me down and cups my face in his hands. "I have never wanted anything more in my life, my darling. I simply needed to know you feel the same."

A bitter taste creeps up my throat. "I do."

He grins and pulls my head forward, smacking his lips against mine.

"Come along," he says. "We should return to the hotel before someone realizes we are without a chaperone."

I take his arm. My face feels like it's been scrubbed with lye.

"Now that that's settled," he says, patting my hand, "I can tell you about my surprise for tonight."

"Oh?"

He nods. "We won't be dining at the hotel this evening. We'll be taking a sunset cruise on my yacht, just the two of us."

"What about a chaperone?"

"There will be several attendants on the boat, including a

footman serving our food." He leans in close and whispers, "I promise to be on my best behavior."

I sigh. "Pity."

He throws his head back and laughs. I give him my fake smile, and he doesn't notice the difference at all. For better or for worse, I'm back in the cage. The least I can do now is enjoy myself before the door closes completely.

CHAPTER TWENTY-SIX

NELL

I HALF WALK, HALF JOG through the lobby.

It's a quarter to eight. The entire hotel is waking around me. There are enough people now, enough sunlight, enough signs of life, to really believe that the entire scene in the ballroom was just a hallucination brought on by stress or exhaustion or *something* logical. It's easy to tell myself I was stupid for getting so freaked out in the first place. For all I know, I was sleepwalking— that's what Dr. Roby thought half of my hallucinations of Mom were anyway, so it isn't like I don't have a precedent for it. I shove aside the images of the bulbs shattering and the bloodied corpses and the man reaching his hand out to me as I march up to the closed ballroom doors, squaring my shoulders and lifting my chin like I have every right to enter.

If TV's taught me anything, it's that people let you get away with a lot if they think you know what you're doing.

I only hesitate for a fraction of a second as my fingers curl around the handle.

It wasn't real.

I take a deep breath, open the door, and slip inside.

The room is still deserted, and there isn't a single scrap of evidence to believe that anything I experienced in here over an hour ago actually happened. There are no ghosts milling in the shadows, no blood on the floor, and all the light bulbs are perfectly intact.

My backpack is lying on the floor where I left it. I walk calmly across the ballroom, but there is nothing calm about the vein throbbing in my neck or the racket my heart is making against my chest. I bend down, grab my backpack, and sling it over my shoulder. A piece of duct tape brushes the inside of my arm. It reminds me so much of the phantom touch I felt earlier that I jump.

No, I tell myself. *Not the touch I felt. The touch I imagined I felt. It didn't actually happen.*

And then, to help my brain really believe it, I say, "There's nothing in this room. None of you are real."

I wait, although I'm not sure what for. No ghosts are going to appear to convince me otherwise. The light bulbs aren't going to burst again. A floorboard does creak somewhere to my right, but it's just the old bones of this Victorian castle settling.

See? I tell myself. *Just a hallucination.*

Of course, that doesn't make me feel any better, considering my mind is playing some massively messed-up tricks on me again, but it's better than the alternative. Dr. Roby's words—*Call if you need anything*—echo through my mind, louder than ever as I head back to my room.

The only thing that keeps me from picking up my phone is my stubbornness, which Mom always said would either get me somewhere or nowhere, depending on my mood.

I don't know if it's the right choice, if I'm choosing some-where or nowhere, but nothing has changed.

I've been in therapy for the past four years. I need to find out if I'm finally okay enough to handle this on my own, and the only way to do that is to try. If I can't handle it, I'll call. But not now. Not yet.

Which is why, when I return to the room, I take a long shower. Even when I'm done washing, I force myself to stand still, to let the water beat across my aching muscles, resisting the urge to check the other side of the curtain, no matter how many times the image of my name scribbled onto the glass keeps popping up in my mind.

When I finally pull back the curtain, there's nothing. The bathroom looks just as it should.

Satisfied, I change into jeans and an old T-shirt, leave my cell phone in my backpack on the suite room floor, and head to the storage room.

This morning, I am more thankful for this job than ever.

It quiets my mind, and I don't find it a coincidence at all that I have yet to experience a hallucination here. Not with Max constantly keeping me on my toes with random plot questions for his screenplay, and not with stacks of articles and letters and photographs I keep losing myself inside, until it's almost like I'm there with them, these people that lived and dreamed and died long before I was born.

I wonder what happened to them all, these names and faces that passed through this hotel, like a train station for souls, a communal stop on the tracks of their lives. My own life feels small when compared with theirs, my troubles insignificant, and the fear that I can't handle this on my own, that I'll never be free of it, dissipates in the faces of these long-gone strangers, until I can almost forget that I have anything to worry about at all.

I find a folder full of articles. They're copies printed off one of those old microfiche machines, and my breath catches in my throat at a caption that reads: MARK TWAIN VISITS THE WINSLOW GRAND HOTEL FOR INDEPENDENCE DAY DINNER.

The newspaper is dated July 4, 1907.

I run my fingers over the photograph underneath the caption. A crowd overflows from the hotel's front porch to greet the famous author as he strides into the lobby. It's not the best picture of him—his face is turned only three-quarters toward the camera, and the focus is a touch sharper around the edges of the photograph than in the middle, so I'm not sure it's the kind of thing the hotel would want to feature in their museum. I lean forward to put the article in my "Keep" pile, but a smudge on the bottom of the page catches my attention.

Not a smudge.

A headline.

YOUNG SOCIALITE MURDERED AT LUXURY HOTEL

And a date: August 6, 1907.

I bring the article closer. Whoever printed it off the microfiche machine must have scrolled a little too far down, capturing more than the intended Independence Day article. I set the paper aside and comb through the folder, searching for the murder headline on another paper, but there's nothing.

"Hey, Max?" I rise and cross the room. "Take a look at this headline. Do you know what it's about?"

Max shoves aside a box of old cocktail napkins and grabs the article from me.

"Oh yeah," he says, scanning it. "Aurelea Sargent. She and her fiancé were murdered in the hotel."

"Murdered?"

Max nods. "The case was never solved, and whatever evidence the police had was destroyed in a station fire in the 1930s." He shakes his head and hands the article back to me. "One of the detectives thought it was a murder-suicide, but the victims' families wouldn't let him put it in the report because it'd cause a scandal."

"Which one did the detective think was the murderer?" I ask Max. "The socialite or her fiancé?"

He shrugs. "No one knows."

I run my thumb over the headline.

"Do you think the historian will want it?"

Max shakes his head. "It looks like it was taken from the library, which means he probably already has access to the original through them. I'd just throw it away. Mom wants this space completely cleared out."

I stare down at the headline a second longer.

"Nell? Did you hear me?"

"Yeah, sorry. Will do."

I carry the article over to the trash bag. But even as I open the bag, I can't bring myself to throw it in.

I know that the people I was reading about and looking at through a black-and-white lens have long since passed away, but I never imagined any of them had lost their lives here, and definitely not in such a horrific way (*blood on the carpet, blood on the walls, blood dripping, dripping down*). I stare at the headline a moment longer before folding the article and shoving it in the back pocket of my jeans.

I try to work for another hour, but I can't stop thinking about the murder, and the bodies lying mangled on the ballroom floor.

Were the socialite and her fiancé killed by the same person, or was it a murder-suicide like the detective thought? And if so, who murdered whom?

My stomach clenches as Max's voice—*Aurelea Sargent . . . murdered in the hotel . . . never solved*—swirls through my mind, tighter and tighter until I almost can't breathe.

For the first time, I leave before lunch.

Max doesn't ask me why.

CHAPTER TWENTY-SEVEN

LEA

THE LOBBY IS BUSTLING WITH men and women, some making their way into the dining room, others waiting to board their carriages for an evening out. I check the grandfather clock behind me. Lon is now ten minutes late in escorting me to his yacht, but I try to keep my excitement to a minimum. It is too much to hope that some dreadful accident has befallen him, requiring him to forego our dinner date and, possibly, our marriage.

I am not that lucky.

Another ten minutes pass before Lon's first mate appears to escort me to the ship, informing me that Lon is stuck in a last-minute meeting but that he will join me as soon as he can. I hide my disappointment behind my well-practiced smile and wonder how much of my life will now be spent feigning happiness when all I feel is a deep, all-encompassing despair.

The soft evening light casts everything in a dusky rose color. The water darkens under the dying sun's glare as red fingers of light rake across the sky. My escort leads me down the docks to Lon's yacht and helps me onto the bobbing deck.

"We'll shove off as soon as Mr. Van Oirschot arrives," he tells me. "Until then, I'll send the footman out with some refreshment."

"Thank you," I say. "That would be lovely."

He tips his hat and disappears into the cabin. I cross the deck and stand at the railing, looking out over the water. How a person can change so much in only twenty-four hours, I have no idea, but I do not feel like the same girl who danced at the ball last night, and I do not feel like the same girl who kissed a boy at dawn. Nor do I feel like the girl who stood outside the hotel this morning and contemplated her escape, only to discover that she is much more fearful than she ever let herself realize.

I am a phantom, a ghost of all these girls. I fade a little more with each passing day, bringing me closer to the moment when I will no longer be defined by the name with which I was born, the name I have carried with me for nearly seventeen years, but by the name Mrs. Van Oirschot, wife of Lon Van Oirschot and mother of his children. Not an individual still seeking her destiny, but a woman trapped in the confines of an arranged marriage. And then, like a dying star, Aurelea Sargent will blink out forever.

Footsteps cross the deck behind me. "May I offer you a glass of champagne, Miss?"

Alec.

I turn. He looks so handsome in this light, the glow of the sunset painting his skin copper, casting shadows beneath his cheekbones and in the dimple of his chin. I nearly forget how to speak. "What are you doing here?"

He takes another step forward, one hand behind his back as the other holds out a silver tray containing one crystal flute. "Mr.

Van Oirschot requested the services of a footman, and since I didn't have anything else to do, I volunteered."

I shake my head and lift the flute from his tray. The glass is as delicate as spun sugar in my hand. "Do you never grant yourself a respite, Mr. Petrov?"

"Please, call me Alec."

His name is like honey on my tongue. "Alec."

He exhales. "What can I say? I am a man with dreams, and dreams require funds."

"What sort of dreams?"

He looks out at the water, a self-deprecating smile curving his lips. "You'll laugh."

"I would never."

His smile widens. His gaze sweeps the deck. The rest of the crew is inside the cabin, preparing the boat for departure, but Alec still lowers his voice. "I want to apply to medical school."

"Medical school?"

He nods. "So many souls were taken from the last influenza outbreak, my father included, but many who fell sick were spared, and it seemed so unfair to me. Why did *they* get to live while my father had to be lowered into the ground? At first, I thought it was simply fate, or luck of the draw, but then I started wondering . . . what if there was a reason their bodies could fight the illness and my father's couldn't? And what if that reason could be used to save those who would otherwise die?"

"You want to find a cure for influenza?"

"Yes, but it's more than that. I want to understand how the body works, how illnesses work, and how they can spread so rapidly and then disappear. I want to help people." He looks down at his feet. "It's ridiculous, though, isn't it? The son of a stable master and a laundress becoming a doctor?"

I take a step closer, and even though I know it is much too

close for propriety, I can't bring myself to care. "It is a noble dream, Alec Petrov," I tell him. "Don't let anyone tell you otherwise."

His lips part, his breath escaping him in a grateful laugh. He starts to say something, but a pipe clangs somewhere to our right. Remembering ourselves, we each take a step back.

"So why are you here?" he asks. "Is this Van Oirschot fellow a friend of yours?"

"Oh." I hadn't even thought about the fact that the boy I kissed this morning and the fiancé who manhandled me this afternoon would be in such close proximity to each other. And so far out from land, too. "Um—"

"Darling!"

Speak of the manhandler.

Lon strides across the dock, three men in suits following in his wake. He hops onto the deck and puts his arm around me, pecking my cheek. "Please forgive my tardiness. Our meeting ran a bit longer than expected, and when I learned that our favorite clients were without dinner plans, I invited them to join us."

One of the men removes his hat and holds it against his chest. "I hope we're not intruding."

I pull my lips back into the radiant smile my mother taught me so well. "Of course not."

A round of introductions quickly follows. The three men are Pittsburgh-based clients, architects looking to extend their contract with Van Oirschot Steel for the construction of future skyscrapers, like the ones being built in Chicago and New York City. Lon mentioned them at breakfast the other day, how there are other steel companies offering lower prices, but the men are holding out for a better deal from Lon and his father due to the spotless reputation of their product.

"Aurelea, this is Mr. Grant"—the man who removed his hat

bows slightly, revealing a bald spot on the top of his head—"Mr. Sully"—a portly man with reddened cheeks and veiny eyes—"and Mr. Cartwright."

Mr. Cartwright, the eldest of the three, pats my hand like a loving grandfather. "How do you do, my dear."

All the while, I feel Alec's presence behind me like a magnetic pull. My body is a live wire, currents of electricity crackling through my veins. It feels so wrong to know him so well and not include him in our conversation. I have to bite my lip to keep from introducing him to the group.

"You there," Lon says to Alec, and I am so thankful for the chance to finally look at Alec that I drop the mask and, for a moment, my smile is real. "Fetch us some martinis, would you?"

Alec bows stiffly. "Yes, sir."

I catch Lon's eye.

"You don't have to talk to him like he's a dog," I murmur through clenched teeth.

The only sign that he hears me is a slight downward tilt of his lips before offering our company a tour of his boat. I hang back as he explains the building process, the amount of money that went into the boat, and how much it takes to keep it up. Alec appears with the martinis and, after distributing them, walks beside me as we tour the deck. Our shoulders brush, followed by our arms, the backs of our hands—

"Very impressive," Mr. Cartwright says. "Surely if you have enough money to build and maintain a beauty like this, you're garnering enough capital to offer your favorite clients a significantly reduced rate."

Lon shakes his head. "Now, gentlemen, I thought we agreed not to bore my fiancée with our business dealings."

"Actually, I don't find it boring at all."

Lon grins at our guests, then takes my elbow and, in a fake-whisper loud enough for the captain in the enclosed wheelhouse to hear, says, "I'm afraid the sums and figures would just go over your head, darling."

The other men chuckle softly.

Heat floods my cheeks. I want to tell him exactly where he can stick his sums and figures, but instead I say, "You're right, of course. I don't know what I was thinking."

"That's quite all right, dear." He pecks my cheek again, then turns back to his clients. "Now, then. Who would like to see the lower deck?"

Next to me, Alec's jaw is tight, and the tray wobbles slightly in his hand. For a moment, I think he's going to punch Lon, but then the men duck inside the cabin, and I lay my hand on Alec's shoulder.

"It's all right," I tell him. "I'm used to it."

"That doesn't make it all right."

I stare at the cabin door. "I know."

———————

After dinner, the men ensconce themselves in a blue-gray haze of cigars, brandy, and poker. I find Alec standing at the stern of the ship, looking out over the water. The sun has long since gone down, and the stars are even brighter here, far away from the hotel and Canvas City lights. They hang suspended above us, thousands upon thousands of them, swirling pinpricks of light shining through a velvety black void.

My heels click against the wooden deck as I approach him.

"I can't remember the last time I saw the stars like this."

Alec's voice is as low and rumbling as the waves. "You don't deserve a man like that."

I rest my elbows on the railing. My bare arm, prickly with goose flesh in the cool night air, grazes the sleeve of his jacket. "What sort of man do I deserve?"

My words are intended to be a flirtatious tease. Instead, they sound tired. Leaden.

Defeated.

"You deserve someone who won't put you down like that, publicly or privately," he says. "Someone who cherishes every second he's blessed to be in your company, who wouldn't value some business deal over you. Someone who . . ." He meets my gaze, licking his lips as if his mouth has gone dry. "Who can't think straight when he's in your presence for wondering what you will say next, and who also can't think straight when he's away from you for wondering when he will see you again."

I lean closer. "And where would I find a man like that, Mr. Petrov?"

Slowly, hesitantly, his hand reaches for mine. Our gloved fingers entwine, and I curse the fabric that keeps our skin from touching.

"I haven't been able to stop thinking about you, Lea," he whispers. "Not for a second."

And even though it is a dangerous thing to admit, with no real future and no real point in doing so, I murmur, "I haven't been able to stop thinking of you, either."

Because if I am a dying star, then I will do everything in my power to burn as brightly as the ones hovering above me before I blink out forever.

CHAPTER TWENTY-EIGHT

NELL

ALEC PETROV WALKS WITH ME on the beach, the sun rising at his back. Our toes dig into the sand, leaving our footprints behind us. Everything else is fuzzy—the water, the beach, the hotel—everything but Alec and the blazing horizon behind him.

He looks different—his hands in his pockets, his shoulders shrugged forward, his face soft and crinkling as he smiles at me. He's wearing a pair of loose-fitting pants rolled up to mid-calf, and suspenders over a blue shirt that looks like soft, thin denim. His hair hangs down into his eyes just like it did the first time I ran into him and he wrapped his arms around me, shielding my skull from the impact of the hard, unforgiving floor.

"Did you enjoy yourself?" he asks, his eyes twinkling like the last burning stars in the early morning sky.

"Yes," I reply.

I have no idea what he's talking about, but his smile widens, so it must be the right answer.

"Your friends are something else," I add, a fuzzy memory surfacing of people dancing in the middle of a packed, sticky floor.

He laughs. "Yes, they are."

I lean in and whisper, "I like them."

He seems taken aback by this, as if he hadn't expected it of me, but then his timid smile turns into a full grin. I close my eyes, thinking he might kiss me, and—

Startle awake.

I roll over in bed, refusing to acknowledge the disappointment burrowing into my chest, and tap my phone.

3:01 a.m.

I try to go back to sleep, but my mind buzzes with this new Alec. His smile, his laughter, his voice, soft and warm and comforting. The way the early rays of sunlight caught in his shirt, outlining the hard ridges of his muscles beneath the fabric, dripping like liquid gold into his hair and on his lips. Those full, smirking lips—

Growling, I jump out of bed and grab my backpack. I know I should go to the ballroom—facing my fears was always an important step in Dr. Roby's process—but I can't quite bring myself to do it.

I go to the dining room instead.

Between my early morning ballet practices in the dining room and hours spent in the storage room, the last week of June flies by. The nightmares still have me waking before the rest of the hotel, but the lack of sleep doesn't bother me. Not when it allows me to continue practicing without getting in anyone's way.

In truth, ballet may be the only thing keeping my sanity intact.

I've woken at three o'clock every morning for the past five

days, adrenaline pumping through my veins, my sheets cold and damp with sweat. Sometimes the dreams are the same as that first night, full of long corridors that never end and that little boy tugging on my hand. Sometimes I'm stuck in the shower, unable to move as messages spread across the fogged-up mirror—*Hello, Nell. I've been waiting for you. Ready to have some fun?*

And, sometimes, I dream of Alec.

Awake, I haven't seen much of him. Max was right—Alec keeps to himself. When I do see him, he's like a ghost, hovering on the edges of our world, and on the rare occasions that he does look at me, it's nothing like the way he looks at me in my dreams.

In sleeping, he walks with me down corridors, flings open the bathroom door and pulls me out of the shower as words continue to inscribe themselves on the glass, runs with me through the moonlit courtyard and out onto the beach, even though I have no idea what we're running from.

He doesn't speak, only watches, listens, protects.

He doesn't let me out of his sight.

In reality, he barely acknowledges my existence, even though we seem to orbit around each other, with me always walking into spaces when he's just walking out, or catching a glimpse of him across the lobby before losing him in the crowd.

If I didn't know any better, I'd swear he was following me.

———

On the morning of the third, Dad recruits me to help decorate the hotel for Independence Day, stringing red and blue ribbons across the hotel's front porch, and I, in turn, recruit Max. We also place Fourth of July pinwheels in the front and back gardens, saving the interior garden for last.

During the past week, this is the place I have seen Alec the most, constantly trimming back the roses, even though they continue to grow and climb. First to the second floor, then to the third.

Then to the fourth.

Every day they swirl higher, and every time Alec snaps the neck of one, three more pop up in its place, taller and more monstrous than the day before. The thorns are as thick as spikes, making each branch look like a medieval torture device, and every single rose is the darkest red I've ever seen—almost black—and there's a heaviness to each petal, a way they dip at the corners, that makes me think of the torn and mangled flesh pumping blood onto the ballroom floor.

Max starts sticking the pinwheels into the ground along the cobblestone path while I search each column, looking for a ladder, a flash of gardening shears—

For Alec.

I spot him on the other side of the garden, but he isn't on a ladder, and the shears lie in the grass at his feet. He stares up at the roses, his arms crossed over his chest. They're halfway to the fifth floor now, with thorny branches climbing up all four sides of the building's interior-garden walls.

Frowning, I hand Max a pinwheel. "I'll be right back."

Max shakes his head, muttering to himself as I walk away. "Five hundred pinwheels. Five *hundred*. Because one or two or even *three* hundred pinwheels just wouldn't say 'Screw you, King George' quite enough for the Grand's liking."

Shaking my head, I cross the garden and stop next to Alec.

He doesn't take his eyes off the columns.

"There's something seriously wrong with your roses."

His eyes narrow as he studies them.

"Only every sixteen years," he says, more to himself than to me.

"Why?" I ask. "What happens every sixteen years?"

He clears his throat.

"Something to do with the weather," he says. "Atmospheric conditions. There's no fighting it."

The words sound off-hand, like he's just stating a fact, but his body's too tense to believe a word of it.

I play along, shielding my eyes against the sun as I stare up at them. "Still. It's weird."

He nods. "It is."

I glance back down at the gardening shears.

"So are you done fighting them?"

His eyes meet mine. "I haven't decided yet."

He looks at me like he's expecting something. An answer I don't know to give.

"Nell!" Max calls out.

I glance back.

"I literally can't do anymore," he groans, his body splayed out on the grass. "My fingers have pinwheel cramp. You have to take over—I'm all washed up."

I laugh under my breath at him and glance back at Alec.

He's gone, and so are the gardening shears, and I start to wonder if I'm imagining him, too.

―――――――――

I learn, as the day goes on, that the Fourth of July is the Grand's second-biggest celebration next to Christmas, and I spend the rest of the afternoon helping Dad wherever he needs me. We share a late-night pizza with a side of café brownies in his office, and it's past nine o'clock before he lets me go, saying he'll still be another hour or so.

I don't want to be alone, so I take the long way to our room. The visions almost never come when I'm around other people, distracted by a million things, like I was today, and I'm not quite ready to let that feeling go. The feeling that I'm okay.

The feeling that I'm safe.

I glance into the interior garden as I pass, even though I don't expect to see Alec there. Every night for the past week, the roses have been cut back to their starting points, but not tonight. Tonight, they swirl around the fifth-floor balconies and curve toward the garden's center, as if reaching for each other across the expanse of dark blue sky arcing above them.

If they keep going like this, they'll create a ceiling over the entire space by tomorrow morning.

But they aren't what stops me mid-stride.

A woman wearing a long, old-fashioned dress and a big, feathered hat stands underneath the lemon tree, holding a closed parasol. Only part of her face is visible underneath her hat, but it's enough of a glimpse to know she's older, mid-forties or so, and that she looks familiar.

I step into the garden.

The woman smiles and then vanishes.

Frowning, I glance back at the lobby. Soft amber light spills onto the twilight-blue grass, as does the tinkling chatter of couples returning from romantic dinners and strolls on the beach, their laughter thrumming across my skin. No one seems the least bit bothered by the woman who stood beneath the lemon tree one second and disappeared the next.

Heart racing, I walk to the tree, my eyes scanning the garden for any signs of the woman. It's still possible she was real, maybe an actress or a reenactor, hired by the hotel for the festivities. That would explain the old-fashioned clothes.

But not the disappearing.

I stop at the tree, close my eyes, and whisper, "You weren't real. You were just an image my mind made up because I'm stressed. I won't see you again."

It's a mantra adapted from the affirmations Dr. Roby gave me as part of his treatment.

Your brain is, for lack of a better term, he said during our first meeting, *misfiring. We need to speak logic and truth to everything you're experiencing. In essence, we need to retrain your brain to see the world for what it truly is, instead of allowing it to accept the false-hoods it keeps conjuring up.*

I start to turn back toward the lobby, but this time, it's the pond that catches my eye.

There's no water pumping out of the lion's mouth. He looks different, too; his brows drawn together, his lips pulled back in a predatorial snarl, displaying fangs that, despite being cracked and weathered with age, look sharp enough to kill. A drop of water drips from one of his canines, plopping into the pond and sprouting ripples along its surface. I watch the ripples cascade over silver-white scales, bloated and floating on top of the water.

A dozen glazed fish eyes stare up at me.

Another drop falls from the lion's mouth. This time, I notice the color of the droplet is darker than the surface of the pond, and that its ripples smear pale pink lines onto the scales of the dead fish. Swallowing, I step forward and hold out my hand. The next droplet falls into my palm.

It's as red as the roses surrounding me.

And warm.

So, so warm.

I close my eyes and let the droplet roll into the crevices of my palm.

"You're not real," I murmur.

I say it over and over again, concentrating on the words as I feel the blood drip down my wrist, gliding lazily down my forearm.

"You're. Not. Real."

But when I open my eyes, the blood is still there. The fish are still floating. And the roses have all turned toward me.

Watching me.

My heartbeat pulses in my teeth. I rip a leaf off the palm tree standing next to me and use it to wipe the blood from my arm. The roses track my movements as I walk away, each one turning as I pass.

I keep wiping at the blood until I'm back in my room and my skin is raw. I toss the leaf out the window, wash my arm in the sink, and turn the TV on so I won't feel like I'm all alone in this room—a perfect target for visions or ghosts, or whatever the hell is actually happening to me—as I scroll through the contacts on my phone, stopping at Dr. Roby's name.

I'm still staring at it when Dad comes in an hour later, my thumb hovering over the call button.

CHAPTER TWENTY-NINE

LEA

IN THE WEEKS THAT FOLLOW, Alec and I spend every spare moment in each other's company, and as the number of Lon's business meetings escalate and my family finds other ventures in the hotel with which to occupy their time—Mother joining several clubs; Benny spending as much time on the beach as Madeline will allow; and Father off hunting and engaging in sport, striking new, influential friendships wherever he can—the more often these moments come to pass.

Canvas City is our refuge.

By day, we swim and fish and delight ourselves with ice cream novelties and greasy bags of buttered popcorn. Tommy, Moira, Fitz, and Clara often join us, and though Clara continues to eye me with distrust, she does not reveal my secret. I do not know if this is because Alec has asked her not to or if it is because she knows I will be leaving the island a married woman at the end of the summer. Whatever the reason, I show my appreciation by sneaking her gingersnap cookies from the hotel, and she even cracks the barest hint of a smile one morning when I bring her a small box of European chocolates Lon gave me the night before.

By night, we dance at the pavilion and play boardwalk games along the main thoroughfare, drinking cheap beers beside a roaring beach fire. The six of us are constellations in the prime of our lives—no longer children but not quite adults. We burn like the sun and glow like the moon. We have no recollection of the past when we are together and no concern for the future. We are only these moments between waking and sleeping. We are only laughter and breath, frivolity and contentment.

We are endless possibilities.

But my favorite clandestine moments occur when Alec and I are alone. Sneaking through deserted hallways and stealing kisses in the fifth-floor linen closet. Wrapping my legs around his waist in the ocean as the waves crash upon us. Twirling in his arms to the music of the Canvas City Band. Seeing myself through his eyes as a woman adored. And I know these moments are dangerous for a number of reasons. I know we could be caught, and I know we could both lose everything. And even if we are not caught, even if we spend the entire summer together and no one but us ever finds out, I do not know how I will be able to say goodbye to him at the end of it, nor to who I am when I'm with him.

All my life I have done what has been expected of me, and once I become Mrs. Lon Van Oirschot, my last vestiges of independence will disappear altogether. But I will still have my memories. I will still have island days and island nights and the image of a boy who looked out at the world and saw only me.

And perhaps my impending marriage has stripped me of all rationality, but the danger inherent in our exploits is not enough to keep me away.

CHAPTER THIRTY

NELL

I'M ASLEEP IN MY BED when he wakes me. I can't see him, but I can hear him calling me.

The man from the ballroom.

"Nell." His voice is soft, distant. "Come to me."

The moon's silver-white rays flood through the open slats of the plantation shutters, painting bands of pale light across the floor. Dad's head is tipped back on his pillow, his mouth open and blubbering with every snore.

I sit up.

The sheets rustle across my body, slowly pulling away from me.

"Nell." The door to our room opens, but no one stands on the other side. "I've missed you."

I stand.

No, I think. *This isn't right.* But my head is fuzzy and the thought slips away from me like a balloon floating into the sky.

I cross the room and step into the hallway. The door closes

behind me as I follow the voice to the end of the hall, my bare feet shuffling drowsily across the carpet.

"Nell," the voice calls from the fifth-floor stairway.

I glance up.

A pant leg disappears around the corner.

I start up the stairs, splaying my hands on the walls to keep my balance.

Hesitate.

I was scared of this voice. In the ballroom.

Why was I scared?

Flickering lights. Ghostly silhouettes of men and women long dead. A hand reaching out, asking me to join them—

Blood. So much blood.

I shake my head. My thoughts are all jumbled.

Was that real?

Is this?

I slump against the wall. I know I shouldn't be doing this—I shouldn't be following this voice—but every time I almost remember why, my mind goes blank.

"Nell," the voice echoes down the staircase, pulling and stretching each word like taffy. "I have the answers you seek."

The voice wraps around me, pushing me back up. My feet climb the last steps, even though not a single part of my brain is telling them to do so.

The hallway is deserted. One of the windows stands open, letting in bursts of cold ocean air. I wrap my arms around my chest as goose bumps prick my skin. I'm wearing the same shorts and tank top I wore to bed, and this feels wrong somehow.

Aren't I always wearing a nightgown in these dreams?

Dream. It's just a dream. And if it's just a dream, then this voice can't hurt me, and if he can't hurt me, then I might as well find out what he knows—what it is my brain keeps trying to tell me with all these visions.

"Nell," the voice calls to me from outside the window. "Out here."

My nails dig into the edges of the window frame as I peer out. It's too dark to see, but there must be a ledge out there, something the man's standing on. The wind pushes my hair back, cutting into my eyes as I lean forward, placing one knee on the frame, my hand reaching out, feeling for the exterior ledge—

"Nell!"

I turn.

Someone's shouting my name, but I can't see them. Everything behind me is black and swirling. The only thing I see is the window and the starlit horizon beyond.

"You're almost there," the ghostly voice drifts on the salt-laced breeze. "Come to me."

I reach out farther, searching for the outer ledge, pressing my other knee onto the frame. My body tips, and my heart lurches into my throat as I rock forward. The horizon disappears, replaced with the sight of the cold, hard pavement five stories below me.

"NO."

Arms wrap around me, pulling me back. A hand curls around my head a second before my spine smacks the floor and—

I slam awake.

Alec is spread out on top of me. Not in my bed, where I should be, but in the fifth-floor hallway.

The air is freezing from the gusts blowing in through the open window above us. The window I almost crawled through. The realization smacks into me like a brick wall.

It wasn't a dream.

Alec's breathing heavily, his hard chest pressing against

mine with every intake. His hair cuts into his eyes as he searches my face. In this lighting, his cheekbones and jawline look even sharper, like razor blades threatening to cut through his skin.

"Are you hurt?" he asks.

My entire body shakes.

"I . . . I don't know."

He wraps one arm around my waist and pushes off the floor, pulling me up with him. His gaze sweeps over me—checking for injuries, I think, but his stare is so intense, it leaves trails of fire on my skin. He keeps me close, as if he's terrified I'll try to jump back out the window if he lets me go.

Finally—and, at the same time, much too soon—he lets go, takes a step back, and closes the window.

"W-what happened?" I ask. "How did you find me?"

"You were sleepwalking," he says, his back to me. "You passed by me on your way up here, so I followed to make sure you were okay."

All the air bolts out of my lungs.

Sleepwalking?

I close my eyes, pinching the bridge of my nose between my thumb and forefinger. "Oh, God. I'm really losing it now. I can't believe I almost . . . Wait."

I open my eyes. Alec's leaning against the window now, his hands curled around the ledge.

He doesn't meet my gaze.

"Why were you awake?" I ask.

"I told you. I'm not a good sleeper."

"Okay, but still. What are the chances you'd not only be awake but close enough to see me? You could have just as easily been on another floor or on the other side of the hotel or—"

"Just lucky, I guess."

I think of all those times I saw him, floating on the edges

of my world. All the times I thought it couldn't have been a coincidence.

"Have you been following me?" I ask.

"Of course not." He pushes away from the window. "Come on. Let's get you back to your room."

He reaches for me, but I pull back.

"What aren't you telling me?"

"Keep your voice down," he whispers, his gaze darting across the hallway. "You'll wake someone."

I don't like it when he bosses me around, and I almost shout back just to piss him off. But the last thing I want to do right now is draw attention to myself, so I do as he says.

"You know what's happening to me, don't you?" I whisper.

"Nell—"

I take a step forward, craning my head back to meet his gaze. "Tell me. Please. I need . . ."

I hesitate.

To hell with it.

"I need to know I'm not losing my mind."

He closes his eyes. His brow furrows, and a muscle in his jaw hardens as he grinds his teeth together.

"I can't."

I take a step back. "What?"

"I can't tell you."

"You can't tell me I'm not losing my mind?" I ask. "Or you can't tell me what's going on?"

"I can't tell you what's going on."

I frown. "Why not?"

"Because then you *will* lose your mind. You need to remember on your own."

"Remember what?"

He doesn't answer.

"Alec. Tell me."

He sighs.

"All right. If you let me take you back to your room," he says, offering me his arm, "I'll tell you."

I roll my eyes and walk past him without taking it. "Fine."

He follows me silently down the stairs. I hate how aware of him I am. Every footstep, every breath. Like he's the sun and I'm breathing in his light.

I turn to him outside my door.

"Now, what *exactly* am I supposed to remember?"

His eyes soften as he stares down at me. Tentatively, he brushes his knuckles across my jaw, sending every nerve ending into overdrive. He leans in, his eyes soft as he presses his cheek against my cheek, his lips a breath away from my earlobe. "You're supposed to remember me."

A shiver runs down my spine. "I don't understand."

"You will," he says, taking a step back. "And you're not losing your mind. You're just as sane as I am."

He keeps backing away, his hands in his pockets and his eyes on me, and I know I need to find words to keep him here, to make him tell me exactly what's going on, but my brain is firing in a thousand different directions. By the time I think of something to say, all that comes out is "Wait."

But he's already gone.

CHAPTER THIRTY-ONE

LEA

"HE'S HERE! HE'S HERE!" a little girl in front of me screams as a carriage pulls up in front of the hotel. She propels herself to the porch railing, leaning over the side to get a better look.

Samuel Clemens—more popularly known as Mark Twain— steps out of the carriage. The crowd gathered on the porch and around the front lawn cheer wildly. Children and adults of all ages hug their favorite books of Mr. Twain's to their chests, hoping for an autograph.

Alec leans over and whispers, "I could push everyone out of the way so you could get closer."

I answer his teasing offer with mock outrage. "Surely you wouldn't be so rude as to push the children, Mr. Petrov."

"Kids are resilient."

I laugh, much too loudly for propriety. A few women glance my way, but then there's a spark and a loud boom as the photographer who's been waiting all morning for Mr. Twain to arrive takes his shot, and the women turn their attention back to the author.

The children surround him as soon as he steps onto the porch. Alec arches a brow at me, but I shake my head. "There is no need to be boorish. I'm sure I'll get a chance to speak with him at the festivities tonight."

Alec sighs. "Just so long as you know I would do it for you, if you asked."

"There isn't much you wouldn't do for me, is there, Mr. Petrov?"

His smile fades.

"There is nothing I wouldn't do for you, Lea."

My lungs burn, and I have to remind myself to breathe.

"Are you doing anything this afternoon?" he asks.

I shake my head. "Why?"

"I have an idea."

Alec packs a picnic lunch and takes me horseback riding to the lighthouse. I wear a dress borrowed from Moira and a wide-brimmed hat over my curls to disguise myself from any hotel patrons who might notice me. Alec wears a newsboy cap pulled low over his eyes, but the holiday crowd is actually a blessing. No one is looking too closely at anyone—they're too concerned with getting in line to tour the lighthouse or picking out the perfect picnic spot.

We eat our lunch on a patch of grass beneath the shade of a tall cypress. Staring out at the horizon, seeing nothing but water and sky, it is easy to believe we are sitting on the edge of the world.

"I want you to meet my mother," Alec says suddenly. "Tonight, after dinner. Do you think you can get away?"

I hesitate. It was so much easier to contemplate meeting Alec's mother that night in the dance pavilion, when Alec and

I had only just met and our feelings for each other had not burrowed into our souls so deeply. Now, the thought terrifies me. What if she doesn't like me? What if my nerves turn me into a bumbling idiot?

"I might be able to," I say, picking at a blade of grass, "but are you sure that's something we should do? The more people who know about us, the more dangerous this all becomes."

"She wouldn't say anything—she would never do anything to hurt me. She asked me the other day what's been making me so happy lately, and I want to show her. I want her to know you, Lea, and for you to know her."

Dread twists my stomach. If we were anyone else, if I were like Moira or Clara, I probably would have met Alec's mother already. We might even share secret jokes about his habits, such as the way he runs his hands through his hair when he's nervous, or the way he shovels food into his mouth, as if he is constantly on the verge of starvation even though he is clearly well-fed. But I am not like Moira or Clara—I never will be—and as much as I want to meet her, to see where Alec comes from, I fear his mother will not find me good enough for her son.

An excuse begins to form on my lips, but then Alec locks those hope-filled eyes on mine and it's impossible to refuse him.

CHAPTER THIRTY-TWO

NELL

I CAN'T SLEEP. I'M TOO wired, and the knowledge that I can't trust myself to not crawl out of a fifth-story window doesn't help matters.

I think about sneaking down to the dining room, but ballet is no longer the refuge it once was. Because if my first guess was right, if I really am just hallucinating all this, then losing myself in dance did nothing to keep the visions at bay, nor did implementing the techniques I learned from Dr. Roby. And if Alec is right—if he was even real and if our conversation even happened—then something else is going on here, and until I figure out what it is, I'm not safe anywhere.

You're supposed to remember me.

Remember him doing what?

I'm out the door at the first hint of sunrise. I grab a to-go cup of coffee and a bagel from the bakery and head for the storage room. The door is locked, so I press my back against the wall and slide down, sitting cross-legged on the floor.

Something scratches the inside of my arm. I reach behind me and feel the corner of a paper sticking out of my jeans, jeans I haven't worn in over a week in favor of shorts and yoga pants. I tug it loose and see the headline once more:

YOUNG SOCIALITE MURDERED AT LUXURY HOTEL

I rub my thumb over the words (*blood, so much blood*), then shove it back in my pocket.

I've long since finished my bagel and my coffee by the time Max and Sofia arrive to unlock the door. I've been staring at the cup for what feels like hours, trying to think. Trying to *remember*. But all I can remember is the scrape on my knee from being tackled off a window ledge and the feeling of Alec's cheek pressed against mine.

I can't tell you what's going on.

Why?

Because then you will lose your mind.

High-heeled shoes and a pair of Converse sneakers stop in front of me.

"Happy Fourth of July!" Max says.

"What?" I blink up at him. "Oh. Yeah. Happy Fourth."

Max's brow furrows. "You all right?"

My voice is gritty like a rockslide. "Couldn't sleep."

Sofia fits the storage-room key in the lock and opens the door. "Maybe you should go back to your room? Lie down for a bit?"

"No," I say, pushing myself up. "I want to work."

She nods. "All right. Feel better."

I follow Max into the room as Sofia's heels click back down the hall. I head for my designated section, but my mind keeps going back to the headline in my pocket, and instead of going through the piles of papers that need to be sorted, I pull the article back out of my pocket, my heart stopping at the word MURDERED.

What happened to you?

My gaze roams up to the Independence Day article above the headline, pausing on the picture of Mark Twain as he ascends the staircase into the Grand.

But it isn't the author I focus on.

In the background, standing on the front porch, behind a kid hanging halfway over the railing and a woman wearing her hair up in a cloudlike poof on top of her head, is a girl who looks . . . weirdly . . . like me.

I lean in closer.

Same heart-shaped face, same pointy chin. Her eyes are squinted from laughing, so I can't tell if they're like mine, but there's a speck on her throat that *could* be a shadow . . . or a very familiar mole.

My hands shake as I stare at the picture. Is she a long-lost ancestor? A doppelgänger? A mirage conjured up by my sleep-deprived brain?

Remember me.

My eyes travel to the boy standing next to her. His face is half-hidden by the older woman's poodle hair, but I would know that smile and those deep-set eyes anywhere.

Alec.

A searing pain shoots through my skull, and it's like my brain is cracking open. I cry out and press my palms to my temples. Images appear on the backs of my eyelids like a movie playing in fast-forward.

Waves crash against a boat as the hotel looms ahead of me. A man with slicked-back hair and a too-wide smile greets me in the lobby, and I take a step back to keep from vomiting all over his expensive shoes. A bellhop who's not really a bellhop, who makes me laugh and lies with me on a moonlit beach and gives me a tiny sliver of hope I can't explain.

"Nell?" I hear Max ask. "Are you okay?"

It feels like someone is driving a pickax through my cornea. I grind my teeth against the pain.

Dancing in the ballroom, my eyes always searching for someone in the crowd. Arguing with the man with the too-wide smile—he wants to hit me, but he would never do such a thing in public, so I stand my ground.

Swimming and fishing and horseback riding and kisses shared in secret, hidden places.

A decision.

A plan.

A gun.

And then the images are gone.

The pain in my skull becomes a dull, persistent ache.

Max lays a hand on my shoulder. "Do you want me to call your dad?"

"No," I say, dropping my hands. They shake like chattering teeth, and I clasp them together until my knuckles whiten. "No, I, um . . . I think I just need some sleep. I'm not feeling very well."

"Yeah, definitely. Take the day off. I can manage without you."

I glance up at him. For a second, he doesn't look like Max. His face changes to someone I don't recognize, and his clothes morph from his skinny jeans and gray T-shirt to an old-fashioned tweed suit. I squeeze my eyes shut and open them again.

Max stares down at me, his clothes back the way they were.

"Okay," I say, stumbling back. "Thanks."

"Do you want me to walk you to your room?"

"No," I say, even as my legs wobble beneath me. "I'll be all right."

I somehow manage to get out into the main basement hallway and up to the first floor without falling, even though the world is tilting around me. My stomach sloshes and a cold sweat beads along my hairline. I think I might puke, but that's the least of my worries.

Everyone passing me—little kids in bathing suits and couples window-shopping and hotel employees—they all change like Max. But unlike Max, they don't go back to normal when I close my eyes. They flicker through different faces and body types, different clothing and different hairstyles. Long gowns and tweed suits change into short flapper dresses and pinstriped jackets. Fifties circle skirts and pleated men's trousers become paisley wrap dresses and fringed leather vests. Big, teased hair and neon fanny packs turn into hoodies and jeans, camisoles and denim shorts.

Around and around they go, like a carousel. I close my eyes and press my hand against the wall, feeling for the turn into the lobby. I hear someone say, "Do you think that girl's okay?" and someone else replies, "Had a little too much fun last night, I think."

Neither of them stops to help me.

Once I feel the corner of the wall beneath my fingers, I open my eyes again.

It's okay, you're okay, everything's okay, I tell myself. *You're going to stop being stubborn and you're going to call Dr. Roby. Whatever it takes, you're going to fix this. It's okay, you're okay, everything's okay—*

Walking into the lobby is like walking into a funhouse. There are too many people, and they're all changing. Men become women and women become men, and it's like each one has a slideshow of photographs superimposed on top of them, flickering through different people from different eras, but the images are changing too fast to get a good look at anyone. I try to take a step forward, but my vision tunnels.

"Somebody."

My voice sounds distant, like it isn't coming from me, and I know it isn't loud enough.

I try again.

"Somebody . . . please. Help me."

I reach out for an old man. He changes into a younger, thinner man with a top hat and glasses, then into a woman with short black hair and dark red lipstick. Into a paunchy man, wearing giant rubber pants and carrying a fishing pole, a platinum blond with pearls around her neck, a teenager wearing sparkly eye shadow and bright green tights, a guy in his twenties wearing plaid shorts and a white polo beneath a mint green sweater.

They're all different people, but they all wear the same expression of surprise mixed with disgust as they pass me by.

I try to inhale, but it's like my lungs have forgotten how to inflate.

"I . . . can't . . . breathe."

The darkness hovering around the edges of my vision seeps inward.

"Nell?"

Alec appears in front of me. His clothes change like everyone else—a bellhop uniform, corduroy pants with suspenders over a blue shirt, high-waisted trousers with a peacoat, bell-bottoms and a button-up, khaki pants with a cable-knit sweater—but, unlike everyone else, his face doesn't change.

It's always him.

My legs buckle.

Alec sweeps me into his arms, cradling me against his chest.

"Don't worry," he says. "I've got you."

His scent—sandalwood and lemon blossoms and clean linen—envelops me, and my heart is racing in my chest, and my body feels heavy enough to plummet to the center of the Earth.

But my lungs fill with air again, and I'm no longer drowning.

CHAPTER THIRTY-THREE

LEA

A *FIREWORKS DISPLAY AND SYMPHONIC* concert on the front lawn follow the big Fourth of July dinner. I feign another headache and convince Mother I need to lie down if I am to be of any use at the ball tonight. She doesn't like it, but the two men who would usually care to know my whereabouts—my father and Lon—are too busy flattering business tycoons and other important men of industry to notice my absence, so she acquiesces.

I meet Alec in the fifth-floor hall by the linen closet, as planned. He greets me with open arms, spinning me around in a wide circle.

I smack his chest. "Put me down. Someone will see."

"Everyone's outside," he says.

My heart speeds up as his hand cups my chin, tilting my head back. He kisses me gently at first, but a moan purrs deep in my throat, and I claw at his back, wanting more. He presses me up against the wall, pinning me with his long, lean body, his muscles hard as granite beneath his clothing. His lips devour mine, until we are the same breath and soul and being.

Alec breaks the kiss. He's out of breath, and every inhale shakes with desire. He leans his forehead against mine and closes his eyes.

"Do you even realize what you do to me, Aurelea Sargent?"

"If it is even half of what you do to me, then you must be losing your mind."

"I've lost my mind and my heart to you, Lea." He opens his eyes. "You've bewitched me."

I smile. "Come on. Your mother's waiting for us."

Alec's mother shares a room with another laundress, but her roommate is downstairs, enjoying the music and fireworks. The room is cozy, containing two beds, two dressers, and two washstands. A small, circular table sits in the middle of the room, with four spindly chairs surrounding it. A pot of tea sits on the table along with a plate of scones I recognize from yesterday's breakfast in the dining room.

Alec's mother, Orya, a small, pale woman with hair the color of bone and eyes the color of salt, inspects me as Alec introduces us. Too late, I am aware of the burning around my lips and nose where Alec's stubble scratched me, and I can only pray the lighting is too dim for her to notice.

"So," Orya says after a moment. "You are the girl who has made my son so happy these past weeks."

Although she has lived in the United States for almost twenty years, her Russian accent laces heavily through every word. Alec told me his father acclimated quickly to American life, losing most of his accent before Alec was old enough to notice the change, but his mother refused to give up even a modicum of her heritage. She held on to her accent as if it were made of gold. She also still celebrates Russian holidays and keep a small cross from the Russian Orthodox Church in her apron pocket.

"Did your mother not want to move to America?" I asked Alec one day while we lay stretched out on the beach in Canvas City.

"It was complicated," he replied. "She recognized her growing family would have more opportunities here, but giving me and my father those opportunities meant saying goodbye to everyone else she loved. Her entire family is still in Russia. They send weekly letters back and forth, but it takes so long to receive them that we're always several months behind on their news, and they're always behind on ours. The correspondence helps, but photographs and words on paper aren't always enough to keep the loneliness at bay."

"Has she ever thought of going back?"

He shrugged. "Maybe, but she knows I would choose to stay here, and I don't think she likes the idea of leaving me, no matter how old or well-settled I am."

Now his mother gestures for us to sit at the table. I take a scone. The pastry is stale and the sugar glaze is dissolving, but I eat it as if it is the best scone I've ever tasted.

An uneasy silence hangs over us.

"Orya," I say, attempting conversation. "Alec tells me you're from St. Petersburg. I've always wanted to travel there. The architecture is so beautiful."

Her eyes narrow. "You may call me Mrs. Petrov."

"Of course." My hands flutter like birds, a nervous habit I thought Mother had trained out of me years ago. "Please, forgive me."

Alec frowns at his mother. I can tell he wants to say something in my defense, but I lay my hand on his knee, stopping him.

Orya notices. "So you two are . . . friends?"

"Yes," I answer. "In fact, we've become quite good friends."

"You have not known each other long," she observes.

I look to Alec. "You don't always need to know someone for very long to know their heart."

She studies me again, and I cannot tell for the life of me what she's thinking. Finally, she says, "This is true."

Alec exhales. He tells his mother of the nights we've spent in Canvas City, and I thank her for his dance lessons, as I promised I would. She listens to us without saying a word. Her face is expressionless. She doesn't touch her tea, nor a single scone. She is a statue, up until the point Alec absently puts his arm around the back of my chair as he tells her about the picnic we shared this afternoon, and then her face reddens and she closes her eyes.

"I am sorry, Alec," she says, "but I have had enough of this."

Alec's brow furrows. "Mother—"

"No," she says. "I cannot listen any longer." She gets up from the table, wringing her hands. "You think I do not notice the engagement ring on her finger? Or the expensive dress she wears? You think I do not know that she is a guest here, and that you are putting your job, your very *life* at risk with this . . . this dalliance?"

Alec jumps to his feet. "Lea isn't a *dalliance*—"

"What else would you call it when you are spending time with a girl who is already spoken for?"

"Please, excuse me," I say, standing. "I should return to the party."

"Yes, you should," Mrs. Petrov clips.

"She doesn't have to go," Alec shouts. He says it again, softer this time, as he turns to me. "You don't have to go."

I glance at Mrs. Petrov. "I think your mother would like some privacy."

He starts to argue, but I shake my head.

"It's all right. We'll see each other tomorrow."

I want to kiss him goodbye, as I have done every night since our first outing to Canvas City, but it isn't proper, and it would only upset his mother more to know that we have been so affectionate with each other.

I say good night to Mrs. Petrov and slip out the door.

"How could you say those things to her?" Alec's voice drifts through the door.

"She is not yours to have," his mother replies, her voice so soft I have to strain to hear it. "The sooner you realize that, the sooner you can detach yourself from her, before you lose yourself completely to someone you can never have."

I want to stay and listen, even as my eyes burn and my stomach twists, but I hear footsteps echoing down the hall, and I know my time is up.

I return to our suite to collect myself, washing my face with cold water and rubbing an ointment on my chin to remove the redness from Alec's kisses. It is only when I no longer feel like I could cry or purge my dinner at a moment's notice that I return to the front lawn and watch the fireworks display with my fiancé, thinking all the while of the boy who's been stealing pieces of my heart for weeks, and of the boy's mother, who managed to rip them all to shreds in a matter of seconds.

CHAPTER THIRTY-FOUR

NELL

ALEC CARRIES ME INTO THE garden. The air is crisp and floral, and it cools my fevered skin. He sets me down on a white bench, slightly damp from the morning dew, and crouches in front of me. His clothes are no longer changing, but the damage has already been done. My stomach pitches as I lean forward, placing my head in my hands.

"I think I'm going to be sick."

"Breathe," he tells me, his fingers tracing delicate circles on my knees.

I angle my head to meet his gaze. "You were in the picture."

He doesn't say anything.

"You were in the picture with . . ."

Say it.

But I can't. It's too absurd.

"With someone who looked like me," I finish.

He shakes his head. "Not someone who *looked* like you." He

glances around the garden, but we're alone, and something about that feels so familiar, like a memory I—

A lemon tree. A shovel.

—can't—

Sweat glistening off tanned, toned muscles. A tug somewhere deep in my stomach that makes my cheeks flush.

—quite—

A knowing smile. A fumbled invitation. And those deep, intense eyes, staring at me like I'm a glass of water and he's dying of thirst.

—grasp.

"What's happening to me?"

He looks away, swearing under his breath.

Finally he says, "You're starting to remember."

"Isn't that what you wanted?"

"I don't *want* any of this."

My eyes sting at the bite in his tone.

"Fine." I splay my hands against his chest and push off him as I stand. I can't think straight when he's this close. "I didn't ask for your help, you know."

I start back toward the lobby, my legs shaky but cooperating.

Alec growls. His hand cups my elbow, stopping me.

"Wait."

I turn to him, my tongue coiled like a whip ready to snap, but my knees betray me, and I fall against him.

For a moment, he stands completely still, his arms tight around me. And then—

His hand cups the back of my neck.

Dancing across a wooden floor. Streaking like a comet in his arms. Spinning, spinning, spinning until I don't know up from down or east from west.

Alec's features soften and his lips, which just a second before had been set in a tight, grim line, look fuller as they part. His arms grip me tighter.

That smile that makes my hopeless heart squeeze inside my chest.

I reach up—so, so slowly—and brush his hair from his eyes. It feels new and wonderful and, at the same time, like something I've done a thousand times before.

Those lips crushing mine, stealing my breath and my destiny and my soul in the gilded light of dawn. Finding me in deserted hallways and empty rooms. Tracing my neck as his fingers trail the ribbons of my corset, and a deep, desperate need to be with him, now, before we have to say goodbye forever.

I breathe his name.

"Alec . . . what's happening to me?"

His smile is heavy. Broken. Defeated. He presses his lips to the top of my head and wraps his arms around me like a shield—like if he let go, I would crumble to dust in front of his eyes.

"Come on." His gaze sweeps the corridors and balconies rising above us. "We can't talk here."

We walk to the beach, where Alec says the surf will drown our voices. But it's still early, and the few people on the beach with us are searching for seashells, carrying on their own conversations, and, somehow, I don't think it's these people he's worried will hear us.

I wait for him to speak, to explain what the hell is going on with me, but he says nothing as he walks next to me, staring down at the sand, his hands behind his back.

"Who's the girl in the picture?" I ask.

He swallows. "Which one was it?"

"Mark Twain. On the porch."

"Ah."

A group of pelicans skim the water, their long, elegant beaks cutting the surface like knives.

Instead of answering my question, he asks another. "What do you remember?"

Sitting in the dining room, suffocating under the toxic expectations that have been placed upon me. Putting on a show for the watchful eyes of the gossiping ladies stationed around the second-floor balcony like frilly, tea-drinking gargoyles. Allowing that man with the too-wide smile and slicked-back hair to take my hand and speak of our future as if he knows what I want and kiss me when we are unchaperoned even though all I want to do is retch from the expensive smell and leering sight of him.

"Flashes," I say. "Snippets. But it doesn't make sense. They feel like memories, but I don't know where they're coming from. The only person I recognize is you, and it's not like we've ever—" *Made out.* No, I am so not admitting that my hallucinations have now included thoughts of Alec and me hooking up. I take a deep breath and start again. "I don't know what's happening to me, but I think I can fix it."

His brow arches, an infinitesimal amount that would've been unnoticeable if I hadn't been watching him so closely. "You do?"

"I've had issues like this before."

He doesn't bother hiding his surprise this time. "You have?"

I nod. "There's a doctor back in Colorado. A therapist. I used to see him pretty regularly. He offered to find me a therapist here, in Winslow, but I didn't think I needed one anymore." I scoff. "What a joke."

Alec stops walking. "What exactly do you think is happening to you?"

"Hallucinations, brought on by—I don't know. Lack of sleep, maybe, or stress from the move or . . . something." I laugh, a fractured sound. "I'm probably hallucinating this entire conversation right now."

He grips my arms. "You're not hallucinating this, and the visions you're getting aren't hallucinations, either. They're memories."

I pull away from him and start walking again.

"They can't be memories. I've never been here before."

"Yes, you have," he says, so quietly I almost don't hear him. "A long time ago."

I turn back. The hotel stands sentinel behind him, a hulking green-and-white figure watching us and the sea, just as it has watched every other person pass this way for more than a hundred years.

"Alec."

He meets my gaze.

"Who's the girl in the picture?"

"Aurelea Sargent."

A *decision*.

A *plan*.

A *gun*.

My tongue suddenly feels like a cracked desert floor.

"The girl who was murdered?"

He nods.

"And the boy?" I ask, because I need to hear him say it. "The one next to her?"

His eyes pin me in place.

"It's me," he says. "And I'm standing next to you."

CHAPTER THIRTY-FIVE

LEA

THE NEXT DAY, MOTHER KEEPS me busy with wedding plans, so I do not see Alec again until our midnight rendezvous on the beach. He looks as exhausted as I feel, as if he also spent the previous night tossing and turning in half dreams. He takes me in his arms and doesn't let go when I pull away. He breathes deeply, as if memorizing every scent and grain and fiber of me.

"Alec? What's the matter?"

He doesn't speak.

"I'm sorry last night went so poorly," I say, fear quickening my words. "Is there anything I can do to make it right?"

He doesn't reply.

"Maybe if your mother got to know me—"

"It wouldn't matter." His arms loosen and he takes a step back, and though the intensity with which he held me terrified me a second ago, it is more terrifying to see the look of decision that replaces it. "She was right. You aren't mine to have."

I shake my head. "No." I try to take his hands in mine, but he shrugs out of my grasp and steps away from me, until it feels like the entire ocean is between us. "Why are you saying these things?"

"Because it's true. This—us—" He swallows. "We can never be more than this."

My mind feels as though someone has stuffed cotton balls between my ears, a foggy barrier muffling his words. "I don't understand. You . . . you knew I was engaged before any of this started."

He doesn't meet my gaze. "I know."

"What's changed?"

"I've fallen in love with you, Lea. That's what's changed."

"But you were fine before last night."

"What do you want me to say? That I pretended for as long as I possibly could that this summer wasn't a lie? That we wouldn't have to say goodbye to each other at the end of it?"

Our voices are rising louder than the surf, and I know it is dangerous to be speaking so openly here, so close to the hotel where anyone could hear, but I can't stop.

"But that's exactly why we shouldn't be wasting our time arguing or thinking about the future. We only have now—*right now*—and this is how you want to spend our time together?"

He closes the distance between us. "You think this isn't killing me? You think I want to say goodbye to you? That ring on your finger is a death knell, reminding me every time I hold you, kiss you, *want* you, that you aren't mine. You will *never* be mine."

"But we have now." Tears cloud my vision. "I am yours *now*."

He runs his hands through his hair, knotting them behind his head. "It's not enough."

My voice is the quiet hush of winter. "It's all I have to give."

He shakes his head. "I'm sorry."

"You're a coward, Alec Petrov," I whisper as he walks away. I take a deep breath, the salt-laced air sharp as knives in my lungs. "Did you hear me?" I shout over the wind. "You're a *coward*."

He doesn't even glance over his shoulder as he heads back inside the hotel, taking my heart and bones and soul with him, leaving behind a mere shell of the girl I used to be as my entire body crumples to the sand.

CHAPTER THIRTY-SIX

NELL

ALEC TRIES TO TAKE MY hand, but I stumble back, kicking up grains of sand. The surf is loud in my ears, a relentless, drumming beat.

"You're just as delusional as I am." I laugh again, but it sounds wrong. Desperate. I turn on my heel and keep walking. "Or maybe this is a dream. Yeah, that's it. I'm still asleep."

"Nell, stop."

"I just need to wake up. I just need—"

My body freezes. I glance down at my legs, confused. I try to take another step forward, but it's like trying to walk through a wall. I tell myself to take a step back, and my body responds, but when I tell myself to go forward—nothing happens.

"That's the hotel property line," Alec says, stopping next to me and staring out at the beach in front of us. "You can't cross it."

"Why not?"

"The curse won't let you."

"*The curse?*" I choke out a laugh. "Okay, now you've really lost it. I can leave anytime I want."

I grind my teeth, pushing all my weight forward.

But it's no use.

I haven't moved an inch.

"Have you tried leaving the hotel since you arrived?" Alec asks.

"Not yet," I admit, "but only because I haven't had any reason to."

He crosses his arms over his chest and gives me a half smirk that makes my heart do a somersault.

Kissing—touching—needing—wanting—can't stop—won't stop—he is the air I breathe and the thoughts I think—he is the blood in my veins and the tears in my eyes—

"And you didn't find that odd?" he asks.

I shake my head, trying to clear it. If this is a dream or a hallucination, then why do these thoughts—these random, yet totally lucid thoughts—feel like the memories Alec says they are?

"I've been busy," I grind out.

"Once you're here, the hotel finds reasons to keep you here until it's done."

"Until *what's* done?"

His smile disappears. "Maybe we should sit down."

"I don't want to sit down."

I know I'm acting like a toddler, but I can't stop. None of this makes any sense.

Alec sighs. "Nell. *Please.*"

It's the resignation, the defeat, in his eyes that softens me more than anything else.

"Fine."

We take a seat on the edge of the tide line. Alec sits facing the water, his knees to his chest. I sit cross-legged, facing him.

He doesn't look at me as he speaks.

"This isn't the first time you've been here, and it isn't the first time you've come back."

My brow furrows. "I don't understand."

But I do. Some small part of me knows what he's trying to say. I'm already putting the pieces together. I can feel her—*Aurelea*—banging at the door of my mind, trying to tell me, to show me, but logic and reason resist her, this other person with these memories and feelings invading my own.

"This is your seventh time coming back since . . ." He hesitates. "Since Aurelea died."

He expects me to believe I've been here, to this hotel, not just once, but *seven* times before?

My voice is small, a hummingbird caught up in a breeze. "Since she was murdered, you mean."

He says nothing.

"How did it happen?" I ask.

He exhales. "I wish I could tell you, but you have to remember on your own."

My eyes narrow. "You're setting me up, right? This is some kind of joke?"

"Nell—"

I push myself up. "I'm so stupid. Do you really hate me this much? And for what? Accidentally bumping into you a couple of times?"

"Nell—"

"I'm sick. *Actually* sick. And you have the nerve to use that against me?"

"I can't tell you what happened," he bites back, "because I have before and it didn't work out so well."

Whatever I was expecting him to say, it wasn't this.

"What do you mean?"

He looks away.

"When?" I lower myself back to the sand. "When did you tell me?"

He hesitates. "The first time you came back. Summer of '23. Your name was Alice then." He picks up a broken sand dollar lying by his feet and runs his thumb over its face, studying the cracks. Then he pulls his arm back and chucks it into the water. "You'll start to get memories from then, too. From all the times you've been back. They'll come slowly, in the beginning, then they'll start flooding your brain like a burst dam. You'll get to a point when you can't deny it anymore. Sometimes it's sooner, sometimes it's later, but it's easier if it's sooner."

"Why is it easier?"

"Because it gives us more time."

The pit in my stomach grows. "More time for what?"

His eyes cut away from the ocean, locking on mine.

"To keep you from dying again."

CHAPTER THIRTY-SEVEN

LEA

AFTER BREAKFAST BENNY BEGS FATHER to take him into Canvas City to compete in the model sailboat race. Father is in a good mood, so he tells Benny to run and get his sailboat. Mother decides to make a day of it, packing a picnic lunch and inviting Lon to accompany us.

"You're unusually quiet today," Lon observes as we take our place among the spectators.

That is an understatement. I am a phantom, a revenant, the smoky tendrils of a snuffed-out flame. I do not speak other than in short, clipped responses to unavoidable questions. Any more than this feels as though it would take an impossible amount of energy. I had hoped Lon wouldn't notice, and for once I actually find myself thankful for his boastful anecdotes and inability to speak of anything other than himself, because it keeps me from having to say much at all. But I suppose he is becoming more attuned to my responses to him, or lack thereof.

"I am preoccupied," I answer honestly.

"Whatever with?"

The sun is mockingly bright. I place my hand over my eyes and search for Benny in the line of children waiting to release their sailboats.

"The wedding, of course."

"Ah." Lon slips an arm around my waist, his fingers curling over my hip. "You know, it's never too late to elope."

"And *you* know we've already discussed how foolish that would be."

He stiffens. My quick tongue has damaged his ego. I know I should apologize, but I just don't care enough to do so.

Instead of pulling away as I expect, Lon moves behind me, pressing his chest against my back and his legs against my legs. Both hands grip my hips as he pulls me against him. "Do you realize," he murmurs in my ear, his breath sour with the smell of his breakfast kippers, "our wedding is only two months away? Theoretically speaking, you could be pregnant during the ceremony, and not a single person would know."

I can't quite hide my sneer as I look back at him. "Just what are you proposing?"

"Come to my room tonight."

A gunshot cracks the air. The sailboats are released. I use the opportunity to step away from Lon, applauding with the rest of the crowd.

"I do not know what sort of girl you take me for," I reprimand him through my smile. Mother is watching us.

"I take you for my future wife," he says. "So what does it matter if we consummate our marriage now or on our wedding night?"

"What if you change your mind and leave me at the altar? I'll be ruined."

"You know I wouldn't do such a thing."

I need to do something. Flatter him. Change his mind. Make him think waiting until our wedding night is *his* idea. But when I open my mouth, my words spill out like venom.

"The answer is no. Now, if you'll excuse me, I am going to go cheer for my brother."

I expect him to follow me to the water, but Mother must sense his anger and the scene he is about to make, because she intercepts him, giving me the escape I so desperately need. I push my way to the front of the crowd and shout Benny's name. His sailboat is currently in fourth place, but he has the widest grin I've seen him wear in God knows how long.

"Your brother?" the girl standing next to me asks, her voice familiar in its bitterness.

Clara.

"Yes," I reply.

"Alec was positively shattered last night." She inspects her nails, picking at the lines of sand beneath them. "I haven't seen him drink that much since his father died."

I keep my eyes on Benny and my voice low. It is dangerous to speak of this here, but I am ravenous for news of him. "What did he say?"

"That he decided to break it off now, before either of you were too far gone. After three drinks, he started wondering if he did the right thing. I assured him that he did."

I can't help myself. I glance at her, expecting her to look gleeful, or haughty, but she is neither of these things. She is solemn, and I wonder if I am imagining the pity in her eyes.

"I know it's hard for you to see this," she continues, "and it isn't your fault. You live in a different world. But Alec was the one who was always going to get hurt here. At the end of the summer, you are going to marry your prince charming and live in a castle, all wrapped up in your jewels and your furs, and Alec will be left with nothing. He'll still be here, living a third-class life surrounded by first-class people who act friendly enough but never care to learn his name."

Not always, I want to say. *He's going to be a doctor.*

But it doesn't matter. It won't change the fact that she is right, that I am a selfish monster of a girl who cared more about the way a boy made her feel now than how she would make him feel in the end.

"That's why I never warmed to you," she says, looking out at the water. "I knew you were only going to hurt Alec—it's what people like you do. But I want you to know if it weren't for that, I think we could have been friends."

My throat is parched, and I have to swallow in order to speak. "Are you in love with him?"

"I don't know," she replies. "But maybe once you're gone, I'll find out. Regardless, Alec deserves to be with me, or a girl like me. A girl he can actually have."

The sailboats cross the finish line. Benny comes in second behind a boy in patched-up coveralls and a dirt-smudged face. Benny shakes the boy's hand, congratulating him on the win.

"If you really care about Alec," Clara says, "you'll stay away from him."

Benny searches for me in the crowd. I force a smile and hold out my arms. Clara disappears as Benny runs to me, wrapping himself around my waist.

"Did you see? I got *this* close to winning."

"You were marvelous, darling," I tell him. "Absolutely marvelous."

Father approaches us, clapping a hand on Benny's shoulder. "Well done, son. You almost had him."

I hand Benny to Father, who lifts him onto his shoulders and carries him over the crowd to Mother. I stand there a moment, watching them.

If you really care about Alec, you'll stay away from him.

Sighing, I pick up the hem of my dress and follow. Lon still looks angry with me, but I appease him with a hand on his arm and a flirtatious smile. I have no idea how I ever thought I could escape my fate, but I am determined to honor Alec's wishes.

I will not make things any harder than they have to be.

CHAPTER THIRTY-EIGHT

NELL

"WHAT DO YOU MEAN, TO keep me from dying again?"

"Every sixteen years," Alec says, his jaw tense, his fists curled, "you come back to me. And every sixteen years, I have to watch you die again."

I laugh. I don't like how maniacal it sounds, but I can't help it. "Okay, now you've really gone off the deep end. I'm going to die because of what? Some curse?"

I think he's going to get angry at me for laughing. That we'll fight and maybe he'll finally give up this cruel joke. I don't know how he knows about my hallucinations, or how he knows them so well as to make up an entire story around them, but that has to be what it is.

A story.

A joke.

A nightmare.

Instead, he looks down at the sand.

"Every time, I don't think I'll survive it," he murmurs, veins tracing his arms like rope, "but then I just go on living. Stuck here until you come back again." He exhales roughly. "*That's* the curse. I have been cursed with an immortal prison sentence, and you have been cursed to return every sixteen years, to relive the events of that summer."

"If that's true, then why weren't you happier to see me? Why were you so distant?" I scoot closer to him, accusation saturating my voice. "If you've been waiting for me for sixteen years, why won't you look at me for longer than two seconds?"

He explodes off the sand.

"You think this is easy for me? You think I *wanted* this? We thought we beat it last time. We were so sure we'd saved you that we actually *celebrated*. We made plans. We talked about our future together as the sun came up." Tears ring his lashes. "You died in my arms, Katie, and there was nothing I could do to stop it. So I'm sorry if I'm not more excited to see you, but I can't have that kind of hope again only to have it taken away from me. You can't ask that of me."

My brow furrows.

The silence stretches between us.

"Nell," he finally says. "I meant to say Nell."

I push myself up. I don't know what to say to him. I still don't know if I'm trapped in a dream or if I'm more messed up than I thought—if I'm talking to air right now instead of Alec—but I do know one thing: Alec believes what he's saying. This isn't a joke or a trick to him. The pain in his voice is too real for that.

"Look, I'm no expert on this or anything," I say softly, "but it sounds like you might have a serious problem. Maybe you should see someone. I could call my therapist and see if there's anyone around here he'd recommend. We could go together—"

Alec crosses the distance between us, so close I can't see anything but him. His entire body tenses as if he wants to shake me, but he keeps his fists curled at his sides. "I don't have a problem.

This is real, Nell, and the sooner you accept it, the easier it will be on both of us."

"Is there any way," I ask, forcing the words out through my too-dry mouth, "that you've . . . I don't know . . . mistaken me for someone else?"

"You've seen the picture. You've been having the visions. You just saw for yourself that you can't leave the property," he says. "You tell me if I've made a mistake."

I stare up at him. Every line of his body spells danger, but even here, in the midst of his anger, I'm not afraid of him. I know, deep in my bones, that he would never hurt me. But how I would know such a thing about a total stranger is beyond me.

Unless what he's saying is true.

Unless I'm not hallucinating any of this.

Unless I really am—*was*—Aurelea Sargent, and he's not a stranger at all.

"So," I say, swallowing, "what happens now?"

"We wait for your memories to come back."

"And then we'll come up with a plan so I won't die again?" I mean for it to come out sarcastically, but the words hang heavy between us.

He grinds his teeth and takes a step back. He stares out at the ocean, avoiding my gaze.

"Alec?" I ask, my voice wavering. "We're going to come up with a plan, right?"

He takes a long time to answer, and when he finally does, nothing about it is reassuring.

"We always do."

———

Once upon a time, when I was a young girl all wrapped up in hope and dreams and fairy tales, I probably would have accepted

Alec's explanation without questioning it. But that girl was blown to smithereens the moment a plane carrying her mother fell out of the sky.

I don't believe in fairy tales. I don't believe in curses. And I sure as hell don't believe in fate. If my mother's death taught me anything, it is that this world is a terrifying place and we're all just biding our time until the next great tragedy befalls us.

That's why I hold on to Dad as tightly as I do and, I think, why he's held on to me. We know that at any moment one of us could be ripped from the other, and there's not a thing we could do to stop it. So, to think that there's some plan, that fate or God or whatever you want to call it would go to this much trouble to bring two people back together every sixteen years to right a past wrong—it just goes against everything I've believed over the past four years.

Which is why I leave Alec on the beach and head back to my room. I need to get my head straight, and I can't do that when he's looking at me like that.

Like every word he's saying is true.

You've seen the picture. You've been having the visions. You just saw for yourself that you can't leave the property. You tell me if I've made a mistake.

It's not even noon yet, so I have the room to myself. My first thought is to lie down on the bed and get some sleep, but even though my body feels like it could collapse at any moment, my brain is too wired to shut down.

I pull up Dr. Roby's contact information. He's probably with a patient now, but he checks his voice mail regularly, and I know he'll get back to me right away if I tell him it's an emergency. That I'm seeing things that aren't there, that I almost sleepwalked right out of a fifth-story window, that I might be having entirely made-up conversations with someone to explain my delusions.

That I might need him to recommend a new therapist after all.

My thumb hovers over the call button.

Swearing under my breath, I exit my contacts, pull up my Internet browser, and type:

Aurelea Sargent, Winslow Grand Hotel

There isn't a lot of information aside from what Max has already told me, and the majority of it comes from urban legend and conspiracy theorists, so I have no idea how much of it is true. But each site agrees on these main points:

Aurelea Sargent and her fiancé, Lon Van Oirschot, were discovered dead of gunshot wounds in Aurelea's suite sometime in the early hours of August 6, 1907, precisely two days before her seventeenth birthday—the same day as *my* birthday, coincidentally enough—and a month from her wedding date. Although several suspects were reportedly investigated at the time, no arrest was ever made. There was also talk of a possible murder-suicide, which seemed even more plausible after Aurelea's friends back home shared that she was not especially fond of Lon. More rumors sprang up of her parents' desperate financial situation, but none of the reports were ever substantiated, and the family quickly shot them down as slanderous hearsay.

Something about this last piece of information tickles the back of my mind—*a trunk full of dresses we can't afford*—but the sensation fades just as quickly as it appears.

Next, I type:

Winslow Grand Hotel deaths

I comb through the sites. Surely if what Alec is saying is true, if I'm Aurelea and I've returned to the hotel every sixteen years only to die every single time, there would be reports of it. Articles. Speculation as to why sixteen-year-old girls keep dying in the hotel.

But there's nothing.

I want to feel smug about this, especially after the whole Aurelea-sharing-my-birthday thing creeped me out, but all this means is that either Alec is just as lost and confused as I am, or my entire conversation with him was a delusion my brain conjured up to calm me down. Was Alec even there, in the lobby? Did he even take me into the courtyard, or to the beach? Maybe I passed out somewhere and dreamed the whole thing.

A knock at the door startles me.

My first thought is that Dad forgot his key, but it's only half past one—I've been researching this for two hours?—and then I think:

Alec.

I pocket my phone and cross the room, casting a quick glance at my reflection in the closet mirror and smoothing my hair before opening the door.

Max's smile greets me. He holds up a brown paper bag from one of the hotel's restaurants. "Hey, sickie. I brought you some soup."

"Wow," I say, trying to hide my disappointment. "Thanks."

He shrugs. "Mom paid for it when I told her you were sick, and I kind of took advantage and bought myself a sandwich, too, but it's the thought that counts, right?"

I force a laugh. "Absolutely."

"So are you up for some company, or should I take my sandwich downstairs and eat all by myself like the mysterious loner that I am?"

"Come in."

We set up our lunch on the small table beneath one of the windows overlooking the roof. Max asks how I'm feeling as he carefully peels the lid off my soup and hands me a plastic spoon.

"Better," I lie. "Just needed to get some sleep."

He brightens. "Thank God. I wanted to see this movie tonight, but all my friends want to watch the fireworks, and I thought maybe you and I could . . . but then you said you were sick, so I figured I'd find you puking your guts out or something."

I'm barely listening. My mind keeps returning to Aurelea. To the visions.

To Alec.

"Nope," I say, absently stirring crackers into my soup. "No puking."

Max unwraps his sandwich.

"So, uh, how about it?"

I frown and glance up at him.

"How about what?"

"Do you want to go to the movies tonight?"

I blink. "On the Fourth of July?"

He nods. "I do it every year. Not very patriotic, I know, but I always have the whole place to myself."

I'm about to say yes. A movie sounds like just the sort of thing to take my mind off everything, and maybe getting out of the hotel would do me some good. But then I remember the beach, the property line, the way my body froze as if someone had turned off my ability to move.

But that was just a hallucination. There's no curse stopping you from leaving the property.

Still, I don't feel like testing this theory in front of Max.

"I think I should take it easy," I say. "I'm still not feeling great."

"Oh." His face falls.

"But . . . we could watch a movie here, if you want?"

His eyes widen. "Really?"

"Yeah. I don't think Dad would care. And I think we'll be able to see the fireworks from here, too, so you can get the best of both worlds."

"Okay," he says. "What time should I come over?"

"Six?"

He nods. "Works for me."

We sit in silence for a few minutes as we eat, until I can't take it anymore and ask the question that's been circling my brain for hours.

"What are your thoughts on reincarnation?"

He blinks. "That's random."

"Not really. I thought maybe you could work it into your screenplay."

I didn't used to be this good of a liar. Mom always knew when I was lying because my ears would turn red, my eyes would start shifting, and my words would come out all jumbled. But somehow in the past four years, with Dr. Roby always asking all those questions and Dad always watching me like a hawk, I learned how to hide my emotions behind lies that sounded too much like truth.

Max scrunches up his face. "I've never really thought about it."

My spoon scrapes the bottom of the bowl. "But do you think it's possible?"

"First rule of storytelling," he says, a glint in his eyes. "*Everything* is possible."

CHAPTER THIRTY-NINE

LEA

THE FOLLOWING WEEK IS THE longest of my life.

I throw myself into wedding planning and bridge club meetings, socializing with Mother's new friends and the families of Lon's business partners, acting the part of proper daughter and fiancée. I'm so good at it, at pushing the pain away every time it crops up, that if it weren't for the iron bands pulling tighter and tighter around my heart, making me feel dizzy and out of breath at the most inopportune times, I wouldn't even notice the fact that I'm missing half my soul.

I smile as Mother discusses our confirmed guests and appropriate seating arrangements. I laugh demurely when one of her new friends asks about my trousseau. I can't stop the tears from welling in my eyes during my first dress fitting, but Mother and my attendants mistakenly assume it is out of love for Lon, and I don't correct them.

At night, I lie awake and try to fool myself into thinking marriage will be the greatest adventure of my life and that I might even grow to love Lon, or at least care for him in some way. I do everything in my power to forget Alec Petrov, but every word, every touch, every kiss we shared haunts me. Fragments of the life I could have had, if only I'd been born someone else.

Love has made me a woman possessed.

It does not help that I run into Alec at least once a day, working as a bellhop, a footman, a gardener, a clerk. His presence flows through the hotel's arteries like blood, impossible to ignore. But I do. Whenever our eyes meet, whenever my heart yearns to close the distance between us and beg him to reconsider, to spend every last moment we have together before the bonds of matrimony forever close me off from his world, I turn on my heel and leave.

In my weakest moments, I wonder if he ever really cared for me the way I cared for him, or if they were just words easily spoken beneath the stars but impossible to hold on to in the light of day. If I wanted to believe in true love so badly that I merely imagined he was falling for me just as quickly as I was falling for him. The only answer I can come up with is this:

I am a silly girl.

Because it is obvious he couldn't care for me as deeply as I care for him, or he would have never been able to walk away. I am a silly girl because, realizing this, how did I ever think I would be able to say goodbye to Alec at the end of the summer? How did I think my soul wouldn't shatter into a million pieces the moment I pledged myself to be true to Lon and left Winslow Island with his wedding ring on my finger? It was a mistake, all of it, from the very beginning. Alec was right.

I was never his, and he was never mine.

"Hurry along, Aurelea," Mother calls at the door. "We don't want to keep the Van Oirschots waiting."

"Coming, Mother," I reply, pinning my hair in place. On Mother's orders, I am wearing the emerald evening gown with the black-lace overlay, even though I desperately attempted to hide it in the back of my trunk after the last time I wore it, when Lon told me it was a dress made for ripping. "Start down without me."

"We most certainly will not," Mother's voice calls back.

I roll my eyes as I search for the dress's matching shoes—which were also stuffed somewhere I'd hoped they'd be forgotten, the location of which I cannot quite remember.

Job well done, me.

I say the only thing I know will please Father, who has been pacing in the entryway for the past twenty minutes. "I'll meet you at the elevator."

Tonight will mark the most important dinner we've attended at the Van Oirschot table, as it will include a group of investors who hinted at a possible business deal with Father. It will not take away our debt—nowhere close—but it is a stepping-stone, one that, combined with my marriage to Lon, will almost guarantee my family's ability to continue enjoying the lifestyle to which they've become accustomed. Not to mention place the Sargent name back in the limelight.

My wager works. Father sounds almost jovial at the thought of me finally getting over my "fear" of the elevator.

"Very well. Come along, Margaret," he tells Mother.

The door closes behind them as they leave.

I find the shoes in the back of Benny's trunk and slip them on before racing out the door. I'm only a minute behind my parents, but my gait is longer than my mother's, and I expect to reach them around the next corner.

Suddenly, a hand snags my arm, pulling me into a short corridor. I gasp.

Another hand covers my mouth.

"It's me."

Alec.

My eyes widen as he turns me in his arms. "What are you doing?"

"I have to talk to you."

I glance at the two suites at the end of the corridor, then behind me, at the busy second-floor hallway. "Do you realize how dangerous this is?"

"Meet me tonight," he says. "At the linen closet."

"I have to go—"

"Lea, *please.*"

And there it is. My name on his lips snaps my resolve as if it were made of toothpicks.

"I don't know if I'll be able to get away."

"I'll wait all night if I have to," he replies.

I stare into his eyes a moment longer. "I'll see what I can do."

With that, I pick up my skirts and step back into the hall, my heart hammering against my rib cage. Somehow, I know something will change tonight. I know that whatever Alec has to say to me will set a course for my future, and that thought scares me more than anything, because I have no idea where it will lead.

But I can't stop myself from finding out.

CHAPTER FORTY

NELL

MAX ARRIVES WITH PIZZA AT six o'clock, as promised.

I am so caught up in my thoughts that I jump when he knocks on the door and momentarily forget why he's here in the first place. My brow furrows as I take in his appearance. He's changed out of the clothes he wore earlier and into a pair of black skinny jeans and a gray sweater over a white button-up shirt. A red beanie rests loosely on the back of his head. He smells like cologne and laundry detergent.

His shoulders slump as he takes in my carefully crafted, I-clearly-don't-care-how-I-look dishevelment. "You forgot."

"No," I lie. I think about turning him away, telling him I'm feeling sick again, but my brain hurts from trying to make sense of everything that happened today, and if nothing else, Max will distract me. I gesture to my ponytail, makeup-free skin, and the same clothes I freaked out in this morning. "I just didn't realize it was such a fancy occasion."

He blushes. "Yeah, I, uh, spilled something on my other shirt. Coffee."

"Oh."

"So . . . can I come in?"

"Uh, yeah." I step aside. "Sure."

I text Dad while Max sets up the pizza and paper plates.

Heads-up. Max came over to watch a movie.

"What do you want to watch?" Max asks, grabbing the remote.

"You pick." My stomach pitches as I eye the pizza. I know I haven't taken in anywhere near as many calories as I need to today, but food is the last thing on my mind. "You're the movie expert."

My phone chirps. I check Dad's text.

No problem. Working late on a project with Sofia anyway. Have fun. ☺

I don't know how, with everything that's going on, I have the strength to be annoyed by this text—especially the smiley face at the end of it—but my teeth clench at the thought of Dad spending time with Sofia. Ringless, boyfriend-less, shares-the-same-obsessions-as-him, drop-dead-gorgeous Sofia.

Max picks an indie movie that, according to him, was highly underrated, and we sit cross-legged on the edge of my bed. I force myself to eat two slices of pizza.

Max eats the other six.

I try to concentrate on the movie, but my thoughts keep circling back to Alec and Aurelea. It isn't until halfway through the movie, when the bed squeaks as Max scoots closer to me, his arm brushing mine, that I realize I don't have a clue what's going on.

"This is the shot I was telling you about," he says, his leg pressing against mine as he leans forward. "See how the wide angle here captures the vastness of the character's struggle?"

"Um, yeah," I say. "Totally."

He leans back again. His shoulder stiffens as it bumps mine, but he doesn't pull away. And then, slowly, the back of his hand whispers across my knuckles.

My breath catches in my throat. I glance down at his hand, lying open next to mine.

Oh. No.

Is this—? Does he—?

Does he think this is a date?

Now I'm tense for a whole different reason.

We spend the rest of the movie like this, our legs and arms and the backs of our hands barely touching. Max shifts his weight a couple times, tilting his hand toward mine even more, but I don't accept his blatant invitation. After the movie's over, Max grabs the empty pizza box and heads for the door.

"This was fun," he says, so quickly the words come out in a jumbled rush. "We should do it again sometime."

I want to ask him which part was fun—when I was so wrapped up in my own problems that I was clearly ignoring him, or when I refused to hold his hand—but I open the door instead and say, "Yeah. Definitely."

"Well." He swallows. "Good night."

"Night."

I don't see the kiss coming until his lips are already on mine.

His breath tastes like tomato sauce and red pepper flakes. It's a nice kiss—soft pressure, no tongue—and under any other circumstances, I probably would have liked it. But all I can think as Max's bottom lip dances with mine is—

Alec.

And then there's an ache in my chest like a bullet burrowing through my heart. I gasp and draw back.

Max frowns. "What's wrong?"

"Sorry."

The pain is gone, but my thoughts are fuzzy with the memory of it.

"I, uh . . ." I shake my head. "I guess I'm still not feeling very well."

"Oh." He clears his throat. "Well, I hope you feel better."

"Thanks."

He turns to walk away, and I know I should just let him go, but I can't stand the look of rejection in his eyes.

"Max."

He glances back at me.

"I had a nice time tonight."

The first echoes of fireworks thunder across the sky. A shower of red sparks falls outside my window, painting everything crimson as a half smile cuts into Max's cheek.

"Me, too."

CHAPTER FORTY-ONE

LEA

MY HEART BEATS A FURIOUS rhythm in my ears as I ascend the staircase to the fifth floor. Mother watched me like a hawk throughout dinner and dancing in the ballroom, so I could not get away until after we had returned to our suite and my parents had gone to sleep. I lay in my bed for what felt like hours before donning my robe and sneaking out of my room, and now I do not know which I fear more—the possibility that Alec is no longer waiting for me, or the possibility that he's been waiting for me all along.

My nightgown rustles against my ankles as I make my way forward, testing the floorboards for creaks. I turn the corner, and there he is. Sitting with his back to the closet, his arms resting on his propped knees, his head tilted back against the door. I take a step forward without thinking.

A board groans beneath me.

Alec's head snaps forward. He exhales at the sight of me, a smile tracing his lips. He pushes to his feet, crossing the distance between us.

"I thought you weren't coming," he murmurs.

"I couldn't get away."

He takes my hands and presses his forehead against mine, closing his eyes and breathing me in. I know I should stop him, remind him why we aren't doing this or remind him that anyone could walk out and find us, but his scent wraps around me and all the reasons why we shouldn't be together can't compete with the overwhelming need to be close to him.

"Come on," he says. "I want to show you something."

He leads me through the fifth-floor corridors and up a half set of stairs to a door. He produces a key from his pocket and twists it in the lock.

The door opens.

Alec flips a light switch, revealing a small, circular room containing one bed, one dresser, a chair, and a washstand. Books are piled everywhere, stacked along the curving walls and fanned out around the bed, their titles gleaming in the lamplight. *The Count of Monte Cristo. Discourse on Inequality. Gray's Anatomy.* There are books on chemistry and theology, art and economics, history and biology. I run my fingers over the books stacked on the dresser, picking up one of my favorites.

Leaves of Grass.

Alec clears his throat. "Mr. Sheffield is always bringing me books to read."

"The Grand's owner?"

He nods. "He's always been kind to me."

"You've read all these?" I ask.

"Yes."

My eyes widen. "You'll be the most well-read medical student in the country."

"I doubt that. Some days I feel as though I'm barely keeping up."

He doesn't say *with people like you*—people born with libraries full of books like these in their palatial homes and access to the finest education money can buy—but I hear the words anyway. They remind me of why I've been staying away from him.

I knew you were only going to hurt Alec—it's what people like you do.

I set the book down. "I shouldn't be here."

I move to leave, but Alec steps in front of me.

"Get out of my way," I tell him.

"Please, just listen to what I have to say."

"It doesn't matter." I try to sound strong and in control, but my throat is closing in on itself, and my words are feeble. "You've already said everything you have to say to me."

"You're wrong." He reaches for me, his hand cupping mine. "I haven't told you that I haven't been able to stop thinking about you. That I ache to be near you. That saying goodbye to you while you're still here, while you're still with me, was the hardest and stupidest thing I've ever done. That you haunt my every waking hour and find me in every dream. You are everywhere, Lea. Trying to ignore you is like trying to ignore oxygen. I'm suffocating without you."

Tears prick my eyes, hot and unwelcome.

"But you were right," I say. "What we're doing here—there's no point to it. Our story ends in heartbreak, and there's no getting around it. Clara helped me see that, and your mother—"

"You spoke to Clara?" he asks.

"Yes."

"When?" His brow furrows. "What did she say?"

I try to move around him. "It doesn't matter now—"

"Like hell it doesn't." He grips my shoulders, holding me in place. "What did she say to you, Lea?"

My lashes flutter as I look up at him. The space between us fills with our rough, shattered breaths. "That I would only hurt you in the end." My throat tightens even more. I swallow, but the tears fall anyway. "She is right."

"I don't care about the end."

"Yes, you do. And so do I."

He shakes his head. "I care about this." His hands move from my shoulders into my hair, his fingers lacing my scalp. "Us." My eyelashes flutter closed as my body melts beneath his touch. He kisses my right eye, and then my left, his lips soft as rose petals. "Now."

"Alec."

His mouth crushes mine as he lifts me, locking my legs around his hips and spinning me until my back is against the wall. His body, so lean and hard and strong, presses into mine, until it is just this: him and me and everything we are, everything we should be, when we are together.

It is hello and goodbye and eternity all wrapped up into one. It is everything we should have had, if only our destinies had not already been decided for us.

CHAPTER FORTY-TWO

NELL

MY MIND IS A BEEHIVE, buzzing as Dad gets home and tells me about his day; buzzing as I get ready for bed, changing into pajamas and scrubbing my face; buzzing as I lie down in my bed and turn off the light.

Remember me.

Remember.

Remember.

When I can't take it anymore, I slide out of bed, grab my backpack, and head to the dining room. It's less conducive to my training than the ballroom, with more tables and less open space, but at least I haven't hallucinated any murderous ghosts in here, which is why I keep going back.

Today's playlist is a mixture of hard rock and heavy metal. Perfect for too-loud thoughts and jittering bones. I thrust all my anger and confusion and self-loathing into my dancing. I spin—faster, faster, *faster*—until my doubts and fears bleed away and I am nothing more than a pumping heart and twisting limbs and ballooning lungs. I am a wild thing, careening across the floor. Dangerous. Reckless. One wrong move, one bad foot placement, and I could fall, shattering a leg and a dream.

But I can't make myself stop.

Right now, more than anything, I need to be less than the sum of my parts.

My phone alarm—the one I set to get back to my room before Dad notices I'm gone—blares in my eardrums. I fumble the device out of my pocket and turn the alarm and my playlist off, then rip my earbuds out and stuff them in my backpack, along with my phone. Hitching the straps onto my shoulders, I turn for the door—

And freeze.

Alec is standing in the corner of the room, leaning against an old piano.

"You always were a beautiful dancer," he says, quietly, as if lost in memory.

I clutch my chest as a pure shot of adrenaline kicks through my veins. "You know, you should really announce yourself when you enter a room."

"Like you would have heard me over that music," he says. "And I could say the same of you."

"What do you mean?"

"I was here first."

"Yeah, like I'd believe you just happened to be hanging out in here at three thirty in the morning."

"*You* were."

"That's not the point."

His grin is too smug for the crack of dawn.

"Fine, I'll bite." I cross the room to stand in front of him, my arms folded over my chest. "What were you doing here at three thirty in the morning?"

"I couldn't sleep."

I arch a brow. "Is that your answer for everything?"

"Insomnia is a well-documented phenomena. Often caused by anxiety or, as in my case, nightmares." He cocks his head. "You wouldn't happen to know anything about that, would you, Nell?"

I ignore his question and give him one of my own. "Even if that's true, why would you come here? You have an entire hotel you could wander around."

"I came *here* because someone took over my usual haunt with her morning ballet sessions."

My brow furrows. "The ballroom?"

He nods.

I remember that first session—the man in the white shirt slipping through the door.

"It was you that morning, watching me in the ballroom. Wasn't it?"

He rolls his eyes. "You make me sound like a stalker, but I'll repeat: I was there first."

Alec. Hovering on the edges of my world before I even realized it. I know I should apologize—for invading his space, or for basically calling him a creeper—but my stubbornness won't let me.

"I'm not going to say sorry. Especially since you could've gone back to the ballroom after I started practicing here."

He sucks his lips between his teeth, as if he's trying not to laugh, but the gleam brightening his eyes gives him away.

"I wouldn't dream of asking you to apologize. Especially since I didn't want to go back to the ballroom after I could tell you were starting to have the visions. I wanted to keep an eye on you."

"Oh, yes, not stalkerish at all," I murmur.

He studies me. "Do you have a moment?"

My muscles recoil. The last time I gave Alec a moment, he

unraveled my brain like a spool of thread, and maybe it isn't fair to blame him for how lost and confused I feel, but maybe it is.

"For what?" I ask, every line in my body screaming *defensive position—back away now if you know what's good for you.*

Either Alec doesn't get the hint, or he doesn't care.

"I'd like to show you something."

And even though I know I should, I can't say no to him.

CHAPTER FORTY-THREE

LEA

FOR THE NEXT THREE WEEKS, when I am not with Alec, I am devising ways to be with him, moments stolen in empty corridors and moonlit gardens. When I *am* with him, I am devising ways to stay just a minute, a half minute, a *second* longer than I know I should. I spend every night in his arms, sneaking back into my room only with the rising of the dawn. Some nights we talk until the sun comes up, trying to squeeze in every conversation we would have had over decades of marriage into our numbered hours.

Some nights we don't talk at all.

Lon is oblivious. He is too busy keeping an eye on potential clients to keep an eye on me, and on the few occasions when we are together, he is too self-absorbed to notice I am not listening to him, or even thinking about him at all. In fact, the only time I acknowledge him is when he tries to get me alone, and then I do everything in my power to stop that from happening, because when it does, when Lon and I are alone, he handles me like an object—a toy he can't yet have. And for a boy who grew up in a world where nothing was ever off-limits, this is a very dangerous thing for me to be.

Alec catches Lon touching me more than once. He sees the way Lon crushes his body against mine when he thinks no one is looking. Dominating me. Controlling me. Possessing me.

I know it takes every ounce of willpower Alec has not to tear Lon off me, especially when I'm saying "No" and "Stop" and "You must be gentle with me, love." Never have I seen someone's knuckles turn so white against their skin as Alec's when he watches us from afar, and this morning, after breakfast, when Lon guided me into the garden and wrenched my hair back to open my mouth to his, eliciting a cry of pain which he muffled with his tongue, I thought Alec was going to kill him.

I'm not even sure where Alec was that he saw it, but the next thing I knew, he was striding toward us, rage contorting his features, giving everything away.

I did the only thing I could think to stop him.

I wrenched myself from Lon's kiss and snapped at Alec, *"What are you looking at, boy?"*

It was an awful voice, the voice my mother uses whenever she bosses a servant around. It was a voice that spoke of superiority and money and condemnation.

It stopped Alec in his tracks.

Lon turned. When Alec didn't immediately answer me, Lon said, "My fiancée asked you a question."

Alec blinked and shook his head, as if he wasn't sure who he even was anymore.

As if he wasn't sure who *I* was.

He cleared his throat. "Forgive me. Your mother is looking for you, Miss Sargent."

I arched a brow. "Tell her I'll be along shortly."

Alec nodded. "Very good."

"Do you think he'll say something to your mother?" Lon asked as he watched Alec walk away. There was no concern in his voice at all, only a mild contemplation, as if he were wondering if it would rain today. "I could have him fired."

Panic shot through me.

"No need," I said, looping my arm through his and starting toward the lobby. "I'll take care of it."

Now, Alec and I are lying on his bed, my cheek resting against the hard curve of his chest. Sometimes we slip into a comfortable silence, when we don't have to say anything at all to appreciate our time together, but tonight, our silence is a monster growing larger with each passing second, breathing up all the oxygen in the room until, finally, Alec says, "I don't like the way he touches you."

I have nothing to say to this. Everything that comes to mind—*I don't, either. It's going to be all right. I can handle it*—feels like the wrong thing to say. Because I may not like it, but there isn't anything I can do about it that I am not already doing. Because it's not going to be all right; in a month's time, I am going to be Mrs. Lon Van Oirschot, and Alec and I will have to do the thing—*goodbye*—that we've been ignoring, pushing it far away from us until we can almost pretend it's not going to happen at all.

Because I *can't* handle it.

I can't handle inviting Lon into my bed every night, wishing it were Alec instead.

But to say any of this is to break the spell holding this room together. Our sanctuary, far away from prying eyes and prattling tongues and the economic lines that divide us. A world of our own making.

So, instead of answering him, I roll onto my stomach and ask, "What flavor shall our wedding cake be?"

It's a game we began playing one night when we were both exhausted but refused to sleep. A game where we plan our wedding that will never take place, our honeymoon filled with destinations we will never see, our life in a well-appointed townhome, close to the hospital where he'll work and to the newspaper for which I will write—a gossip column, perhaps, or an advice column (those have always been my favorite to read).

We've built a life worthy of dreaming about here, in this room. A life that will never truly start but that I will hold on to long after it has ended.

But Alec doesn't play the game tonight.

"Mr. Sheffield called me into his office today," he says.

I push up onto my elbows. "Does he know?"

"No," he says. "At least, I don't think he does. He wanted to speak with me about my future. He's known I've wanted to become a doctor for some time, and while he says it is an admirable ambition, it will take me years to save up enough money to attend medical school."

"But you've been saving since you were eleven. Surely you must be close."

He shakes his head. "I'm another two years away, at least."

"Two years isn't so bad."

He brushes a curl from my face. "He offered me a scholarship—"

I sit up, beaming. "Alec, that's wonderful!"

"—to study business," he continues. "He says I'm the brightest employee he has working for him, including all the bigwigs in his offices, and that I know more about this hotel than the builders themselves. With some formal education, he thinks I could be his right-hand man, possibly even taking over ownership someday."

"But"—my brow furrows—"you're going to be a doctor."

"It's a once-in-a-lifetime opportunity." He sits up and takes my hands in his, his thumbs circling my skin. "I wouldn't have to pay for school. I could take all the money I've saved up so far and use it to take care of you, and when I graduate, I'll have a good job waiting for me with guaranteed upward mobility." He swallows. "I could support you, Lea. We could be together."

"No."

"No?"

I shake my head and push myself off the bed. "No. You're going to be a doctor. I don't care if I have to work in a shirtwaist factory; you're not giving up your dream."

"You say that like you have any idea what it entails, but you haven't worked a day in your life."

His voice isn't cruel, but his words sting anyway.

"I know," I say, "but I am more than capable. At the very least, I could do some secretarial work."

He angles his body to sit on the side of the bed, his elbows on his knees. "But you wouldn't have to do that at all if I took Mr. Sheffield's offer. I may never be able to offer you everything *your fiancé* can"—his hands curls into fists at the thought of Lon—"but I can give you a good life."

I move in front of him, running my hands through his hair. "We can make a good life together."

He tilts his head up to look at me, and then his arms circle my waist, pulling me against him.

"Are you saying what I think you're saying?" he practically breathes.

Am I? The thought of running away has always been a terrifying one, like throwing myself into unchartered winds and praying for a safe landing. But with Alec, I don't have to worry about finding land. He is the ground beneath my feet.

"Yes," I whisper. The word has no more sound to it than the

gentle *whoosh* of candle flame, and yet it cracks through the air like a whip.

It is the sound of decision striking destiny.

Alec beams up at me, then crosses the room to his dresser, pulling open the top drawer and fishing out a small, decorative box.

"I was hoping you'd say that."

He drops to one knee in front of me, and I clasp my hands over my mouth.

"Alec?"

"Aurelea Sargent," he says, taking my trembling hand. "I cannot promise you everything I want to. I cannot promise you an easy life, nor can I promise you riches or jewels or a home to call your own—not for some time, at least. But I can promise you that I will work hard to give you those things. I can promise you a life of love and laughter and unending devotion. And I can promise you that if I am forced to walk through this life without you by my side, I will only ever be half a man, because my heart will be with you wherever you go."

He opens the box, revealing a paper ring made sturdy by a thicker paper lining and strong adhesive. Across the paper is a familiar, slanting font from one of Alec's favorite book of poems, the one he's read to me night after night as we lay together. A single line from Walt Whitman's "To a Stranger":

I am to see to it that I do not lose you.

My tears break my lashes, streaming down my cheeks.

"I cannot promise you a proper ring now," he says, "but I can promise you that, one day, I will give you the ring you deserve."

"Are you blind?" I choke out through my tears. "This is the most proper engagement ring to have ever been crafted, Mr. Petrov."

"Is that a yes, Miss Sargent?"

I laugh. "It has always been a yes, Alec."

He exhales through a grin so wide, I fear it may break his face in two.

"But I want to make one thing clear," I say, stopping him before he can say anything else. "I will not marry you on the promise of money or jewels or a house of my own. I have had all those things already, and I know their true worth." I slide off the bed and bend down on my knees across from him, threading my fingers behind his neck and meeting his gaze. "I will marry you because I could not survive a single day without you, and because I know that as long as we are together, nothing in this world can stop us."

Alec wraps his hand around my neck and kisses my forehead. "I love you."

I hold him tight against me. "I love you, too."

He squeezes me one more time, then pulls the ring from the box and carefully fits it onto my finger.

"When should we leave?" I ask.

"Tomorrow night, during the ball—just like the first night you snuck out to go with me to Canvas City. If we're lucky, no one will notice you're gone until morning. If not, we should still have several hours before your parents return to their suite."

"Where will we go?"

"Tommy's cousin is a priest in Savannah. We'll borrow his uncle's car, and he and Moira will ride with us to be our witnesses. As long as we're married before your parents can find us, there'll be nothing they can do to stop us."

"You've already figured all this out."

"I've been talking Tommy's ear off about it for days." He arches a brow. "*Mrs. Petrov.*"

I sigh, quite certain a name has never sounded so sweet. "I don't know if I can wait that long to be your wife."

He frames my face in his hands and kisses me. "You are already my wife, Lea. I prayed to God for you and committed myself to you long ago. This is just a formality."

I don't know how I'm going to wait until tomorrow night to start my forever with him. For the first time since meeting Alec, I count the minutes until the sun comes up, praying for time to hasten, to get me out of this room and through the day. Into a ball gown and then into a car.

Into Savannah under the cover of darkness, and then, finally, *finally*, into my husband's arms.

CHAPTER FORTY-FOUR

NELL

WE CLIMB THE STAIRS TO the fifth floor, then up another, familiar half set of stairs that Sofia told me was off-limits when Dad and I first arrived here—the stairs that lead to the hotel's tallest tower and to a door that, for some reason, kicks my heart into a gallop.

There is no key card reader. Instead, the knob bears an old-fashioned lock. Alec fishes an iron key with jagged teeth out of his pocket and opens the door, revealing a small, circular room lined in floor-to-ceiling bookshelves. The only furniture in the room is a single bed with a sturdy wooden frame and matching dresser, and a bedside table with a lamp. But I only notice these things in a peripheral way, because as soon as my eyes catch on the pictures, I can't look away.

Polaroids hang from the ceiling like snowflakes on strings, the plastic film over the pictures gleaming in the lamplight as they twist in a cold gust of air-conditioning. My brow furrows as I watch them.

"Alec?"

I look back at him over my shoulder, waiting for an explanation, but he just closes the door and leans his shoulder against the wall, arms crossed as he stares at the floor, his hair falling like a curtain over his eyes.

More pictures sit on the dresser in frames. Sepia and black-and-white photographs transition into the pastel colors of faded film and then into sharper, more saturated pigments, the kind from the photos of Mom's and Dad's childhoods, before everyone took all their pictures with their phones.

Every single photograph bears my face.

I pick up the oldest picture, a small, oval miniature in shades of brown. The girl who looks like me smiles, but it isn't the smile she bore in the Mark Twain photograph. It's tight, controlled, well-practiced. My thumb sweeps across the glass.

"Aurelea?" I ask, forcing the words out through the lump in my throat.

Alec doesn't answer.

I put the picture back and gaze at the other frames on the dresser. All the girls staring back at me wear different clothes and hairstyles depending on the decade, but there's no mistaking they're all the same.

All me.

I take a deep breath and turn to the Polaroids.

My smile, the one I haven't seen myself wear in four long years, flashes back at me through a hundred tiny windows into another life. Alec and I, roasting marshmallows over a fire on the beach; Alec carrying me on his back through the garden; a close-up of our faces bent together, our heads framed by the pillowcases on Alec's bed.

Images flicker—

A *decision*.

A *plan*.
A *gun*.
—colliding into one another—
A *decision*.
A *plan*.
A *gun*.
—slowing—
Remember.
—shuffling—
Remember.
—focusing—
REMEMBER.

CHAPTER FORTY-FIVE

LEA

LON IS PARTICULARLY INSUFFERABLE TONIGHT, drinking glass after glass of champagne and holding me too tightly as we dance, so that I can see the glittering lights of the ballroom reflected in the mirrorlike film over his eyes. I can practically hear the sloshing fizz inside his stomach. But wearing my mask of pleasantries is easier tonight than ever, for through it all my heart beats the words *I'm leaving you, I'm leaving you, I'm leaving you.*

At eleven thirty, I complain of a headache and excuse myself from the ballroom as planned. Father is talking business with Mr. Van Oirschot's associates, and Mother is clucking away with her friends, neither one of them showing any sign of fatigue or restlessness. It is a safe bet that they will be here for another hour, at least.

Lon isn't happy to see me leave, but he's too drunk to put up much of a fight. Especially when one of his friends puts an arm around his shoulders and offers him a brandy.

Our suite is empty—Benny and Madeline are having a

sleepover in one of his friend's rooms—so I don't have to worry about keeping quiet. I change into my traveling clothes and pack quickly, grabbing only the barest of necessities: a few skirts and blouses and fresh undergarments, my hairbrush and pins, my lavender-rose perfume, and a bar of soap. When I'm done, I snap the valise closed.

Lon's engagement ring winks at me in the soft, electric light.

I stare at it for a moment. Contemplate keeping it and hawking it in a jewelry store somewhere. The money from this ring alone could pay for Alec's education now, enabling us to use the money he's saved to find some small place to call our own. But I don't want to give Lon any more reason to come after me than he'll already have, so I slide the ring off my finger. The phantom weight it leaves behind is nothing compared to the weight that has been lifted from my heart.

I set the ring—my *tether, my shackle, my cage*—on the bureau and fish Alec's paper ring out of its hiding spot in my steamer trunk. The featherlight weight of this ring sings like freedom. Freedom to be myself. Freedom to love whomever I choose. Freedom to make my own way in this world.

Alec has given me all that and more, but I have given him that, too. Apart, we were dark clouds grazing, heavy and sullen, across a prosaic sky. Together, we are the storm that can challenge the winds and tides and landscapes of our lives.

Together, we can create our own destiny.

The clock reads eleven fifty. Tommy's car will be waiting for us at the hotel's back entrance at exactly midnight. He will only stay five minutes; any longer could attract unnecessary attention and possibly ruin our chances of another escape should this one go awry. I spare one last glance around my room, at the House of Worth dresses hanging in my wardrobe and the exquisitely constructed furniture surrounding me. So much extravagance in one room. So many nice things with which I have been blessed throughout my life, and yet, in the end, none of them really mean anything. Not when compared to rights so basic and yet so evasive as the freedom to live however, and love whomever, I choose.

With a sigh, I pick up my valise and turn.

"Going somewhere, darling?"

Lon stands in the doorway, his gaze roaming down my traveling clothes to my valise, and then to the engagement ring lying on the bureau.

"What are—" My voice trembles. I take a deep breath and start again. "What are you doing here, Lon?"

He studies me, an unreadable expression crossing his face.

"When you left," he says, taking a step into the room, "I thought it the perfect opportunity for us to spend a little time together. Alone." He chuckles as he runs his thumb over his bottom lip. "But it seems you have other plans."

Deny it, my mind cries, a protective instinct. And maybe I would have been able to if I hadn't changed yet. If my wardrobe weren't in disarray from packing. If his ring were still on my finger.

But there's no denying this.

"Where did you think you could go," he asks quietly, "that I would not find you?"

"Wyoming," I lie. "There's a teaching position in a farming community there."

"You were going to cross half the country by yourself?"

"Yes."

His eyes lock on the paper ring on my engagement finger. "I don't appreciate being lied to, Aurelea. It's the bellboy, isn't it?"

My eyes widen.

He huffs out a laugh. "Yes, I know about you two. Those

gossiping, second-floor biddies told me all about it. You aren't half as clever as you think you are, darling."

"But—" My head is spinning. I can't think straight. "But we never—"

We never showed our affection for each other in public spaces, other than on the beach and in the Canvas City dance hall at night, when we knew—or thought we knew—no one from the hotel would be able to spot us. Which means they couldn't possibly have seen anything that I couldn't explain.

"We're friends, Lon," I say. "That's all."

He scoffs. "*Friends*. Yes, I thought you might say that. But it's in the way you two look at each other that gave you away to those old crones, and then you were spending all that time together. Fishing and picnicking. Really, I'm surprised you found the energy to spend any time with me at all."

I take a step back toward the window, a plan forming in my mind. "If you really thought I was going around with some bell-boy behind your back, why didn't you do something about it?"

"I assumed it was a passing fancy," he says. "A summer fling. I'm not ashamed to admit that I've had my fair share of maids this summer, so to expect complete chastity from you would have made me the worst sort of hypocrite." He takes a step forward, his muscles bunching. A predator waiting to strike. "But it seems he's filled your head with thoughts of leaving me, and I can't have that."

Gritting his teeth, Lon starts forward. I swing my valise as hard as I can at the window, shattering it on impact. Glass tinkles like rain as it falls to the floor. Lon hesitates, shock registering across his face.

I pick up a jagged piece and hold it out in front of me. My hand shakes as the glass cuts into my palm. "Stay away from me."

His eyes glint dangerously in the lamplight. "Oh, I am going to have so much fun taming your wild ways, my dear."

"Lon—"

He lunges.

My hand swipes through the air, the glass cutting a red, angry line across his cheek. He whirls away from me, clutching at the wound. His fingers smear the blood like paint.

For a moment, we stare at each other in silence, both of us recognizing that a line has been crossed here. He cannot overlook my insubordination.

I run.

He fists a chunk of my hair, yanking me back. I swipe again, but this time Lon ducks, swinging around me. One hand circles my neck. The other clamps down on my wrist, twisting until the glass falls from my fingers, clattering to the floor. Then he's groping me, tearing at my bodice, his liquor-soaked breath whispering horrible things in my ear.

Three quick knocks sound on the door outside the suite, followed by two slow ones.

Alec.

Lon pushes me onto the bed. I scramble onto my back, raking my fingernails across his eyes. His breath hisses in his throat, his drunken movements wobbly on the mattress. I jerk my knee up hard between his legs.

He shouts and falls to the side, clutching himself. I take my chance, jumping off the bed and rushing for the door, even though I know our escape is impossible now. Lon will follow us. We probably won't even make it out of the hotel before we're detained by security guards and concerned citizens, scrutinizing my ripped dress and the blood on my palm.

But I can't stay here.

I unlock the door—Lon must have flipped the lock when he came in—and turn the handle. The door opens just an inch before Lon barrels into me, knocking me to the floor. My head cracks against a corner table. Stars explode across my vision, blurring the world around me as Alec bursts into the room, landing his fist squarely across Lon's jaw. Lon scrambles back, but Alec doesn't stop. His fists are like mallets, beating Lon's face into a pulp.

Rage has turned him feral.

I try to sit up, but my head swims, and darkness seeps back across my vision.

Everything disappears.

When my vision returns, Lon is ducking Alec's blows, jabbing back, gaining his balance. Alec roars and barrels into Lon's chest, knocking them both to the ground. I can hear them fighting on the floor—the smacks of fists carving flesh—but I can't see them past the furniture.

The fighting stops suddenly, and something metallic clicks. It is a familiar sound, one I've heard countless times in my childhood, whenever Father would shoot at targets in the back garden of our country home in preparation for his hunts, but it sounds wrong here, in this small, crowded space, where there are no animals to kill.

Alec pushes himself off the floor, his hands held out in front of him. Lon appears next, holding Father's hunting rifle, lining up his sights.

"I won't let you have her," Lon snarls.

Alec's voice is soft. Calming. "You don't want to do this."

"If you leave now," Lon says, "I'll let you live. If you don't, I will put a bullet in your heart and tell the police I found you in my fiancée's room, forcing yourself upon her."

A muscle in Alec's jaw ticks. "I'm not leaving without Lea."

Lon laughs. "I beg to differ."

A familiar, determined gleam flashes in Lon's eyes as a grin slithers across his cheeks, and all I can think is *He won't shoot if I stand in front of Alec*. He might be able to explain Alec's death as self-defense, but he wouldn't be able to explain mine.

Ignoring the pain throbbing through my skull, I push myself off the floor—*don't shoot*—and jump in front of Alec as a crack of gunfire pierces the air.

For a second, I think he missed. But then a sharp, burning sensation like liquid fire bores through my chest, and I glance down to find red blossoming on my blouse.

Everything happens slowly—Alec catching me in his arms as I fall. Alec screaming my name. Alec cradling my body against his.

Lon also screams, but he doesn't come near me. Instead, his breathing turns rough. His expensive shoes click across the hard-wood floor as he paces, muttering to himself. Panic grips me as I realize I didn't save Alec at all, that Lon could still reload the gun, that he might, even now, be searching for bullets. I try to look for him, try to see what he's doing, but Alec frames my face with his hands, forcing my eyes back on him.

"Look at me," he says. "Stay with me."

I try to reach for him, but my hands and forearms are numb. So are my feet, all the way up to my knees. I shiver as winter howls through my bones.

I have never been so cold.

There's another crack of gunfire, so loud my punctured heart jumps, and then something hard thuds against the floor. But Alec is still holding me, still whispering my name, which can only mean—

Lon shot himself.

The taste of gunpowder mixes with the copper on my tongue.

Alec rocks me like a baby, his tears dripping onto my chest. My brain tells me I should feel them, but I don't.

I don't feel anything.

Alec pushes my hair from my face. "Don't leave me."

But I'm already going, falling, fading. Blood gurgles in my throat, thick and viscous and impossible to breathe around.

"I love you," I try to murmur, but everything sounds so distant, and I don't know if he hears me. I try to say the words again. I can feel my lips forming them, but then my breath rattles in my throat and I'm sinking

sinking

sinking

into nothing.

PART TWO

CHAPTER FORTY-SIX

NELL

WE SIT ON THE BEACH, my back pressed against Alec's chest as he leans against a palm tree, watching the sky beginning to lighten in the east.

It is the dawning of a new day. August 6, 2003.

We made it.

My name is Katie, and I have lived six other lifetimes in one hundred years. Lea, Alice, Evelyn, Penny, Gwen, Sara, and then me. I have witnessed decades no other sixteen-year-old girl has seen outside of books and movies.

1907. 1923. 1939. 1955. 1971. 1987.

Each life vastly different from the one before it, and yet all ending the same way. Here, at the Winslow Grand Hotel, at the hands of what I once considered a curse, but now, with Alec's arms wrapped around mine and the promise of a future breaking on the horizon, I recognize it as the blessing it's been all along—a second chance given to us over and over again to make things right.

And finally, *finally*, we've figured it out.

Alec rests his chin against my head, his arms tightening around me as he breathes me in.

"I can't believe you're really here," he murmurs.

I turn in his arms, propping myself on my knees to face him. I press my forehead against his.

"I'm here," I say. "It's over."

We don't know what will happen when the sun comes up. We don't know if Alec, who looks eighteen but has actually walked this Earth for 130 years, will start aging like a normal person again, or if all those years will descend upon him like a thief, stealing his youth and the years he never had. If he will disintegrate in front of my eyes or vanish as if he was never there at all.

I won't believe it.

I won't believe that, after all these years, I would survive this and he would not. Because then what was the point? Why would we find each other again just to lose each other in the end?

He holds me tightly as we watch the sun come up, as if he can stop the world from splitting us apart simply by refusing to let go. And when the sun finally breaks the horizon, painting the sky pink and lavender and orange, it is the most beautiful thing I have ever seen.

Because Alec is still here.

And so am I.

Alec jumps up, pulling me with him and spinning me around. He howls at the sun just like the night we howled at the moon on this same beach in 1907, and in his joy, he drops to his knees, letting me go.

As if in slow motion, I feel his arms pull away from me—feel the link between us sever. My heart squeezes in my chest, coming to a grinding, agonizing halt.

And then . . .

I fall, slowly, swiftly, down to the sand.

The last thing I see is Alec bending over me, screaming, but I can't hear him over the ice fracturing my veins.

Stop, I think as my vision begins to darken, my breath clogging my chest. *Stop*.

But the darkness fills my eyes like smoke, choking out the light.

Another life,

another chance,

another future,

gone.

———————————

I remember.

Not everything. There are still gaps—patches of fog, transitions and bridges I can't quite connect—but it's enough. Alec stares at me from across the room, waiting for me to say something.

His name is a prayer on my lips.

"*Alec*."

I launch myself into his arms. I expect him to squeeze me tight, pulling me to him like the moon pulls the tide. I expect him to kiss my head, my cheeks, my lips. To wrap us up in each other and say hello and goodbye in the span of a single breath, just as we have done so many times before.

But his arms stay at his sides.

I pull away from him.

His eyes betray his thoughts: *Move slowly—speak softly—stay on guard*.

"You kept the pictures," I say, prompting him to speak.

To reassure me.

To let me in.

"I wanted to tear them down."

"But you didn't."

I remember stringing them up on an unseasonably cold and rainy morning that August, in the summer of 2003. When Alec asked me what I was doing, I told him it was my backup plan, in case I didn't make it. A reminder to him that I would return, that it wouldn't be goodbye forever.

But I was so certain our plan would work. This was supposed to be a just-in-case. Something we would laugh about later.

Instead, they have hung here, over his bed and over his life, for sixteen years.

I can't have that kind of hope again only to have it taken away from me. You can't ask that of me.

I take a step back.

"You aren't happy I'm back," I whisper. "Are you?"

"Of course I am. I just . . ." He runs his hand through his hair and exhales a rough, jagged breath, tears filling his eyes. "I don't have the strength to lose you again."

I take his hands in mine, like he did to me that night in the fifth-floor hallway, when he begged me to spend as much time together as we could before the end of that summer more than one hundred years ago, unknowingly setting our destinies in motion.

"We don't have a choice."

He closes his eyes and takes a deep breath, wrapping an arm around me and pulling me to his chest. We stand like that, memories and grief wrapping around us, whispering doubt and fear into our hearts.

But we have to believe. In ourselves. In second chances. In love.

We have to fight.

"What do we do now?" I ask.

"I don't know," Alec says, resting his chin on top of my head. "God help me, I don't know."

CHAPTER FORTY-SEVEN

NELL

DURING THE NEXT HOUR, ALEC and I sit huddled in his room, going over the memories flooding my brain. He fills in the missing pieces, the fragments that blur together over so many lives, and the cogs that time has lost. His voice becomes stronger as he speaks, as if taking action in this simple matter has given him a surety, a purpose, something to do other than stand there and wait for the end to come. But he still won't meet my gaze, and he flinches at my touch like a wounded bird.

He has been hurt too many times, and I don't know how to heal his pain.

In 1923, the first time I came back, my name was Alice. I was a bright young thing, a jazz baby of the Roaring Twenties. After spending my formative years under the looming threat of war and saying goodbye to my brother, John, forever on the day he sailed for Europe to fight in the trenches, I lost myself in witchy absinthe and glittering parties. My parents were worried about me, but I didn't care. It was the only way I could deal with watching so many boys I once knew and loved—or even the ones I knew and hated—leave for the front and never return.

I was going to enjoy every last second of my life in honor of them, even if I couldn't always remember those seconds, and even if, in the dark of night, when my head was spinning and sobs wracked my body, a small part of me knew it was nothing less than cowardice on my part. A way to hide from everything that had happened, and everything that would never happen, now that John was gone.

When my parents decided a family vacation at the Winslow Grand was exactly what we needed to help us move on, I didn't argue. What could be better than summer days spent on the beach and summer nights spent dancing to the ragtime beat of the Canvas City Band?

For Alec's part, he had spent sixteen long years trapped in the hotel, unaware that he wasn't the only one cursed. When I walked like a ghost back into his life on a cool June morning, he didn't know I needed to remember my life as Aurelea on my own. He sought out every opportunity to get me alone, to convince me that I had been at the hotel before. At first, I thought he was mad, but when the memories started flooding back, blurring the lines between fantasy and reality even more intensely than the green spirits I kept hidden in a flask, I was the one who ended up losing my mind.

Lon's ghost didn't help. Chasing me, haunting me, just as he's doing now, in 2019. Trying to kill me before Alec and I even got the chance to make things right.

In 1923, Lon's plan worked. I jumped to my death before the curse came full circle.

In 1939, my name was Evelyn. Convinced my coming back was just a part of his curse, a way for fate to torment him and not a chance for us to make things right, Alec stayed away from me, thinking it would protect me from reenacting what had happened to us thirty-two years before. But the memories came back anyway, and when the world changed and I found myself back in 1907—because that's what happens on August 5; we always go back and relive the day exactly as we experienced it the first time leading up to Lea's death just after midnight on August 6—I didn't know how to stop what was coming, and neither did Alec.

I died the same way I did in 1907, with a bullet in my chest and Alec hovering above me.

In 1955, my name was Penny. My family lived in a small house in the suburbs. We wouldn't have been able to afford a summerlong trip to the Grand if we hadn't won it through a mail-in raffle. That time, Alec tried to keep me from setting foot inside the hotel, not knowing then that it didn't matter. The moment I stepped onto hotel property—actually, the moment I was reborn—it was already too late.

In 1971, Alec tried to save me by shielding me from the gun. But, in the end, the bullet found its way to my chest, and when Alec flashed back to the present day, he returned alone.

In 1987, Alec tried to hide me from Lon when we went back in time. Surely if Lon couldn't find me, he couldn't kill me. But even in our alternate 1907, Lon was a part of the hotel. He could whisper to the walls, and they would whisper back.

He always knew where we were hiding.

And then, finally, in 2003, we decided to change our escape plan from that fateful night. Instead of leaving at midnight, we waited until one o'clock, by which time Lon had imbibed so much alcohol, we were certain he didn't have the strength to return to his room, let alone follow me to mine. My bag was already packed and hiding beneath my bed. When I complained of a headache and left the ballroom, Alec met me on the second-floor balcony. We walked to the room together, and he guarded the door while

I changed. But Tommy's car wasn't there when we tried to leave. And when we decided to walk to the ferry instead, we couldn't leave the property.

That was how we'd ended up on the beach, watching the sunrise, thinking we'd finally broken the curse. That we were just waiting to return to the present, as Alec had done so many times before. Because I was there. I'd survived.

We were wrong.

"There was obviously something we were supposed to do that we didn't," I say now as I watch the early morning sunlight catch in Alec's hair, revealing strands of mahogany threaded through the brown. I want to thread my fingers through it so badly, but every time I come near him, he sucks in a breath, and a scarring truth rips my heart:

He doesn't want me here.

He shakes his head, a dark, cruel laugh escaping his lips. "We didn't miss anything. We just aren't meant to make things right."

"Yes, we are." I reach for his hand, but he pulls it away from me. I curl my knees into my chest.

"Tell me what happened to you," I say, my voice quiet. "The first time I died."

He's silent for a moment.

Then, softly, "Your parents came back to your suite. They found me holding you. I guess it had been hours, but it felt like seconds. I told them what happened, but they didn't believe me, or they didn't want to believe me, which might as well have been the same thing. I became the only suspect. They wanted to take me into the station for questioning, but when they tried to remove me from the building . . ."

"They couldn't," I whisper.

He pushes off the bed and looks out the window, his back to me.

"Mr. Sheffield, the hotel's owner—he always cared about me. Treated me as if I were his own son. When he saw something was wrong, he offered the police a private office inside the hotel to conduct their interrogation. They still wanted to take me into the station when it was over, but Mr. Sheffield had a lot of sway at that time. I don't know what he did or said to convince them of my innocence, but it worked. They searched for other suspects, but, of course, none were found."

I slide off the bed, the mattress springs squeaking beneath me. Tentatively, I step forward. I want to wrap my arms around him, to comfort the boy who endured so much pain all those years ago. Who has continued to endure that pain every day for the past 112 years. Instead, I stand next to him, studying his face as he watches the people passing by beneath us.

"How have you been able to live here so long without anyone finding out?" I ask.

His lips twitch. "Oh, people have noticed. Haven't you heard the rumors?"

"I have," I say. "But that's all they are. Rumors. You'd think after more than a hundred years, someone would have some proof."

"Mr. Sheffield saw to that. There was a lot of turnover in hotel staff, even back then. Those who didn't stay more than a few years weren't a threat. Those who did were told in no uncertain terms not to question the fact that I hadn't aged, or else they would be seeking employment elsewhere. I know part of it was to protect me, but it was mostly to protect the hotel. Think of the circus this place would become if my secret ever got out." He turns away from the window and the world he can't touch. "Over the years, the number of people who knew my secret dwindled, and for the sake of the hotel, the truth of my immortality has since been contained to one person."

My brow furrows. "Who?"

"The general manager."

"Sofia?"

He nods. "I imagine some of the older employees have guessed, the ones who have worked here for decades. But you'd be surprised how protective people can be of the Grand. No one would ever say or do anything to ruin its reputation."

"Is that why there isn't any record of other sixteen-year-old girls dying in the hotel? Have they kept it a secret somehow?"

He leans back against the wall, his arms folded over his chest.

"Alec?"

"They didn't need to keep it a secret," he says after a beat. "It's part of the curse. No one"—he shakes his head, swearing under his breath—"no one remembers you when you die. Not your family, not the hotel staff. No one . . . except me."

All the air rushes out of my lungs.

"What—? How—?" Too many questions cloud my brain. I can't think around them. "No one remembers me at all?"

He swallows. "It seems as though you'll only get to keep your life if you survive going back. If you don't, it's like you never existed."

"So my father . . ." My stomach twists. "If we don't beat the curse, he won't remember me?"

Alec doesn't meet my gaze. It's all the answer I need.

"I have to go," I say, pushing away from the windows. The sun's been up for at least an hour. "Dad's probably wondering where I am."

Alec catches my wrist, stopping me. I look back at him. More than one hundred years of pain and love and loss are written on his face as his gaze meets mine.

"I can't lose you again, Lea."

I give him a small smile I hope is encouraging, but it feels too sad as I cup his cheek in my hand.

"I'm not Lea anymore," I tell him. "And I'm not Katie, or Alice, or anyone else, and I'm not going to end up like them, either. I'm Nell." My eyes sting, and the lump in my throat chokes my words. "I have my own destiny."

I kiss him, tears breaking through my lashes. His mouth parts for me, his bottom lip gently kneading my own. We break apart and I wipe away my tears.

"We'll figure this out," I say. "Just . . . don't give up."

He smiles back at me, but his eyes say he already has.

I squeeze his hand, then open the door and slip out into the hall.

In the eight lives I have lived, from Aurelea Sargent to Nell Martin, I have loved each and every one of my families. They were nowhere near perfect, and some of them were downright dysfunctional, but even as Lea, even with an abusive father and a mother who cared more for her daughter's social standing than her happiness, I was still the blood of their blood, and they were still the people who shaped my life. The Sargents remembered me, but the others? They all went on with their lives as if I never existed. Some of them are probably still alive, living God only knows where, and if I showed up on their doorsteps today, they wouldn't recognize me.

And yeah, maybe if Mom was still around, Dad would be okay if this didn't work out, if I just disappeared, but we have been the glue holding each other together for the past four years. How lonely will he be if he wakes up one day without a daughter? Will he be able to cope, or will he slip back into the depression that threatened to pull us both under just a few short years ago? Is his flirting with Sofia a sign he's finally ready to move on? Or is he only ready because he has me to lean on?

When I was Alice, I believed my parents would be better off without me. I was such a disappointment after John, and I wasn't there for them the way I needed to be. I was too wrapped up in my own grief.

But now I know it wasn't true. They needed me then, and Dad needs me now. This is bigger than me, bigger than Alec.

We can't fail this time.

CHAPTER FORTY-EIGHT

NELL

I SEND A QUICK "CHECKING IN" text to Dad as I head for the gift shop, a plan starting to take root in my mind. I take the back staircase and cross to the interior garden, intending to use it as a shortcut, but pull up short at all the joggers and early risers crowding the grass. They gawk up at the roses, taking pictures and shaking their heads, their mouths hanging open.

Above me, the roses cling to one another, their thorns and branches interlocking into a latticework ceiling, nearly blocking out the sun. Only a small circle of sky remains in the middle, creating a spotlight on the grass beneath. The rest of the garden is so dark, the staff has kept all the exterior corridor lanterns lit to see by.

"Incredible," a woman in neon-pink jogging shoes murmurs to her husband, shaking her head.

There's something seriously wrong with your roses.

Only every sixteen years.

I hurry past them, weaving through the crowd, then dart into the gift shop, where I pick up a Grand-themed notebook and pen before heading to the storage room.

Max isn't here yet, so, sitting with my back pressed against the door, I take out the notebook and bullet point every single thing I remember from each night I died, starting with Aurelea and ending with Katie. Then, in big bold letters, I write:

WHAT ARE WE MISSING???

I stare at it a moment, then circle it three times for emphasis. Sighing, I take out my phone and type *Lon Van Oirschot* into the search engine.

This search brings up a lot more hits than the search for the murder, although each one gives a more detailed account of Lon's grandfather, Alfred Van Oirschot, who made his fortune in fur trapping and real estate, and Lon's father, who took his inheritance and invested in promising new technologies, most notably railroads and steel, than on Lon himself. The contributions Lon had started making to the company are overshadowed by his "tragic" death. Aurelea's name is only mentioned in half of the articles. The other half simply mentions "his fiancée" being killed as well.

Max plops down onto the floor next to me.

"Hey, ballerina. Whatcha reading?"

I click out of the browser and snap my notebook closed.

I can barely concentrate as I work, my hands moving over old papers and photographs and trinkets without really noticing what I'm doing. My mind keeps buzzing as new memories pop up—flashes of sound and color all jumbled, each life bleeding into the next—and my hands keep itching to write it all down. To make sense of what I'm thinking. To figure out what Alec and I have been missing every time.

My pulse pounds like a drum in my ears as the room starts to feel too small, my mind too cluttered. I am all too aware of every wild heartbeat and every wasted second.

I'm about to tell Max I'm taking a break when I spot them peeking out from beneath an old cash register—a stack of familiar black ledgers with looping gold lettering inscribed on the spines. Heart pounding, I open the flashlight app on my phone and check the spines.

I find the one I'm looking for halfway down the pile.

Mother guiding me into the lobby for the first time, exclaiming, "Oh, Aurelea, isn't it beautiful?" Father heading for the reception desk, signing his name in a ledger. Lon appearing in front of us, that awful scent of too much cologne and coffee and cigars making my head spin.

"Hey, Max. I think I found something."

Max walks over and takes a look at the spines. "Nice. Mom'll definitely want to put some of those in the museum."

"Here," I say, grabbing one side of the register. "Help me move this."

We slide the register off the ledgers and slowly lower it to the ground. Our fingers brush, and Max's mouth quirks into a crooked smile that makes me feel all queasy inside. I was so wrapped up in everything that happened this morning that I completely forgot about our kiss, but now it comes roaring back to me.

I drop the register a little too forcefully.

Max arches a brow but doesn't say anything. He starts reaching for the ledgers, but I grab the one I had my eye on before he can get to it. It reads:

WINSLOW GRAND HOTEL REGISTRY: JUNE 1906–DECEMBER 1908.

It doesn't take long to find Lon's signature, dated May 31, 1907. Exactly one week before Lea arrived. Just the sight of it makes my entire body tense. My fingernails dig into my palms. What I wouldn't give to hit that smug bastard right across the face.

"Here's something," I say, angling the ledger toward Max's corner.

Max leans over me, his shoulder resting gently against mine.

I clear my throat and point halfway down the page. "Lon Van Oirschot's signature."

"Whoa." His eyes scan the page, his brow furrowing. "Did you find Aurelea?"

I study him for any sign that Sofia has told him my secret, but he's either a really excellent liar, or he has no idea.

"She wouldn't have signed it. But here"—I flip forward a few pages—"this is her father."

My heart wrenches at the sight of his signature.

Edmund Sargent wasn't a great father. He wasn't even a good one, unless you define "good" as keeping a roof over my head and food in my stomach, which I guess some people might. But I still cared for him, and whether that care came from love or from some deep, psychological warfare, I never wanted to let him down. Yes, my marriage to Lon was his ticket to regaining his fortune, but before that, before our relationship became that of a butcher selling off his prized meat to the highest bidder, there were the rare birthdays in which he came home from work early to celebrate. Christmas mornings filled with toys he'd lovingly selected. Dancing in the foyer whenever he'd made a particularly profitable business deal.

He was my father, and I'm sure losing me in such a horrific way hurt him, regardless of the anger and indifference he'd often shown me.

Maybe he would have never forgiven me for running off with Alec, or maybe he would have come around eventually.

Maybe my whole family would have come to accept Alec, in time. Maybe it wouldn't have had to be an "either/or" thing for the rest of my life.

Thanks to Lon, I'll never know.

Max bumps me with his shoulder. "Now I know why you practically snatched this one out of my hands."

I sigh. "I haven't been able to stop thinking about her."

"I know what you mean," he says. "It's hard to believe something so awful could happen here."

He turns back to the other ledgers.

"Max, wait."

His brow furrows. "What's up?"

The queasiness increases.

"Can we talk?"

He wriggles his eyebrows at me. "Isn't that what we're doing?"

"I mean . . . about last night."

"Oh." He frowns. "Um, yeah. Sure."

I bite the inside of my lip. "When I asked you over last night, I didn't know—I mean, I didn't think it was a . . . a . . ."

He takes a deep breath. "This is about the kiss, isn't it?"

"Well. Yeah."

He rolls his eyes. "I'm sorry. I don't know what came over me. I just . . . I like you, Nell, and the moment felt right, but maybe it wasn't. I knew you weren't feeling great yesterday, and then like a jerk I went and kissed you—"

"I didn't stop you," I say, because it's true. Because, for a brief, fleeting moment I'd *wanted* to kiss him. Wanted to prove to myself that the feelings I was having for Alec weren't real. Wanted to pretend I was a normal girl living a normal life—not a girl who could no longer tell what was real and what wasn't, nor a girl whose destiny had already been decided for her.

"It's just that," I continue, "there's . . . someone else."

He smacks himself across the face. "Of course there is. I should have known. I just figured since you'd moved and everything—" He shakes his head and exhales. "So are you guys doing the long-distance thing?"

I blink, surprised.

I'd never even considered Max would think I meant someone back home, in Colorado, but it would be easy to lie to him. It seems less hurtful somehow, more humane, for the boy in question to be one Max doesn't know and never has to meet. But there's too much of a chance that Max will see Alec and me together, and I'll be damned if I ever have to hide our relationship again, in this life or the next.

"It's not someone back home," I say. "It's Alec."

Max stares at me.

"Alec Petrov," I clarify.

His jaw drops. "*Petrov?* But . . . how? When? The last time you mentioned him, you were complaining because he'd treated you like dirt."

His shock is enough to convince me he has no idea of my past or of my connection to Alec.

"Yeah, he did," I say. "But then we got to know each other."

His eyes narrow. "Don't tell me this is one of those 'reformed bad boy' things, where you think he's changed, but he'll just end up treating you like garbage anyway?"

"It's not. I can definitely promise you that."

He doesn't look like he believes me.

"Look, I'm not saying this just because I'm jealous—which I am, for clarity's sake—but because I think you're awesome, and regardless of last night and whatever happens next, I want to be your friend. Just . . . watch yourself around him, okay? I don't want to see you get hurt."

If he only knew.

"I will." I give him a small smile. "I really am sorry."

He shakes his head. "You don't have anything to be sorry about, ballerina."

"Really?"

"Really," he says, giving me a dazzling smile that almost hides the pain. "We're good."

CHAPTER FORTY-NINE

NELL

I LOOK FOR ALEC AFTER work, a million half-conceived ideas of how we can beat Lon flooding my brain. All of them are broken, fractured pieces of a plan that don't fit together and don't make any sense on their own, but at least it's a start.

I find him on a powerlift in the garden, its platform raised up to the fifth floor, tearing down the roses with ten other workers.

"They've been at it for hours and have barely made a dent," an old man wearing a straw sun hat tells me. "I've been a gardener for fifty years and I've never seen anything like it."

Alec wipes the sweat from his brow and glances down at me. I take a step toward him, but then I see Dad standing underneath the platform, talking to a crowd of guests and gesturing up to the platform.

Dad's gaze locks on mine.

"Excuse me for a moment," he says to the guests, buttoning his suit jacket and making his way over to me. "Hey, kiddo. Done with work for the day?"

I nod.

Dad notices me looking up at the roses and shakes his head. "Can you believe it? Sofia says it happens every few years."

"Every sixteen," I murmur under my breath.

"Incredible." Dad puts his arm around my shoulder. "Want to get some dinner? I'm starving."

I glance up and meet Alec's gaze once more.

"Uh, yeah, sure," I tell Dad.

"Excellent."

Dad leads me out of the garden, talking about the day he's had while, behind me, branches snap and roses flutter to the ground like snow.

———————

I'm standing in my old room—the one from 1907.

Everything looks the same as it did all those years ago.

And I'm wearing the nightgown.

This is a dream, I think.

But everything feels too real to be a dream.

It even smells the same, like the ocean, and Mother's perfume, and a hint of candle wax from Benny's light box down the hall. I run my fingers along the textured grooves in the armoire, appreciating the familiar silkiness of the polished brass handles.

A warm gust of breath encircles my ear. I close my eyes, a tear escaping my lashes, as Lon leans his strong, predator's body against my spine.

"Beautiful, isn't it?" he whispers. "This world we inhabited? I could have kept you wrapped up inside it all your days."

I grit my teeth. "For what price?"

His hands brush my shoulders, his fingers ghosting up my neck, encircling my throat. "Everything comes with a price, my dear."

I step away from him before his hands can close over my windpipe.

"You don't know anything about me if you think I'll let you win without a fight."

He chuckles softly. "There is really no point in it. I will *never* let you win." His jaw hardens. "Now, then. Give your fiancé a kiss, and perhaps I will forgive your past transgressions."

He starts forward.

I back into the door, my hand fumbling for the knob. I close my palm over the cold metal and wrench the door open, stumbling back into the parlor.

My corpse lies in the middle of the room, surrounded by a pool of blood seeping into the floorboards. Lon's body is slumped against the far wall, his skull blown out across the wallpaper.

"You cannot escape it," Lon says, appearing next to me. Looking down his nose at the carnage he wrought.

Something warm and wet blooms on my nightgown, sticking the fabric to my chest. I glance down at the thick, red liquid pumping from my rib cage.

A familiar voice echoes across the room.

"You're going to end up like all of us, darling."

She's standing across from me, although she looks nothing like she did when she was alive. She is a corpse long buried in the ground, her clothes in tatters, her hair dry and bristly as straw. Next to her are Father and Benny, their rotting flesh hanging from their bones and burial suits like shabby curtains.

"Mother?"

"There is no escaping death," Aurelea's mother—*my* mother—says.

A figure flashes in the corner of the room. A tall, blond woman wearing the same sweater and pencil skirt she wore when she boarded a plane four years ago. She smiles at me, but then her image flickers like bad TV reception, and suddenly her smile is pulled too wide, exposing her shattered jaw.

"Mom!" I try to move forward, but my feet are rooted to the ground. My own blood slowly creeps down my chest, my sleeves, my waist. Lon takes a step closer to me, wrapping his arms in the scarlet liquid pouring across my torso, congealing into thick, dark globs as it trails down my gown, until the fabric is no longer white and airy but red and heavy with blood.

Lon nuzzles my neck, pushing my hair aside.

"I will not let you have your happily ever after, my darling," he tells me. "Not when you have so selfishly stolen mine."

Father steps forward, his arms outstretched. A cockroach climbs out of his ear, plopping onto the frayed shoulder of his burial suit. "It's time to come home, sweetheart."

Benny takes my hand, his lips cracking and his dead eyes glassy as he speaks. "It only hurts for a second, Lea. Then it's like flying."

Tears well in my eyes. I bend down to his level and cradle his cold, bony cheek in my palm. "I'm sorry I had to leave you, Benny."

He smiles at Lon as if they are in this together. But then Benny leans forward, cups his hands around his mouth, and whispers the same word he said to me in the linen closet.

"*Run*."

I bolt awake, my heart pounding.

The room is pitch-black. I grab my phone from the bedside table and use its light to stumble to the bathroom as I hyperventilate.

The first thing I check in the bathroom's light is my pajamas, but there's no blood on them, even though I can still feel the heat and thickness of it sticking to my skin, and there's no blood pouring from my chest, even though I can still feel it pumping to the floor.

My whole body starts to shake. I knock my head against the door and slide down to the cold tile, my hands brushing away blood that isn't there.

I don't want to cry. I don't want to give that sick bastard the satisfaction. But the tears come anyway, hot and fast and suffocating.

Outside the door, Dad's mattress squeaks, and I hurriedly turn on the faucet to cover my sobs. The last thing I want to do is try to explain this, even though I'm sure Dad would understand if I told him it was because of a nightmare, or if I said it was because of Mom, which wouldn't even be a lie. But he would worry, and I don't want him worrying about me.

Not anymore.

I pause, staring at my phone. Red fingerprints cover the screen. I turn my hand over—the one I pressed to my chest in the dream.

Dried blood swirls through the cracks in my palms, flaking like bits of old paint onto the tile.

CHAPTER FIFTY

NELL

"NELL?" DAD ASKS. "EVERYTHING OKAY?"

I glance up from my uneaten bagel. Dad sits across from me, worry lines etching his face. The rest of the room comes into focus slowly, replacing the images of my decomposing family and a nightgown made of blood.

"Huh?" I ask.

Dad's frown deepens. "Are you feeling all right?"

"Oh. Uh, yeah." I shake my head. "Bad dreams."

Dad takes the last bite of his egg sandwich. "Anything I can help with?"

"That's okay," I say, picking at my bagel. "They didn't make sense."

He nods, then leans back in his chair, his hands behind his head as he stares out the windows at the sun rising over the beach. "Don't you just love it here?"

The thing is, I do. I didn't when I first came here, on the ferry in 1907, when it was nothing more than the place where I would spend my last remaining months as a Sargent before losing my last scraps of freedom and becoming a Van Oirschot. But all that changed when I met Alec. Canvas City; the beach; the secret, hidden places in the Grand where Alec and I could be together without fear—*that* is the Winslow Island I fell in love with.

And regardless of what has happened since—regardless of the fact that Lon is here, too, watching me, invading my thoughts, threatening every breath I take—this hotel has brought me back to Alec. It has given us more time than Lon's bullet intended for us to have. It is a magical place.

I don't want to leave it again.

"So, kiddo," Dad says. "Four weeks until your seventeenth. Have you thought about what you want to do?"

My birthday. August 8. Two days after Aurelea was killed. Three days after Alec and I go back to 1907 and do it all over again.

I want to believe I'll be here to celebrate it. I want to believe we'll actually do it this time. Break the curse. But this is Lon's game. He's played it seven other times, and he's never lost. I can practically hear his voice telling me not to plan anything, that I'll be long gone before then and Dad won't even remember he had a daughter to mourn.

So, in a giant middle finger to Lon, I say, "Yeah. Let's have a pizza party, just you and me."

"Are you sure that's all you want?"

I gaze out the window, at the lush palm trees and bright, tropical flowers swaying in the breeze. At the pristine sand and the whitecapped waves lapping the shore.

At the dark figure standing behind me, reflected in the glass. "Absolutely."

I'm not much use to Max, not that he really notices. Even though he said it wouldn't change things, he's been ignoring me since our talk yesterday. Any other time it would bother me, but it turns out Max is really productive when he isn't wasting his time flirting.

He picks up the slack for me without even meaning to.

It's not that I don't try to get work done, but my mind is a century in the past, and every time I try to focus on the documents and photographs in front of me, a new idea flashes like a camera in my mind and I sneak out my notebook to write it down.

Memories keep coming to me, although most of them are sketchy and inconsistent. One second I'm remembering something from my days as a flapper, the next I'm remembering teasing my hair in the mirror and seeing Lon's face staring back at me.

I'm still not sure if some of my ideas come from these memories, if they've been tried or discussed before, but I write them down anyway, and by the end of the day, I have five. Five solid ways to try beating the curse. And I don't have a single clue if any of them will work.

But Alec will.

I find him in the inner garden. The thorny ceiling is gone; the roses have been trimmed back to the third-floor balcony.

"Been working around the clock," I hear someone say as I pass.

I stop at the bottom of the platform and shield my eyes as I look up.

"Alec?"

He glances down at me, rubbing his forearm across his damp brow. For a moment, just like every other time I've seen him, his eyes betray the joy he feels at seeing me. But then, almost immediately, that joy is wiped away, replaced with so much pain and fear and doubt that my heart cracks under the weight of it.

I glance at the other workers, then mouth, *"Can we talk?"*

He nods and sets down his gardening shears. He climbs down the ladder, then takes my hand and leads me away from the onlookers, back inside the hotel.

"I've come up with some ideas," I say, holding the notebook out to him, "on how we can . . . you know."

He takes a deep breath and nods. "Let's go somewhere else."

I follow him to the beach. I know this time who it is he doesn't want overhearing us.

Lon is everywhere in that hotel.

"Okay," Alec says once we're standing by the tide line, the crashing surf and giddy screams of children wading in the water drowning our conversation. "What are you thinking?"

I open the notebook, creasing the binding back.

I clear my throat. "What if we tried exorcising Lon from the hotel?"

"Like a ghost?"

I give him a pointed look. "More like a demon."

He shakes his head. "I don't think it would work. Lon's spirit isn't choosing to stay here. He's just as trapped as we are. If anything, all it would do is make him angrier."

"Okay . . ." I pull out a short, stubby pencil from my pocket and cross out the first idea. "What if we took modern technology back with us? Something that could help?"

Alec crosses his arms over his chest. "Like what?"

"I don't know. A gun? Something we could use to fight back?"

"Every time we've gone back, it doesn't matter what clothes I'm wearing or what I have in my pockets—I always return wearing the exact same thing I wore on August 5, 1907, and nothing else ever travels back with me."

I sigh. I hadn't known for sure that taking a gun back with us would actually help, but it made me feel safer to know that if

Lon attacked me again, I would have something other than my fists or a glass shard to level the playing field.

"So you don't think it would work?"

Alec looks out at the horizon and shakes his head again.

I cross that one off my list.

"What if we don't run away?"

"You mean, if we let Lon think you're going to stay with him this time?"

I grimace. "We've tried it before?"

He nods. "When we go back, Lon acts like he did that day. He says the same things, keeps the same schedule. But he knows why we're there. He *will* still seek you out." He swallows. "He'll still kill you."

"What if we kill him first?"

"The curse won't let us," he says. "Everything stays the same until Lon comes for us, and then all bets are off."

I throw my hands up. "Can you at least *try* to be a little more helpful?"

He doesn't say anything. Just stares at me with defeat already in his eyes.

Finally, he murmurs, "What do you want me to do? Lie to you?"

My eyes burn, but I blink away the tears. "My life is on the line here, Alec, and you don't seem to care."

His jaw hardens. He takes a step forward, until my nose is practically in his collarbone. He stares down at me, his breathing rough, his eyes sharp as icepicks. "Do *not* say that I don't care. I care too much, Nell. *Far* too much. That's why I can't do this again."

"Fine," I bite back. "Then I'll do it without you."

He stares at me a second longer, as if there's so much more

he wants to say, but he doesn't see the point. He curses under his breath.

And then he walks away from me.

I don't call after him.

He's too far gone for me to reach.

CHAPTER FIFTY-ONE

NELL

I WILL NOT CRY.

I won't.

I won't.

I *won't*.

I repeat this mantra in my mind as I head back to my room. Up the stairs, twirling four flights around the elevator shaft, remembering how it felt to stand inside that gold cage, my heart beating so hard against my chest, as if it also wanted to run away and never stop running. Remembering how lost I was, until I met Alec. And now . . .

Now, I'm alone again.

I take a right at the fourth-floor landing, into the exterior hallway overlooking the garden. Someone's opened the windows to let in the breeze, and I pace in front of them, letting the fresh, rose-scented air cool my fevered skin.

I'm okay, everything's okay. I'm going to figure this out.

I have one last idea in my notebook, and I still have a month left to think of something else if it doesn't work. It's too early to give up yet, even if Alec already has.

Footsteps thud behind me. I stop pacing and force a smile, expecting to see another guest, but when I turn, there's no one there.

The hallway's empty.

Frowning, I take a step forward. "Hello?"

The doors slam shut, followed by the windows. The glass bends inward, as if someone is pushing against them from the other side, until the pressure's too strong. Glass shards explode into the hallway, winking in the sunlight as the windows shatter, one by one. The force knocks me into the wall. Fractures of glass scrape my arms, my legs, my face. I scream as I fold into the fetal position, crossing my arms over my head.

I don't look up until the last tinkling shards hit the ground. My mind's already searching for a logical explanation—an earthquake? A strong gust of wind?—even though I know there is nothing logical or earthly about this.

The high-pitched, staccato whine of screws being loosened echoes down the hall. I push myself up and run for the doors.

Locked.

I try to shove them open, but they don't even rattle.

Cursing, I glance up.

The light fixtures are all hanging sideways, each held to the ceiling by one last screw. For a moment, the whine stops, leaving them dangling over me.

And then, slowly, the screws screech again as they're twisted out of their fasteners. I press myself against the wall and watch them turn, pulling out one by one as if an invisible hand is removing them. But instead of falling, the fixtures hang suspended in midair. I'm too busy watching them to register the glass shards tinkling around me, rising above me, joining the fixtures along the ceiling, all pointing with their jagged edges down, until it's too late.

Lon's laughter bubbles off the walls.

"You can't escape me, Aurelea," he says. "I'm everywhere."

I hear someone else say my name—"Nell!"—but the voice sounds far away, and I can't tear my eyes from the ceiling. The fixtures and glass wobble.

I cover my head and scream as they fall.

"Nell."

Someone shakes my shoulder, but I keep my head tucked in the crook of my arms.

"Nell."

A woman's voice.

"It's all right," she says. "He's gone."

My brow furrows. Slowly, I look up and meet Sofia's gaze.

The hallway looks just as peaceful as when I first entered it. The windows are all still open and intact, a gentle breeze whooshing through them, and the light fixtures are firmly planted against the ceiling. I push up from the floor and inspect myself for the cuts and puncture wounds I'm certain will be there, but there's nothing. Not even a scratch.

And then I remember what she said.

He's gone.

"You've known it was me?" I ask her. "This whole time?"

She nods. "I've just been waiting for you to remember."

"But how did you recognize me? Alec said no one remembers me after—" I can't finish the sentence. *After I die.*

"Alec's pictures of you," she says. "And I knew it had been

sixteen years since the last time you were here. It wasn't hard to put together."

"Did anyone else see me in here?"

"I don't think so," Sofia says. "But quite a few people will have heard you. No matter. I can give my staff an explanation for anyone who asks." She sighs. "I know it's terrifying, but try not to let him get to you. He can only hurt you if you let him. Until you go back, of course."

Easy for her to say. She didn't almost sleepwalk right out of a window or wake from a nightmare with blood on her hand.

"Right," I say. "Thanks."

"If there's anything else I can do for you, let me know."

I nod.

She starts to walk away.

"Actually," I say, stopping her. "There is one thing."

"Yes?"

An older couple ambles into the hall, the woman's cane tapping against the floor as they pass us, her husband holding on to her other arm and slowing his pace for her. We nod at each other in greeting.

Once they disappear around the corner, I take a step closer to Sofia and lower my voice. "When I go back . . . if I don't make it . . ."

Sofia's features soften. "Yes?"

"Could you look after my dad? I know he won't remember me, so I guess he won't really have anything to be upset about, but we've kind of been a team, him and I, so he might get a little . . . lost . . . without me here."

Her lips twist into a sad smile.

"Of course I'll look after him. Just make sure Alec reminds me."

Right. Because she won't remember he had a daughter in the first place. "Thank you."

She puts her hand on my shoulder. The touch is so nice, so motherly, I flinch away from it without thinking.

She quickly hides her frown.

"Don't give up hope," she says. "You've been given this chance for a reason. There is something you can do to beat him. You just have to figure out what it is."

I'm surprised she feels so comfortable talking about Lon here, where his spirit just made such an impressive display and where he could still be nearby. Watching. Listening. Plotting. But, of course, she isn't worried about him coming after *her*, or anyone else.

He only wants me.

She gives my shoulder one more tap, then heads back inside the hotel. I turn and walk the other way, toward my room, my resolve strengthening with every step.

I will *not* let myself be a victim in this.

And I won't let Alec be one, either.

CHAPTER FIFTY-TWO

NELL

I WAIT UNTIL MIDNIGHT. THERE'S no moonlight to see by, so I judge how deeply Dad's sleeping by the volume and consistency of his snores. When I'm sure he's too far gone for a sonic boom to wake him, I slide out from under the covers and grab the sweater I left at the edge of my bed and the key card I left on the TV stand. I slide my feet into a pair of well-worn flats, then slip quietly out the door, closing it softly behind me.

The hotel isn't as quiet at midnight as it is before dawn, not with some of the late-night vacationers only just returning to their rooms from the lounge. For the most part, I'm able to keep thoughts of Lon out of my mind as I walk the halls, only hurrying my footsteps when I hear the floorboards creak behind me or when a light bulb flickers overhead.

I reach the stairs to the tallest tower and knock on the door. No answer.

He could be in the ballroom or roaming the halls. Or he

could actually be sleeping, for once. I knock again, harder this time.

A throat clears behind me.

"Looking for someone?"

I turn.

"Were you following me?"

A muscle in Alec's jaw ticks. "I wanted to make sure you weren't sleepwalking again."

"You've been watching my room?"

He nods, not quite meeting my gaze.

I step down off the landing, drawing closer to him. "Even though you've already given up?"

His eyes flash, but he doesn't deny it.

I take his hand. "Come on. We need to talk."

The moonless sky reminds me of the night Alec and I spent on Lon's yacht, although the streetlamps and far-off city lights dull the stars shining above us. Sand slips over my feet as I lead Alec to the tide line. His palm skims across mine as we walk, shooting electric sparks through my veins.

I take his other hand when we reach the surf, forcing him to face me.

"What do you see when you look at me?" I ask.

He shakes his head. "Nell . . ."

I squeeze his hands, frustration and loss and heartbreak all crashing over me in equal measure. "Come on, Alec."

He grits his teeth.

"I see you dying in my arms, over and over again. I see every single day I have lived without you for the past 112 years. I see the world changing all around me, a world I can't touch or feel or participate in outside these walls." His breath shudders, and an agonized, bitter laugh escapes his lips. "Did you know that my mother died a year after Lea?"

My breath catches in my throat.

"No," I say. "I didn't."

"I still didn't know I wasn't aging then. I didn't know when I said goodbye to her and promised I'd see her again that it might not come true. I didn't know that I would watch my family in Russia—the only family I had left—all grow old and die through letters and photographs, while I didn't age at all. I didn't know I would watch the same thing happen to Tommy and Moira, and Fitz and Clara, or that I would have to lie to them and tell them I moved away so they wouldn't catch on to my immortality. I didn't know all four of them would stay on the island, or that I would see them sometimes, on the beach or in the hotel restaurant. That I would count every new wrinkle and every grandchild and, eventually, read all their obituaries. I couldn't even attend their funerals, Nell. Do you know how painful that was?"

"I can't imagine," I say, my voice small, my words so insignificant in the shadow of his loss.

He tips his head back as tears line his eyes. "I didn't know when I lost my mother that I would also eventually lose my ability to care about anyone or anything, because I would learn that it hurt too much to do so. I only knew that I was an orphan, and I couldn't find solace in the one person who could've given it to me, because she'd already been dead for 383 days by the time my mother drew her last breath. And the worst part of it all is that I have no one to blame but myself. Your death, the curse—it's all my fault. It's *always* been my fault. If I had just left you alone from the beginning like I should have—"

"I would have never known true love," I interrupt him. "I would have led a miserable existence with a husband who would have broken my spirit and kept me under his thumb from the moment I said 'I do.' Even if I had lived to be a hundred years old, it wouldn't have been a *life*. You freed me, Alec. I lived more in those two months with you than I did in the sixteen years before it."

"You deserved more than two months."

"And I'll get it," I say. "We can have forever, Alec. We just need to break the curse."

Tears slide over his lashes, silently trailing down his cheeks. "You're always so optimistic. In the past, it made me optimistic, too. But this curse isn't a chance for us to be together. It's the price I pay for my crime. This is my purgatory, and for one night every sixteen years, I descend into hell to watch you die again and give my pound of flesh. That's all this is. All it's ever been."

I shake my head. "No. I refuse to accept that. I don't keep coming back just to torment you, Alec. If that were the case, I'd come back as a ghost, or a memory. Something intangible. But I live full lives *every time*. I get new names and new parents and new memories. I get new dreams and new scars and new reasons to live. I'm not Lea, and I'm not Katie, or anyone else who's come before me. They're all a part of me, and they always will be, but I'm *Nell*." Tears burn my eyes, but I keep going, my voice unwavering. "I lost my mother in a plane crash four years ago. I want to be a professional ballerina, and I want to watch my father grow into a happy, old man. I want to *live*, Alec. But I can't do that without you." I press myself against him, moving his arms around me. "Please, don't give up now. Don't let this be how we end." I wrap my arms around his neck and stand on my tiptoes until he presses his forehead against mine. "Come back to me."

His body tenses. "Nell . . ."

"Shh," I whisper. "Believe in us again, Alec." I pull my face away and stare up at him, threading my fingers through his hair. "Believe in me."

He hesitates, and for a moment I think I'm too late, that he's too far gone.

But then he curses under his breath and crushes his mouth against mine, stealing my breath and salting my lips with his tears. His arms tighten around me, making us as close to one person as we can possibly be. I sob my relief, gasping for breath even as I kiss him back, crashing myself into him, unleashing every moment of love and fear and heartbreak and joy I have felt with him, in this life and in the seven others I've led. So many thoughts jumble in my brain—*I love you, I missed you, don't ever let me go again*—but one rises above the others.

Home.

I am finally, gloriously, *home.*

"I'm sorry," Alec says, raining kisses and tears on my neck, my shoulder, my collarbone. "I'm so sorry. I'm here now." He squeezes me. "I won't give up on us."

We hold each other for a long time, listening to the crashing of the surf and our entangled breaths.

Here, in this moment, time has no hold on us.

CHAPTER FIFTY-THREE

NELL

WE SPEND EVERY DAY TOGETHER after that. Our mornings are taken up by our work—Alec roaming the hotel, filling in wherever he's needed, while I spend my time in the storage room. Not that I get much done. I try to focus, but half of me is always thinking of ways to break the curse, and the other half is obsessed with spending as much time with Alec as I can.

I make a silent promise that if we survive it this time, I will put in double shifts in the storage room to make up for my wandering mind. I want to be here so badly to see the museum when it opens, it is a physical pain that keeps me up at night and stalks me throughout the day.

I wonder one morning, while trying to focus on photographs of the Grand from the First World War, what will become of me and Alec if we never break the curse. Will I still return here one hundred, two hundred, three hundred years from now? Will the Grand even be standing?

Will the world?

What would become of an immortal like Alec if the world ended and he were the only one left? My heart clogs my throat as I imagine him all alone in the universe—a fate worse than death—and then I have to force the thought away. It's too horrific to contemplate.

It must not just be nightmares but thoughts like these that keep Alec up at night.

We spend most of our afternoons and evenings together, when Dad's too busy at work to notice. We discuss different ideas, plans to break the curse, but the only one Alec thinks might work is number five on my list, which is to run away before midnight, sometime in the afternoon perhaps, when Lon is playing golf with his father, too far away to stop us. It will be almost impossible to sneak away undetected by my parents and the hotel staff, and we aren't even sure if we'll be able to leave the property, but it's a chance we're willing to take.

Our time together isn't all work. We play just as much as we plan.

Swimming in the ocean, collecting sand dollars along the tide line, stuffing our faces full of sweets from the bakery. We spend every night in each other's arms, and every morning before dawn, Alec watches me practice my audition routine in the ballroom. Sometimes I lose focus, wondering if it's even worth practicing when I don't know if I'll be here come September, but Alec doesn't let me think like that. He applauds whenever I do something especially impressive and shouts his encouragement, saying things like, "How does someone even jump that high? Did you come back part kangaroo this time?"

As long as I'm not alone, Lon doesn't attack me in the daylight, and I'm almost never alone. Instead, he steps up his assault in my nightmares, so that Alec has to shake me awake every time I scream.

But tonight's dream is different.

I'm not even certain it's a dream, or if it's something else entirely. All I know is one second I'm lying on Alec's bed, listening to him read *Leaves of Grass*, my head tucked in the crook of his shoulder. The next, Lon is standing over me.

I expect Alec to react, to push me behind him, away from Lon's prying eyes and sinister sneer. Instead, Alec continues reading, oblivious to Lon's presence in the room.

That's how I know this isn't real. Alec would never let Lon get this close to me.

"Enjoying yourself?" Lon asks.

I push myself off the bed, but Alec doesn't notice.

"Get out," I order him. "You're not welcome here."

Lon *tsks* his tongue against the roof of his mouth. "That is where you're wrong, my darling." He disappears, then reappears behind me, his breath in my ear. He holds out a rose so red, it's almost black. "I am welcome everywhere."

"No," I say, turning to face him and pushing his rose away. "You're not."

I know I should be afraid of him, but my anger has become stronger than my fear.

Lon chuckles, a dark, deep sound that reverberates through my bones as he squeezes the rose. The petals pulverize in his palm and blood drips through his fingers.

"Well, well. It seems the princess has grown a spine. How precious."

He reaches up with his bloodied hand and traces his fingers along my jaw, tipping my head back.

"You know," he says, "I've always admired the fire in you, Aurelea. It's so much fun to snuff out."

I jerk my chin out of his grasp.

"Not this time, Lon," I bite my words, my voice filled with all the venom and hatred I feel for this man. "You're going to lose."

Amusement tilts his lips. "And what makes you think that?"

"We've discovered something." It's a lie—we haven't discovered anything other than another idea that may or may not work—but Lon doesn't need to know that. "The missing link. The curse is going to break, and you will be left with nothing."

His eyes narrow. "I don't believe you."

My smile grows, and I know my eyes must be alight with the vengeful joy bubbling up inside me. "Believe what you like. It doesn't change the fact that, four days from now, you're going to lose, and Alec and I will walk out of this hotel, together." I take another step closer, relishing the fear and doubt swirling in his eyes. "We'll grow up, get married, have children, and live a long, happy life together, and you won't even be so much as a passing thought in our minds ever again."

Lon's face contorts with rage. He thrusts out his arms, shattering the windows circling the tower. The shards fly inward, just as they did that day in the exterior corridor. But I don't let them scare me this time. Instead, I lie back on the bed, curling myself against Alec's side. "Go away, Lon. You're not impressing anyone."

I know this newfound courage won't last forever. I know that when we go back to 1907, we will be in Lon's world, and he will be able to kill me just as he has done every time before. But, for now, I am in my world, safe in Alec's arms, and I will not let him intimidate me here.

Lon sneers. "I've only begun to reveal the tricks up my sleeve. Sweet dreams, darling."

I slam awake.

Alec stops reading. "Did you fall asleep?"

I sit up, a shiver tingling my spine. The windows are all intact, just as I knew they would be.

Alec puts his arms around me and leans back against the headboard, pressing his lips against my temple.

"It's all right, now," he says. "I won't let him hurt you."

I want to believe that, but Lon's final words echo through my mind, and when the alarm on my phone blares for my morning practice, I'm still awake.

CHAPTER FIFTY-FOUR

NELL

I'M STILL THINKING OF LON'S warning the next day while eating breakfast by myself in the café. Dad had a guest emergency, and Alec is on morning rose duty with the rest of the gardening staff, so I take the opportunity to sketch out every possible exit route and diversionary tactic I can think of to give us an edge over Lon when we return.

"So this ballet movie we're making," Max says, plopping into the seat across from me. "Should we go for something sexy, like Natalie Portman and Mila Kunis in *Black Swan*, or something classy, like Moira Shearer in *The Red Shoes*?"

"What'd you do?" I ask, closing my notebook. "Watch every ballet movie ever made?"

"Just about."

I arch a brow at him.

"What? I have a lot of free time on my hands."

I take a sip of my coffee. "Something classy, for sure. Maybe it should be set at a boarding school. You can't get classier than that."

"Boarding school," Max says, tapping the notepad app on his phone. "Got it."

"In Paris."

He keeps typing. "Obviously."

"And everyone should drink champagne all the time."

"You're making fun of me now, aren't you?"

"Only a little."

"Well, just you wait. One day this script is going to arrive on your doorstep and you are going to *love* it."

"I can't wait," I say, grinning.

Max gives me a small smile in return. "It's good to see you happy again. I feel like it's been a while."

"It's good to have you talking to me again," I reply.

"I wasn't avoiding you, if that's what you're thinking."

"Are you sure about that?"

He shrugs. "Okay, maybe a little, but you have to understand that the male ego is a very sensitive thing. We need time to lick our wounds when a beautiful girl rejects us. But I've also been really getting into our work here. It seems like I get an idea for a new plot twist every day."

"So the screenplay's coming along?"

He leans back in his chair. "Ten new pages last night."

"That's fantastic," I say, although I feel a little weird knowing Max's screenplay is based on Alec.

He glances over his shoulder at the people eating their breakfasts around us, then leans forward and whispers, "Seriously, though. Petrov's treating you all right?"

"You think that's why I've been so crabby lately?"

"Well . . . yeah."

I shake my head. "Alec's amazing. I've been dealing with something else."

"Oh," Max says. "Okay."

He doesn't look entirely convinced. I put my hand on his arm and say, "Really. I'm good."

Max stares down at my hand a second. When he looks back up, his charming, crooked smile is a little too straight, and there's a sudden glint in his eyes I've never seen before.

"Well, the question remains," he says, lowering his voice. "When are you going to ditch that loser and give me a chance?"

I force out a laugh, thinking it must be a joke.

But Max stares back at me with determination.

My brow furrows. "I thought we talked about this."

"We did, but I'm bringing it up again."

I don't know what to say. I don't want to hurt his feelings. Max is the only true friend other than Alec I've made on this island. Probably the only friend I've had in four years. "I thought I was clear . . . I'm interested in Alec, and that isn't going to change."

He grits his teeth.

"It's nothing against you," I say quickly. "You're a really great friend, Max."

He stares at the desk, saying nothing.

My heart pounds in my chest. "Max?"

His hand lashes out, pinning my wrist to the table.

"He's not right for you. Don't you see that?" His grip tightens. "I mean, it's pretty clear to everyone else that you belong with me."

Everyone else?

"Max, you're hurting me."

"I won't see you run off with him."

"Run off? Max, what are you talking about?"

"He doesn't belong in our world, Lea."

I inhale sharply.

"What did you just call me?"

Max leans forward, his breath in my ear. Lon's voice slithers out of his lips. "You can't escape me, darling. I already told you. I'm *everywhere*."

A little kid runs by us, banging a boogie board against the seats. Max blinks, his hard, cold eyes softening. He glances down at my wrist as if he doesn't remember grabbing it. He clears his throat as he lets go.

"Nell?" he says, uncertain. "What were we just talking about?"

A line of blood leaks from his nostril.

I hand him my napkin. "Your nose is bleeding."

He presses the paper against his nostril, then pulls it away, staring at the red splotch.

"Did I hurt you?" he asks.

I eye him warily. "You should go."

He winces as if I've slapped him, but he doesn't argue.

"Are you . . . will you be at work today?"

I glance down at the table. "I don't think so."

Max stares at me a moment longer, then slowly scoots his chair back and stands.

"I'm sorry if I—" He shakes his head. "I'm sorry."

I can tell by his expression, and by the set of his shoulders, that he has no clue what just happened. I want to tell him it's all right. Want to go to work with him just as I do every day, to let him know I'm still his friend, that he didn't do anything wrong.

But if Lon can use him to get to me, then I am no longer safe in a room alone with him.

And he isn't safe with me.

I find Alec in the garden, stuffing compost bags full of roses. The other workers are in the exterior hallways, cutting through the branches that coil over the windows in a latticework of thorns, choking out the light.

"We've got a serious problem," I whisper.

Alec takes my hand and leads me inside the hotel. I wait until we're alone before telling him about Max's Linda Blair moment.

"All that was missing was the pea soup," I finish.

I don't know if Alec gets the reference, or if he's ever even seen *The Exorcist*, but I don't think he heard anything I said after I told him how forcefully Max grabbed me anyway.

Alec clenches his fist. "I'm going to kill him."

I roll my eyes. "Max wasn't hurting me. Lon was."

"Fine," Alec whispers back. "I'll hurt Lon through Max."

I give him a pointed look.

He sighs. "I know, I know. I won't actually hurt him."

"Has Lon ever done anything like this before?"

"Possessed someone?" He shakes his head. "I don't think he's ever felt like he's had to, which means he's either finding new ways to amuse himself, or . . ."

"Or?"

"Or he thinks we might actually be a threat this time."

CHAPTER FIFTY-FIVE

NELL

WANTING TO STAY AS FAR away from the storage room and Max as I can, I help Alec in the garden for the rest of the morning. We spend the afternoon battling the surf, allowing the water and the sand to clean the dirt and sweat from our bodies. I try not to think about Lon, or Max, but my phone keeps buzzing with apologies.

I'm sorry, Nell.

I don't know what I did wrong, or why you're mad at me.

How can I make it right?

"I don't know what to say to him," I tell Alec. "I can't say it's fine when it isn't."

Finally, I tell Max to get some rest and maybe stay away from the hotel for a few days.

He doesn't reply.

Dad and I have dinner together at six o'clock. I try to be present, to take in these last moments with him before I go back to the past, but I'm worried about Max. I'm hoping that if I stay away from Max, then so will Lon, especially now that he's made his point.

But I'm wrong.

So, so wrong.

"Mr. Martin?" Max asks, running up to us in the fourth-floor hallway as Dad and I head back to our room.

Dad checks his watch. "Max? What are you doing here so late? Burning the midnight oil?" He glances at me. "Or are you here to see Nell?"

I know it isn't Max as soon as he smiles.

"No, sir. I'm sure she gets enough of me at work." He winks, making my insides crawl. "My mom sent me to find you. There's a guest at registration who needs help with something."

Dad sighs. "The job of a guest relations manager is never done. Would you put this in the mini fridge for me?" he asks, handing me his box of leftovers.

"Sure," I say, my voice wobbling under Max's stare.

"You have your key?" Dad asks me.

I don't want to say yes with Max standing right there, but I don't have any other choice. I nod.

"All right," Dad says. "You two kids have fun."

And then he's gone, and it's just me and Max standing in a deserted hallway.

Max watches me with eyes that aren't his.

"If you come near me," I tell him. "I'll scream."

He laughs. My stomach flips at the cold, hollow sound.

"Oh, my darling," he says, taking a step forward. "You should know by now that I *like* it when you scream."

I kick him between his legs as hard as I can. He falls back, but I don't wait to see how hurt he is.

"Sorry, Max," I say, whipping my key card out of my pocket and running for my door. If I can just get inside and lock it, Lon won't be able to get to me without leaving Max's body.

I jam the key into the reader.

"Come on," I whisper, waiting for the light to flash.

Max is already up and moving toward me.

The light blinks green. I wrench open the door and practically throw myself inside, pushing the door closed behind me—

Max's hand blocks the door.

"Max, let go," I tell him. "I don't want to hurt you."

He drives his shoulder into the door. I press my back against the other side, pushing with all my might, but my legs are tired from my morning training sessions, and they shake under the pressure. I reach into my back pocket and grab my phone. Alec doesn't have a cell, so I call the only person I can think of.

She picks up on the first ring. "Hello?"

"Sofia." The door bangs against my spine as Max rams himself against it. "Are you still in the hotel?"

"Yes, but I was just leaving. What's up?"

"Find Alec," I tell her. "Get him up to my room now."

She hesitates. "What's going on?"

The door slams into me again, harder this time.

"It's Max," I tell her. "Lon's possessed him. You have to get Alec up here now."

"Oh, God," she murmurs. "I'll be right there."

The door smacks into me again, knocking me off balance. My legs crumple underneath me and I fall to the floor as Max bursts into the room. I scramble forward, but Max fists his hands in my hair, yanking me to my feet.

"You think you've won?" Lon says through Max's lips. "You think I can't touch you here? You think I can't hurt you?"

He throws me against the wall. I cry out as pain radiates

down my side. He tries to grab me again, but I push off the wall, grabbing the table lamp from next to the lounge chair. I hold it above my head, ready to strike.

"Max, if you're in there," I say, "if you can hear me, I don't want to hurt you. You have to fight him, okay? You have to come back."

"He can't hear you," Max replies. "And even if he could, I don't think he would stop me."

I hesitate. "What do you mean?"

Max grins.

"The boy cares for you," he says with Lon's voice. "It was all too easy to manipulate those emotions. The rejection he felt from you, the anger and jealousy that someone else got to you first. He left his heart wide open. That's why I could possess him. Why I could put on his skin just as I put on every wall and floor and ceiling of this hotel. He *wanted* to hurt you."

"Max isn't you," I spit. "He wouldn't hurt me because of that."

"Why not?" he replies, taking a step forward. "You hurt *him*."

I raise the lamp higher. "Not another step."

"It's only fair that he hurts you back."

"Max!" I scream. "Max, please, don't let him do this. Fight it!"

"I already told you." He rolls his neck, cracking every bone. "Max doesn't want to fight it." I whip the base of the lamp at his head, but he ducks at the last second, the lamp grazing his shoulder as he hooks his arms around my stomach and tackles me onto the bed. I try to push away from him, but he's already on top of me, circling his hands around my throat.

"I don't care what you think you've found," Max says, clamping down on my windpipe. "You can't win if you're already dead."

I gasp for breath, but his hands are too tight—nothing's getting in. I beat my fists against his arms, his chest. Try to wrap my hands around his throat. Black spots explode across my vision. I try to hit him again, but my arms are getting heavy, my lungs screaming for air.

"Nell!" Alec yells from the doorway. I can't see him, but I hear him run across the room. His fist connects with Max's jaw. I take a deep, painful breath as Max's hands leave my throat.

Sofia screams, running for her son.

"Stay back," Alec tells her, grabbing Max by his shirt and hauling him up.

Lon's self-satisfying smirk twists Max's lips.

"Leave the boy alone," Alec says, "or I swear to God—"

"What are you going to do?" Max asks. "Kill me?"

Sofia moans. I push myself off the bed, my head swimming.

"It's all right," I rasp at her. "Alec won't let anything happen to him."

"You can't stay in there forever," Alec says. "Max might be strong enough to throw *Nell* around, but I'm a different story. I'll lock you in a closet and you won't be able to leave unless you let him go."

Max's sinister gaze drifts to Sofia. "You'd let him do that to me, Mommy?"

Sofia shudders.

Alec knocks him against the wall. "Get. Out."

Max arches a brow.

"Fine," he says. "But this isn't over." He focuses on me. "Three more days, my love, and we'll be together again."

I grit my teeth. "Go to hell, Lon."

"Only if I can take you with me." He winks, and then Max's eyes roll up into the back of his head and his body goes limp in Alec's arms.

———

By the time Max comes to, Sofia has agreed to take the rest of the week off for an impromptu vacation with Max somewhere up the coast until this is all said and done.

We don't want to give Lon the chance to use him again.

"The last thing I remember clearly was trying to leave the hotel," Max says, pressing an ice-cube-filled hand towel to his jaw, "and then everything else after that is a blur." He looks up at me, his eyes widening.

"Did I . . . ?" He sucks in a breath. "Did I do that to you?"

He gestures to my neck, where bruises from his fingers have already started to form. I run my hands over the tender skin. I have no idea how I'm going to hide them from Dad.

"No," I say, my voice croaky and awful. "You didn't do this."

He shakes his head. "It's fuzzy, but I remember having these thoughts and . . . and wanting to find you . . ."

Sofia steps forward and puts her arm around him. "Come on. Let's go home."

She stops at the door, asking Alec to take Max into the hall before turning to me. "I'm sure Alec has told you there are rules regarding who can know your secret?"

I nod.

"But the rules don't apply to you or Alec. It's *your* secret to tell. You can share it with whomever you wish, and, if you don't mind, I would like to tell Max tonight, once we're away from here. I can't stand to see him looking so confused and guilty when I could explain to him what's really going on."

"You think he'll be able to handle it?" I think of how much Lon said Max cared for me, and of how easy it was to manipulate those emotions.

"You just let me worry about that," Sofia says.

"He won't remember me if I don't come back," I say. "So he

293

might not remember any of this, either. You could wait. See what happens."

She shakes her head. "I won't have you talking like that. You're coming back this time."

I give her a small smile.

"Of course you can tell him," I say.

She pulls me into a hug, holding me tight, like Mom used to. "Good luck."

A lump forms in my throat. "Thanks."

Alec and I walk Max and Sofia to the elevator. Max doesn't take his eyes off me as the operator closes the cage door, nor as the elevator descends. I watch him back until he disappears from view.

"I can't leave you alone now," Alec murmurs. "Not if Lon can possess anyone to attack you."

"I don't think he can possess just anyone. You said yourself he's never done it before, and Lon pretty much told me he could possess Max because his heart was open to it. I think I'll be all right."

Alec puts his arm around my shoulder and presses his lips to my temple. "*Think* isn't good enough."

"We'll make it," I whisper. "It's almost done."

He swallows. "That's what I'm afraid of."

CHAPTER FIFTY-SIX

NELL

ALEC AND I WORK ON our plan until we have it scheduled to the minute. On the morning of August 5, 1907, I will be with my mother and the wedding planner, without a free moment to myself until after lunch. Alec will use this time to seek out Tommy. He doesn't think it will be like the last time we tried this, when we couldn't leave after midnight, because Alec *had* left the property that morning while running errands. It was only after midnight, on the morning of August 6, that he could no longer leave the hotel.

He hopes he'll be able to convince Tommy to get his uncle's car to the hotel at precisely fifteen minutes past one in the afternoon, at which point my mother will be taking her nap and Father, Lon, and a myriad of business partners will be on the golf course, unable to monitor my movements. It's a big ask—Tommy didn't exactly get his uncle's permission to "borrow" the car in the first place, and the only reason he agreed to it originally was with the promise that, after witnessing our predawn wedding ceremony in Savannah, he would be able to get the car back to his uncle's house before he even knew it was gone.

If we can't get Tommy's car, we'll have to board the ferry and find some other means of transportation in Charleston. Alec isn't sure if we'll actually have to drive all the way to Savannah as originally planned to break the curse or if simply leaving the island will be enough, but he doesn't want to leave anything up to chance if we can help it. He thinks he remembers a bus depot in Charleston on Meeting Street, so we decide to start our search there if need be.

I spend my last day the same way I've spent my other days: a quick bite to eat with Dad after my morning ballet practice. But this time there are thick splotches of concealer hiding the fading bruises on my neck. Work with Alec until lunch, and then swimming with him in the afternoon, breathing in the smell of salt and sand and coconut sunscreen.

I count every breath in my lungs. Focus on every image my eyes take in, storing them in my mind like snapshots from a camera. I dig my toes in the sand and feel every grain ripple over my skin. I am alive with the knowledge that tomorrow may be the last day of my life.

Alive, and terrified.

I ask Dad to take the night off from work and eat room-service pizza with me for dinner. He reminds me that my birthday pizza party isn't for a few more days, but I tell him I just need some time with him. He doesn't ask any more questions.

We watch an old Jimmy Stewart movie—one I think I may have seen in another life—and talk about his job, my training sessions, work. It isn't a very deep or important conversation, but that doesn't matter. We could talk about seahorses for all I care. I just want to hear Dad's voice.

When he falls asleep watching a *Frasier* rerun, I turn off the TV, pull the covers over him, and press a kiss to his cheek.

"Love you, Dad," I whisper.

I sneak out of our room and spend the rest of the night in Alec's arms. For the first time in weeks, we don't talk about the plan. We don't go over our minute-by-minute schedules or try to find new ways to get around the curse. We just hold each other, listening to our numbered heartbeats.

At 11:59, Alec's arms tighten around me.

"Ready?" he asks.

I bury my face in the crook of his shoulder. I don't want to watch the clock change to midnight. "Never."

"I love you," Alec says.

I open my mouth to tell him I love him, too, but a white light envelops us.

The world spins.

And then I'm holding on to nothing.

PART THREE

CHAPTER FIFTY-SEVEN

NELL

I OPEN MY EYES TO warm morning sunlight streaming across my face. I reach across the bed for Alec, but several truths hit me at once:

I am in a different, larger bed.

The room is square instead of round.

And Alec isn't here.

My heart pounds as I glance around the room, at the mahogany four-poster bed and matching armoire, the antique ceramic pitcher and bowl sitting atop the dresser, the old-fashioned light fixtures and the large traveling trunk pushed into the corner of the room.

I look to my left, catching my reflection in a vanity mirror. My hair is longer, falling in ringlets over my shoulders and down my back, and I am wearing a nightgown made of sheer lace and pink ribbon. I pull the collar away from my throat.

The yellow-green bruises that were there yesterday are gone.

I lift my hands and stare at the soft, unblemished skin, free of the scar beneath my thumb that I got from a bike crash when I was eight.

August 5, 1907.

I made it.

I have done this six other times, and yet it still takes me by surprise, being back in this room, where so many nightmares and daydreams chased me that final summer of my life as Aurelea Sargent. When I'd had no idea what fate awaited me after this night, and all I knew was that I was in love with a boy who society told me was all wrong for me and terrified of the fiancé society had thrust upon me. When I stood at a precipice, where one side held a familiar life of comfort and subservience and the other held excitement and unknown territory, and—above all else—true, selfless, all-encompassing love.

This morning, in that life, I had chosen to jump. To trust in that love. To trust in fate. I'd had no idea that Alec would not be able to catch me. Benny's laughter drifts through my closed bedroom door. I suck in a breath at the light, tinkling sound of it. In my time, Benny has long since died, along with the rest of my family, but here, on this day, he's just a kid with a full life ahead of him.

My door opens suddenly. Mother fills the frame, looking whole and healthy, with pink skin and silky hair and full cheeks—not at all like the corpse I had seen in my nightmares. She stares down at me with a mixture of annoyance and amusement. "Still abed at this hour?"

"What time is it?" I ask, my voice rough, my heart aching at the sight of her.

"Half past nine," she replies, crossing to the armoire and pawing through my dresses. I already know which one she will choose. "I think the white lace with the blue ribbon feels appropriately bridal for a meeting with the wedding planner. Don't you agree?"

I nod, pushing myself out of bed.

Mother hands me the dress.

"Hurry up," she says. "Your breakfast is getting cold."

I wait for her to leave the room, pulling the door closed behind her, then pour the pitcher of water into the basin and wash my face.

I comb out my hair next. It has been more than one hundred years—or sixteen years, depending on how you look at it—since I've twisted and pulled my hair into such an elaborate topknot, but my hands perform the movements as if no time has passed. Next, I change into the gown, carefully tying the ribbon around my waist. Then, without thinking, I pinch my cheeks and bite my lips to give them some color.

You can take the girl out of the Edwardian era, but you can't take the Edwardian era out of the girl.

Benny is finishing his breakfast of toast and fruit preserves when I step into the parlor, his bouncing blond curls shimmering like spun gold in the sunlight.

"Benny."

His name is a breath on my lips, barely audible, but he glances at me anyway. And even though he couldn't possibly know that it has been a lifetime since I've seen him or that he has been nothing but a rotting corpse in my dreams, he pushes away from the small table and runs to me, throwing his arms around my waist.

I wrap my own arms around his slight frame.

"Good morning," I say, tears stinging my eyes.

"Morning," he says brightly, looking up at me with that smile and those dimples I love so much. "Nanny and I are going down to the beach. Want to come?"

I blink away the tears before they can fall. "I'd love to, but Mother and I already have plans." And even though I know it won't happen, even though it breaks my heart, I say the same thing I said to him more than a century ago. "Tomorrow?"

He nods. "Tomorrow."

Madeline shoos him into his room to change into his swimwear. I watch him go, curls bouncing all over the place.

Mother eyes me warily.

"You're acting strangely this morning," she observes. "Are you feeling well?"

"I feel fine, Mother," I reply, taking a seat at the table and reaching for a scone.

I have to stay calm and not let any of this affect me. I can't give Mother a reason to change our schedule today. Everything must stay exactly the same if our plan is going to work.

Following the hotel's event planner around the courtyard as she describes her vision for our wedding breakfast is surreal. Not because I remember every detail, from the proposed flower arrangements to the monogrammed bone china, which I do, but because I remember the feeling of claustrophobia I got every time the planner would speak of my wedding day, the clawing anxiety that threatened to suffocate me behind my well-practiced smile.

But this morning was different. This morning, I knew I was going to run away with Alec at midnight, leaving all this behind, and I was nervous for an entirely different reason—wondering if it would work, counting the hours until we could be together, praying that, come dawn, I would be Mrs. Alec Petrov.

Now, I'm anxious and jumpy for the same reasons, only this time our plan has changed, and I know what awaits us if we fail.

"Why are you fidgeting?" Mother asks me out of the corner of her mouth as the planner shows us a mock table covered in pristine white linen, an all-white flower arrangement draped in pearls at its center. "Do you have somewhere else to be?"

"No," I whisper back. "Sorry."

I focus every fiber of my being on staying still for the duration of the meeting, even as a million questions run through my mind.

Will Lon still play golf this afternoon, trusting the day to unfold exactly as it did a century ago?

Was Alec able to secure the car to get us to Savannah?

Will I ever see my dad again?

At half past eleven, Mother and I thank the planner and head inside the lobby. The room is crowded with faces, some familiar, some not. Overhead, the old bats sit in their chairs along the second-floor gallery, watching the lives playing out beneath them. I narrow my gaze at them, wondering if they have already told Lon about Alec and me. It takes everything inside me not to give them the middle finger as I walk by.

Instead I snap my gaze forward, ignoring them. And then—my breath catches in my throat—there he is, striding toward me in the same bellhop uniform he wore the first day we met.

Alec.

He doesn't meet my gaze, and I quickly look away from him. But he passes close enough to press a note into my hand. I keep it hidden from Mother until we are seated in the dining room and she is busying herself with the lunch menu. Concealing the paper beneath the tablecloth, I read the words hastily scrawled onto it.

No car. Meet at same time. 2:00 ferry.

It was already decided that if Alec couldn't get the car, we would need to take the two o'clock ferry, as we wouldn't be able to walk to the dock fast enough to make the one thirty, so nothing has *really* changed, but it still feels like it has.

For some reason, plan B does not feel as solid as plan A.

Mother picks over a light lunch of soup and salad, and we return to our suite half an hour later, each retiring to our rooms. I don't pack a trunk as I did the first time—there's no point, and it would only draw attention.

All I can do is wait.

CHAPTER FIFTY-EIGHT

NELL

ALEC IS ALREADY WAITING AT the back entrance when I arrive.

He's changed out of his bellhop uniform and into his suspenders and cotton shirt. Something forgettable that won't stick out to anyone. It was more difficult to find something equally forgettable in my wardrobe, so I settled for the blouse and skirt I wore the first time Alec took me dancing in Canvas City, plaiting my hair down my back and topping it with a simple straw hat pulled low over my eyes.

I want to run to him, to wrap my arms around him and breathe in his scent, and I can tell by the look in his eyes that he wants to do the same thing. But we quickly look away from each other and keep to opposite sides of the hall, as if we are two individuals who happen to be in the same space instead of what we really are—two halves of one whole, seeking escape.

"Ready?" Alec mutters under his breath.

I nod, just a fraction of an inch. Almost imperceptible, but Alec picks up on it.

He turns for the double doors.

He'll go through first and start for the docks. I'll follow thirty seconds later. He'll wait for me around the corner, away from prying eyes, and then we'll walk to the ferry together, as if we're just a normal couple going for an outing in the city.

He closes his hand over the knob and pulls.

The door doesn't open.

My breath catches. I look away, focusing my gaze on the clock so no one will notice my concern.

"Try again," I murmur.

He does, but the door doesn't budge.

I give up worrying about other people and cross to the doors. I twist the handle of the other door, but it's locked, too.

Alec meets my gaze.

"No," I whisper.

Lon's laughter echoes down the hall. Other people passing by don't seem to hear it, but to us, it's deafening.

"You thought you could change the rules and I wouldn't do a thing about it?" Lon's voice whips through the hall.

Alec grabs my hand and moves in front of me.

"Well," Lon continues, "I can change the rules, too."

The doors burst open, and Alec's hand is ripped from mine. He flies through the doorway, landing hard on the gravel below.

"Alec!" I try to run after him, but the doors slam shut in my face. I bang on them and twist the knobs. Wedge my fingers into the seam and try to pry them open.

Alec bangs on the other side of the doors, screaming my name, but he can't get through.

"Don't give up, Nell," he yells. "I'll find another way in."

"Now, then," Lon says, a chuckle lilting his words. "Time to have a little fun."

Like a painting doused in water, the wallpaper starts to run, colors bleeding into one another until I can't even make out the door anymore.

"Alec, something's happening," I shout.

His answer through the doors is warped, muffled, as if I'm hearing him from underwater. The colors take on new lines, new shapes. I close my eyes, my stomach pitching at the sight of it.

When I open them again, I'm standing in the crowded ballroom. Night presses into the windows surrounding me. I'm no longer wearing the casual blouse and skirt. Instead, I'm wearing the ballgown I wore on this night all those years ago.

Lon stands in front of me, a smile tilting his lips.

"May I have this dance?"

He doesn't give me the chance to refuse him. He steps forward, taking my hand in his and wrapping his other arm around my torso.

"Sixteen years is too long to wait to touch you again, my love," he whispers in my ear.

The clock strikes eleven. Thirty minutes until I run for my room to pack and change. Fifty minutes until Lon finds me there. One hour until he shoots me, then shoots himself.

Lon whirls me around the dance floor, *spinning, spinning, spinning* until I feel sick.

I can't find Alec anywhere.

———————————

Everything is the same as it was that night, even down to the liquor on Lon's breath and the slurring of his words. Mother and Father stand off to the side of the dance floor, socializing with Lon's business partners and their wives. Benny and Madeline are safely tucked away in his friend's room for his sleepover, and Alec is still nowhere to be seen.

But when the clock reads half past eleven and the orchestra

switches to Debussy's "Rêverie"—the same song I heard the first time I entered the dining room in June 1907, the same song I heard more than a century later in the ballroom, a ghostly melody coming from nowhere—Lon bends forward and, his voice clear of all drunkenness, says, "I believe that's your cue to run."

I stare up at him, uncertain of what I should do. If I run to my room now, this night will end as all the other nights before it. But if I don't, if I stay here, I'm not certain that will change anything, either.

I have to find Alec.

I wrench my hand from Lon's grip and take a step back.

His face splits into a too-wide smile.

"Go on, Aurelea," he says. "*Run*."

I grit my teeth against the urge to do as he says. Instead, I find Mother, just like I did all those lifetimes ago, and tell her I'm heading back to my room early due to a headache. She isn't happy with me, and in the past, the disappointment in her eyes would have gutted me. But tonight, I'm too busy memorizing her, here, like this. Alive and whole and healthy. *This* is how I want to remember her. How I want to remember Father and Benny when this is all over. Even if it's only for the last few minutes of my life.

I meet Lon's gaze once more, silently letting him know I'm not afraid of him, that I haven't given up, and calmly walk out of the ballroom.

As soon as I'm away, I kick off my shoes, pick up my skirt, and run for the back entrance. The halls are mostly deserted, save for a few hotel employees and couples in dark corners. They stare at me as I race past them, but I don't care.

I'm not sticking to this ridiculous script anymore.

I reach the double doors and try to open them, but the knobs don't even twist in my hands, and the doors don't show any sign of budging. I try to pull out the screws in the hinges, but they don't move an inch. It's as if the doors have been welded shut, and Alec doesn't answer when I call his name. I run back toward the lobby, past a very confused clerk at the reception desk. I try the doors at the front entrance, but they're sealed tight, too.

I rattle them, cursing Lon, but the doors stay shut.

Through the windows in the doors, I see Alec running toward me. He pounds on the doors from the other side, but no matter how hard we try, we can't open them.

"I'm looking for a way in," he shouts at me through the glass. "Just try to hide from him until I can get there."

"Alec—"

"Don't look at me like that," he says. "Don't look at me like this is goodbye. This isn't goodbye, you hear me?"

He shakes the doors again. My eyes burn at the sight of him, trying so hard to get to me. Both of us knowing he won't get in if Lon doesn't want him to.

The clerk yells, "Hey! What are you doing there?"

I wipe the tears off my cheeks and, in my most snobbish, authoritative voice, say, "Open this door."

The clerk furrows his brow.

"Is it locked?" he asks, moving around the reception desk.

Lon's disembodied voice surrounds me.

"Now, now. You're ruining my fun, Aurelea."

"Please, hurry," I tell the clerk.

"How about we put you where you belong, *hmm*?" Lon asks.

The world starts to blur around me again.

I turn back for the door. "Alec!"

The last thing I see is Alec trying desperately to get to me—

And then I'm back in my room, my valise on the bed, Alec's paper ring on my finger, and Lon standing in the doorway, his hands already in fists.

CHAPTER FIFTY-NINE

NELL

"HERE WE ARE AGAIN," LON says, slinking toward me.
"You, ready to leave me for a pauper. Me, the lovestruck fiancé
who didn't see it coming."

I know I should be afraid of him, but my anger is stronger
than my fear. This man, who hurt me and groped me to display
his dominance, who killed me in a fit of jealous, alcoholic rage,
who set all this in motion instead of just letting me go, letting me
be happy, *dares* to say he loved me?

"You were never lovestruck, Lon," I tell him, my voice shaking. "You were a child who didn't want to lose his favorite toy."
His eyes flash in warning, but I keep going. "You are still that
child. Unable to let me go."

"Oh no. It's deeper than that now," he says through gritted
teeth, moving closer. I keep the water pitcher in my periphery,
but I don't dare look straight at it. "Do you know what it's like
to kill yourself, Aurelea? The agony I felt in that moment? The
overwhelming need for release? I didn't know where my soul

would end up—hell, most likely, although I was certain I could argue my case with God if need be—but it seemed a better alternative than the complete devastation I felt the moment I killed you. But do you know where I ended up instead? *In this damn hotel.*" He pounds the wall with his fist. "Stuck inside its walls. A never-ending purgatory. You really think, after all that, I would let you have *your* happy ending?" His nostrils flare. "I wouldn't even *be* here if it weren't for you."

"You did this to yourself, Lon. You have no one else to blame."

"Don't you dare—"

He raises his hand, but I'm quicker than he is, grabbing the pitcher instead of breaking the window as he expects. I swing it as hard as I can at his head, the porcelain cracking against his skull. He falls into the side of the bed, grabbing his temple where blood has already started to seep from the wound.

I run into the parlor, barreling for the door.

Lon appears in front of me. "Going somewhere?"

I skid to a stop.

He laughs. "You can fight back all you want, darling," he says. "It won't change how this ends."

In another life Alec would be at the door now, waiting to take me to our getaway car. He would find a way into the room to try to rescue me. But Alec isn't at the door—he's not even inside the hotel—and there's no one to save me but myself.

I turn around, searching the room desperately for Father's hunting rifle. It has to be around here somewhere. Where else would Lon have found it?

"Looking for something?" he asks, appearing once again in front of me.

I run for the door again, this time getting there before he can stop me. But when I try to open it, it doesn't budge.

Lon chuckles. "I suppose there are some benefits to being stuck inside these walls. Every single one bends to my will."

His image blurs, across the room from me one second and in front of me the next. His hands bracelet my throat, pushing me against the door. His eyes are manic, blood dripping from his temple and into his lashes, but his voice is deathly calm as he whispers, "I will *never* let him have you."

I bring my knee up hard between his legs. He bends forward at the pain, his fingers loosening just enough for me to twist out of his hold.

I dart into Benny's room. He's always leaving his windows open. There's a chance I could sneak through one, and if I dangle from the ledge, the fall won't be as high—

But Lon's already there, fisting his hand in my hair and throwing me to the ground. I smack into Benny's light box, aflame as always. He never did remember to blow out the candle. The light box rolls across the floor, throwing crescent moons and North Stars across the walls in a dizzying swirl.

"You've learned some new tricks in this life, Aurelea," he says. "I'll give you that. You're even more of a fighter now than you were then."

I try to push myself up, but Lon lands a kick in my ribs, knocking me down. White-hot pain radiates through my side. I curl up in the fetal position as he kicks again. Smoke tinges the air and, in a distant sort of way, I realize how out of place that smell is in a hotel that doesn't allow open flame.

You have to get up, I tell myself. *You can't let him win. Get up, get up, get up*—

He swings his leg back to kick again, but I roll out of the way, springing to my feet. I cry out as the pain in my side flares. Lon stalks me, but I'm not looking at him. A ball of orange flames ignites behind him, climbing the curtains.

Benny's light box sits at the bottom of it.

I'm so distracted, I don't see Lon's hand coming. It smacks across my face, my vision bursting black and white with stars. I whirl on impact, staggering forward. I grip the only weapon I can find—Madeline's knitting needles, sitting on her bedside table—and hide them with my body. The flames are growing now, higher and fatter, feeding on the curtains and the tinderbox walls. Perspiration sprouts across my forehead and in the crooks of my palms. I squeeze the needles tighter.

Lon clamps his hands down on my shoulders, turning me around. I bring the needles up, aiming for his eyes. He blocks just in time, grabbing my hand, but I sink my teeth into his forearm, drawing blood. He yelps, part pain, part anger, as he lets me go. He brings his other hand up to smack me, but I'm already darting for the parlor.

Where's the gun?

The smoke is growing thicker now, spilling into the parlor from Benny's room, stinging my eyes. I can hear Lon's footsteps behind me, but I keep looking for the rifle. Lon was standing along the far wall, by the settee, when he pointed it at Alec, so it must be—

Lon barrels into me, knocking me to the floor. I bring the heel of my hand up into his nose with a sickening *crack* and try to crawl away from him. He pulls at my skirt, sliding me back. I lash out, scratching and kicking him everywhere I can reach.

It's enough to pull away from his grip.

I keep low as I crawl forward, the smoke thickening into a black cloud above us as the flames curl over Benny's door and onto the parlor ceiling. And then I see it.

The rifle.

It's propped against the wall, half hidden by the side table on which Father's cleaning kit rests. He must have been polishing the barrel and set the gun there to be put away later. I glance behind me, looking for Lon, but he's nowhere to be seen. I backtrack toward the gun, staying as close to the floor as I can, the flames growing hotter above me. I push the table aside and reach for the gun—

Lon's hand closes over the barrel of the rifle just as mine closes around the stock. I tug the rifle toward me, but Lon has a better grip. My fingers slip, and I grab the only thing I can reach.

The trigger.

Lon's eyes widen. He pushes the rifle forward, jamming the butt into my cracked ribs. I cry out but don't let go. Lon tries to get a better hold on the rifle, and my hand slips away from the trigger. I stand to get better leverage, my fingers scrambling, but the smoke is so thick, I can barely make out Lon or the gun. I feel the rounded metal of the trigger guard, my finger sliding back as Lon rips the gun away from me—

CRACK.

The gunshot echoes across the room. Lon and I stare at each other, our eyes wide.

And then Lon's knees buckle.

He falls to the floor, blood blossoming on his white dress shirt.

I take a step back, the rifle trembling in my hands. I have no idea if I've killed him—if you can even kill someone who's been dead for more than a century.

Blood pools around him. I drop to the ground, out of the smoke, but I don't let go of the gun. He tilts his head toward me, meeting my gaze, and I half expect him to disappear again and reappear in front of me, completely whole. But he takes a deep breath, and a single word rattles from his lips.

"Aurelea."

His body twitches. A breath escapes—

And then his eyes go dim.

The doors and windows burst open, creating a wind tunnel that stokes the flames. Fire explodes across the room, engulfing the walls, the ceiling, the furniture. The wind dies as the pressure in the room equalizes, but the damage is already done. I try to crawl forward, toward the open door, but the smoke is so thick, I can't tell if I'm going the right way. My lungs burn—from the smoke or from my cracked ribs, I'm not sure which—but I suddenly can't breathe. Every gasp for air fills my lungs with smoke, suffocating me. My head grows dizzy and my vision blurs and everything . . .

starts . . .

fading . . .

away.

"Nell!"

Alec appears in the open door. A beam falls from the ceiling, crashing to the carpet. Alec vaults over it, skidding to a stop in front of me.

"Alec—"

"It's all right," he says, scooping me into his arms. "I've got you."

He carries me over the beam and out into the hall, both of us coughing up smoke. Other guests run past us as a warning bell and the shouts of "Fire! Fire!" echo through the halls, but most of the guests are streaming out of the ballroom, everyone rushing for the doors.

"Hold on, Nell," Alec says, running away from the bottle-necked crowd, toward the back entrance. "We're going to make it."

I feel myself slipping in and out of consciousness, but the smoke in my lungs is clearing with every breath of clean air, and I believe him.

We're going to make it.

"Hold on," Alec says, kicking open the doors.

I wrap my arms tighter around his neck as he carries me out of the hotel, down the steps, and onto the gravel drive, where an old-fashioned fire truck screeches to a stop.

"All right there, you two?" one of the firemen asks as he rushes past us.

I try to tell him yes, we're okay, but he's suddenly swallowed by a white light. I close my eyes against the brightness.

"Alec?"

"It's okay," he murmurs into my ear. "I love you, Nell."

All the sound around us—the firemen shouting orders and the people screaming as they flee the hotel and the crunch of gravel beneath bootsteps—swirls together, growing louder and louder, crashing and bleeding into static.

CHAPTER SIXTY

NELL

ALL AT ONCE THE LIGHT dims and the world quiets, until there is nothing but the *whoosh* of the ocean and the gentle hum of a summer breeze and Alec's breath warming the nape of my neck.

I open my eyes.

We're outside the back entrance, but the drive beneath us is asphalt, not gravel, and there's no fire truck in front of us. Instead there's a parking lot full of modern cars.

Alec and I glance at each other, the same question in our eyes.

"Do you think—?"

"Are we really—?"

We laugh, but neither of us finishes the question. I'm too afraid this is a dream. That if we acknowledge it, we'll lose each other again.

Alec brushes the hair off my face.

"You had bruises," he says, "from where Lon . . ." He swallows the words he can't say. "And your skin was red from the fire, but it's fine now. Not even a scratch."

I take a deep breath, my lungs free of smoke. "It's like nothing happened."

Gently, Alec sets me on my feet, and, for the first time, I realize we're both wearing the clothes we wore in his room, before we went back in time. I'm in a pair of yoga pants and a tank top, while Alec wears a gray Henley and black sweatpants.

"Has this ever happened before?" I ask him.

He nods.

"But I've always been alone."

We stare at each other, knowing this is a good sign but neither of us quite willing to believe it. What if we messed it up somehow with the fire, so we got kicked back here just to go through it again?

Is it even the day we think it is?

The world is painted the blue-gray palette of early morning, but a golden light breaks the horizon along the beach to our left. Wordlessly, Alec takes my hand and leads me to the beach.

A jogger runs toward us. I stop her with a wave.

She pulls out her earbuds.

"This is going to sound really weird," I say, giving her an apologetic smile, "but could you tell us the date?"

Her brow furrows. "The fifth."

Alec's hand tightens around mine.

"Of August?" I ask.

The woman blinks. "Yes."

A lump forms in my throat.

"What year?"

At first, she smiles at us like we must be joking, but the smile disappears as she takes in the desperation in our eyes.

"Oh, uh . . ." She clears her throat. "2019."

"Thank you," I murmur.

She nods, pops her earbuds back in, and jogs away from us.

I turn to Alec.

2019. Not 1907.

August 5. Not August 4. Not July or June or any other past month.

We didn't get kicked back just to go through it again. If we had, it would be the fourth, and we'd be waiting to return to 1907 once more at midnight on the fifth, to relive the day leading up to the murder. If it's the morning of the fifth, and we're here, not in 1907, then that can only mean . . .

A beaming smile breaks across Alec's face.

"Did we do it?" I ask him.

"Wait," he says, tugging my hand. "There's one more test."

We walk along the beach, the dawn setting the sky ablaze. I marvel at the feeling of Alec's hand in mine, at the air filling my lungs and the sand squishing up between my toes. Every second I'm breathing feels like the most precious gift I have ever received, and I don't know why I never realized it before, but if this is real, if we really broke the curse, I never want to take it for granted again.

Alec stops.

"This is it," he says. "The property line."

"Are you sure?"

His jaw tenses as he stares at the line I'm sure he's walked a million times during the past century, and it's all the assurance I need.

I press my lips to the back of his hand.

He looks at me.

"Together?" I ask.

He nods.

"On three," I say. "One. Two. Three."

We step forward, both of us tensing, expecting the property line to stop us, but our legs go right through, followed by the rest of our bodies.

Alec hesitates, just for a second. Then he turns to me, tears in his eyes, and he picks me up, spinning me around.

"You're here," he shouts, his body trembling around me. "You're really here."

We stay like that for a long time, holding on to each other, unwilling to let go until the sun is so high, I realize Dad must have woken up by now and that he's probably wondering where I am.

I wipe the tears from my eyes and look up at Alec. "Do you want to have breakfast with my dad and me?"

Alec smiles. "Absolutely."

He puts his arm around me as we take the long way back to the hotel. Not along the beach, but down a residential side street, Alec's hand trailing flowers and his feet slapping against pavement and his eyes taking in a world that he hasn't been able to touch or see or smell for more than a century. I watch the wonder in his eyes and feel the tightening of his hand in the fabric of my shirt, unwilling to let me go for even a second, and all I can think is *home*.

We're finally home.

EPILOGUE

NELL

February 2020

IT SEEMS LIKE EVERYONE ON the island has turned out for the museum's grand opening. The lobby is so packed with men in fine suits and women in cocktail dresses that the poor waiters can barely move through the crowd with their hors d'oeuvres and champagne flutes.

I reach into my purse and check the time on my phone again.

"Sorry I'm late," Alec whispers in my ear.

I smile as he wraps his arms around me and presses his lips to my temple. "How was your exam?"

"Great," he says. "There wasn't anything on it I wasn't expecting."

"Still on track to graduate a year early, then?" I tease.

He smirks. "Yeah, but I'm aiming for two."

I roll my eyes. Aside from being the freshman that *everyone* knows at the College of Charleston for testing out of all his general education requirements, Alec's professors have already said he's a shoo-in for the Medical University of South Carolina upon graduation. Of course, with his grades and test scores, he could get into any medical school he chooses.

I spot Dad and Sofia through a break in the crowd, standing near the courtyard doors alongside Max. I take Alec's hand and make our way toward them, my eye catching on the engagement ring on Sofia's finger.

I would be lying if I said it wasn't weird when Dad and Sofia started dating, or when he told me he wanted to marry her. I don't think a small part of it will ever *not* be weird, seeing Dad's arm around her instead of around Mom, eating Sofia's meals instead of Mom's, swapping Christmas gifts with her and sharing our lives with her instead of sharing them with Mom.

But I can't deny Sofia and my Dad just . . . spark. I didn't want to see it at first, but it's there. And now that she isn't subtly trying to figure out whether or not I've remembered my past lives yet, which she admitted afterward was probably on the stalker side of creepy, she's been totally normal. Or at least as normal as someone obsessed with hotels can be.

I know they'll make each other happy.

"Hey, Max," I say now as we stop next to them. "Any news from USC?"

After we came back, we confirmed the story Sofia told Max about us, even though he didn't believe it at first. We had to show him our picture from 1907, and all the other ones Alec had held on to in his room. With our blessing, Max took our story and wrote a screenplay based off it, which he attached a sample of to his application for the USC screenwriting program. I would be shocked if they turned him down—he's already been accepted to several universities across the country off that script alone.

I think he wants to eventually shop it around Hollywood,

but I'm not worried. It's too out there for anyone to believe it actually happened.

"Not yet, but fingers crossed. Hey, man," Max says, bumping Alec's fist. "How's it going?"

"Good," Alec says, bumping Max's fist right back, even though I can tell from his grimace that he'd much rather shake hands the old-fashioned way, and I bite the inside of my cheek to stifle my laugh.

"Oh," Max says suddenly, turning back to me. "I'm such an idiot! Your audition was today!"

"It was," I say, coyly.

The Charleston School of Ballet held auditions today for the spring recital, a student showcase attended by recruiters from all the top ballet academies across the country. A principal role only increases the chances of getting into a good academy after high school and, from there, a good company.

"And?" Max asks. "How'd it go?"

Alec squeezes my hand. I texted him as soon as the audition was over.

"I got the principal role in the *Romeo and Juliet* routine."

"They gave you Romeo?" Max asks.

I elbow him in the ribs.

"Just kidding," he says, throwing an arm around me and pulling me into his side. "Congratulations."

Dad grins proudly at me and slides his arm around Sofia.

I hate that Dad's the only one in our new family unit that doesn't know the truth about me and Alec. I think about telling him sometimes, but I know it would be hard to believe, and I don't know if he can handle the thought that I could have died last summer. Maybe I will tell him someday, when we're both older and have enjoyed full lives, when it won't be as scary, but I know it would terrify him now, still so close to Mom's death.

That's another reason I'm thankful for Sofia. I know she will never replace Mom in Dad's heart, and I know she would never want to. But to see Dad finally moving on makes me feel like I don't need to stay so close to home. I don't know where Alec and I will end up, but there are prestigious medical schools and ballet companies all across the country, and for the first time since Mom died, I am no longer afraid of the unknown.

Whatever happens, I know it will be amazing. Because I'm here. I'm alive.

And so is Alec.

One of the workers waves at Sofia to come up to the front of the room, where a big red ribbon blocks off the entrance into the museum.

"That's my cue," she says, handing Dad her champagne flute. She crosses to the front of the lobby and turns on a microphone

"Good evening, everyone," she says, "and thank you all for joining us on this very special night. This historical exhibit has been almost two years in the making, and it wouldn't be possible if not for two very special young people who were willing to give up so much of their free time to help put it all together. Would Nell Martin and Max Moreno please join me up here?"

I raise my brows at Max, and he winks.

"Let's go get 'em," he says.

The crowd applauds as we make our way forward. Sofia instructs us to place our hands on the giant scissors along with her own.

"Now then," she says, "without further ado, I declare this exhibit, A Walk Through Time, officially open."

We cut the ribbon, and the crowd applauds again. We wait for Dad and Alec to join us before heading inside.

The exhibit is just how Sofia imagined it would be, like being fully immersed in the Grand's long and vibrant history. Life-size pictures of hotel guests throughout the years surround the displays, along with videos of past presidents and celebrities who frequented the Grand. Music from each decade filters through hidden speakers (my idea), changing from classical to ragtime, swing to fifties rock 'n' roll, and continuing on through present day.

Alec and I stop at the *Fire of 1907* exhibit. There isn't much information on the fire, other than a newspaper picture of the damage and an accompanying article stating that the fire was, luckily, contained to one suite. A light box was believed to be the source of the fire, with the cleaning polish the staff regularly used on the walls and furniture acting as the perfect igniter, causing the fire to rage into an inferno in a matter of seconds. Thanks to the Grand's alarm system, there was only one reported death in the fire. A picture of Lon Van Oirschot accompanies the exhibit, along with a brief biography detailing his family's history. Sadly, the biography reads, he was to be married at the end of the summer, an engagement cut short by his untimely death.

No one knows what happened to his fiancée.

The suite itself was quickly rebuilt, and tour guides often ask people to guess which suite it was from the hotel's exterior, but the reconstruction was so seamless, no one can ever tell.

Alec squeezes my hand and whispers, "Want to go somewhere?"

I meet his gaze.

"Always."

Alec leads me to the beach. It's a full moon, washing the sand and whitecapped waves silver in its glow. There isn't a single cloud in the sky. We slip off our shoes and walk to the tide line. It's our place, where we once laid on the sand and let the water rush over us. Where we shared our first kiss. Where we fell in love.

"I lied about the exam being so late," he says. "I took it this morning."

"Why did you lie?"

"Because," he says, reaching into his pocket and pulling out a black velvet box, "I had to pick up this."

My heart stops.

"I know I can't give you an official engagement ring yet without giving your dad a heart attack," he says. "But I thought this could suffice for now."

He opens the box. Inside is a band that looks like it's made of glass, with a silver inlay around its edges. He pulls out the ring and holds it up to the moonlight so I can see the paper inside and the Walt Whitman quote inscribed on it.

I am to see to it that I do not lose you.

"I give you this ring, Nell Martin," Alec says, gently slipping it onto my finger, "as a token of the promise we made to each other in another life, and as a token of the promise I make to you now, to love and to cherish you until the day I die, and then for an eternity after that."

"Oh, Alec." Tears sting my eyes. "It's perfect."

I wrap my arms around his neck and press my lips to his. And as the ocean crashes around us and the moon watches us from above, those twelve words—*I am to see to it that I do not lose you*—wrap around us, binding us in an eternal vow. To never take our lives for granted. To never lose each other again. To choose each other, each and every day.

To choose love.

Again, and again.

To choose love.

ACKNOWLEDGMENTS

To God, first and foremost, always and forever. The only reason this story exists is because You saw me when I was at my lowest and crafted the most amazing adventure to give me hope and renewal. I will forever sing Your praises for how You've saved me, not just once, but again, and again, and again. You are at the center of every word of this book. Thank You for everything.

To my incredible editor, Anna Roberto, for once again working your magic in bringing the absolute best out of my writing. You somehow always see what I'm trying to do and give me just the right guidance to help me get there. Your value is immeasurable. Also, to Rich Deas, for creating yet another stunning cover that perfectly captures the essence of this story; to Brittany Pearlman, for working tirelessly to get my books into readers' hands (you are amazing!); and to everyone at Feiwel and Friends for all of the hard work you put into bringing this book, the book of my heart, out into the world. I am eternally grateful.

To my dream agent, Andrea Somberg, for being the first cheerleader of every project and my constant defender. I could never thank you enough for making my wildest publishing dreams come true. My heart skips a beat every time I get an email from you!

To Mom and Aunt Georgia, for bringing me along on the trip that inspired this story, and to Grandma, for nudging me to take your spot on the trip when you couldn't go yourself. It will forever be one of my favorite memories, not only for how it gave me this story, but also for how God used it to restore my soul.

To Dad, for taking me to the Ohio Theater and other cool, creepy places when I was younger. I'm not sure if you knew you were fueling a love for the old and the potentially haunted when you did so, but those buildings and those places deepened my understanding of the world that hides beneath the veil of this one, and they are an important piece to the puzzle that makes up the stories I write. I would not be the person nor the writer I am today without those places.

To my sisters, Heather and Jenny, for being just as obsessed with the supernatural as I've always been, giving me a tribe of misfits and dreamers within my own family to which I could belong. I was always free to be myself around you, even if others didn't always understand me. And to Sarah, for always asking me about the stories I was writing, making it feel like my dreams were attainable from a very young age, even when I didn't believe it myself.

To Tracy Wilson, for making sure my ballet references made sense. It turns out that when you haven't taken a ballet class since you were five, you tend to forget some things. You're the best!

To Nathan, for being the center of every romantic hero I write. I'm so blessed that, just like my young adult characters, I got my epic love story in high school, and I'm so thankful I get to continue living it every single day. You are the true other half of me, my soul mate, my home.

To Emerson. I was praying for you when God gave me the inspiration for this story, and I was pregnant with you when I wrote it. You have been on this journey with me every step of the way, my beautiful girl, and I thank God every day for you. I love you so very much. And to our baby boy on the way, you have also been a part of the writing of this story, and there's a good chance you may even be born on the day this book comes out. Daddy and I are so thankful to God for you, and we already love you to pieces. We can't wait to meet you.